HOURGLASS

DANILO KIŠ

Hourglass

Translated by Ralph Manheim

faber and faber

First published in the USA in 1990
by Farrar, Straus and Giroux, Inc., New York
and simultaneously in Canada
by Harper and Collins, Toronto
First published in Great Britain in 1990
by Faber and Faber Limited
3 Queen Square London WCIN 3AU

Printed in England by Clays Ltd, St Ives plc
Originally published in Serbo-Croatian as *Peščanik*
Ralph Manheim is hereby identified as translator of
this work in accordance with Section 77 of the
Copyright, Designs and Patents Act 1988

A portion of this book originally appeared, in
somewhat different form, in *The New Yorker*.

A CIP record for this book is available from the British Library
ISBN 0-571-14304-0

Ex voto in the old style

TO MIRJANA

Was it thus in the days of Noah? Ah, no.

—*Anon., seventeenth century*

HOURGLASS

PROLOGUE

[*1*]

The flickering shadows dissolve the outlines of things and break up the surfaces of the cube, the walls and ceiling move to and fro to the rhythm of the jagged flame, which by turns flares up and dies down as though about to go out. The yellow clay at the bottom of the cube rises like the floorboards of a sinking boat, then falls back into the darkness, as though flooded with muddy water. The whole room trembles, expands, contracts, moves a few centimeters to the right or left, up or down, all the while keeping its cubical shape. Horizontals and verticals intersect at several points, all in vague confusion, but governed by some higher law, maintaining an equilibrium that prevents the walls from collapsing and the ceiling from tilting or falling. This equilibrium is due no doubt to the regular movement of the crossbeams, for they, too, seem to glide from right to left, up and down, along with their shadows, without friction or effort, as lightly as over water. The waves of the night dash against the sides of the room-boat. Gusts of wind blow soft flakes and sharp icy crystals by turns against the windowpane. The square, embrasure-like window is stuffed with a disemboweled pillow; bits of cloth stick out and dangle like amorphous plants or creepers. It is hard to say whether they are trembling under the impact of the wind blowing through the cracks, or whether it is only their shadow that sways to the rhythm of the jagged flame.

Slowly the eye becomes accustomed to the half darkness, to the swaying of the room without clear contours, to the flickering shadows. Attracted by the flame, the gaze makes for the lamp, the only bright spot in the vast darkness, aims for it like a disoriented fly, and comes to rest on this one source of light, which twinkles like some fortuitous distant star. Blinded for a moment as if entranced by the light, the eye sees nothing else, neither long shadows nor swaying surfaces nor dangling rags, nothing. It sees only that light, that jagged flame, somehow outside of space, just as stars are outside of space; then slowly it begins to decompose the light, to refract it within its prism, to discover all the colors of the spectrum in it. And only then, only after decomposing, dissecting it, does the eye discover, in the slow waves of paler and paler light that spread around the flame, all that remains to be discovered amid the folds of shadow and emptiness: first the lamp chimney, the flame's glass envelope, at first glance imperceptible, abstract, a mere echo of the flame, an echo beyond which the darkness abruptly begins, as though the light were cut off by the glass, thrust into a pit, buried in darkness, and not only in darkness but in some peculiarly dense substance, having an entirely different specific weight from the envelope surrounding the flame. But that lasts only a moment, the time it takes the eye to grow accustomed not to the darkness but to the light. Then, little by little, the eye discovers its mistake and perceives the soot on the walls of the chimney, ranging in color from black-brown to silvery as on a blind mirror, sees that the glass envelope is not the boundary of the light, and also discovers, not without surprise, that the silvery tinge of the soot is also an illusion and that the resemblance to a blind mirror is not a trick of the mind but a trick of the light, clearly visible in the round mirror behind the lamp chimney, which reveals another flame, identical with the first, almost unreal, but unmistakably a flame. If the eye did not distinguish it before, it was only because the *mind* resisted the illusion, because the mind refused to accept the appearance (as in the picture where the eye perceives a white vase or an hourglass or a chalice, until the mind—or is it the will?—discovers that this vase is an empty space, negative, hence an illusion, and that the only positive, that is, real thing in the picture, is the two profiles turned toward each other, face to face as it were, as in a mirror, a nonexistent mirror, the axis of which passes through the axis of the no longer existent vase-hourglass-chalice into a double mirror, so that both faces, and not just one, become real, for otherwise the second would be only a reflection, an echo of the first, in which case they would no longer be symmetrical, let alone real; so that both faces would be Platonic archetypes and not just one, for otherwise the second would be a mere *imitatio*, a reflection of a reflection, a shadow; and consequently these two faces, on prolonged scrutiny, move closer to each other, as though wishing to unite and so confirm their identity).

Grown accustomed to the light as the mind has grown accustomed to the illusion, the eye now begins to burrow in the darkness and half darkness; freeing itself from the magical attraction of the flame, it sees the oil lamp as well as the trembling shadow, and distinguishes great dark cubes of shadow. The side that is hidden by the mirror is already in total darkness (and the flame issues

from that darkness, as though fed by it), while to the left and right of the lamp appear large gray shifting surfaces, too luminous to be shadows, too diffuse to be light. But then the mind comes to the help of the eye and discovers, as though by touch, the hard surface of the grayish-white walls and at the same time, clearly dividing shadow from light, three beams in the ceiling, three long beams duplicated by their shadows, which, like sticks immersed in water, are truncated by lateral shadows of uncertain origin. Having got its bearing in space, found a reliable point of reference and located true north, the eye finds the large shadow of the kitchen stove, confused with the stove itself, a double stove, made up of black, rusty cast iron and of tenuous shadow, an eight-legged stove that rocks on its long legs like some shivering dog. Behind the lamp's mirror, behind the flame-reflection, there is darkness, a blind window—that is where the cold, the sharp sound, and the muffled jangling of glass come from. On the other side, across from the blind window, there is a wooden chest, only one side of which is visible; it wobbles, but does not fall over. The shadow breaks in uneven waves against the lower part of the chest; at this point there is a bulge, a meter or possibly a meter and a half wide, in the clay floor, more like a cicatrized wound than like a grave. More sensed than seen, in the corner, leaning against the dark side of the chest, squeezed between the eroded wall and the boards of the chest, is what the eye has been looking for: a schoolbag with rounded sides.

Circling the room like a moth, colliding with hovering shadows, with walls and beams, the eye returns to the light, where lie as though hidden (since the eye discovers them last, because it has not looked for them near the flame, because it has not looked for anything near the light) various objects scattered over a table hitherto rendered invisible by the shadow or the light. To the left, next to the lamp, pads of quadrille paper; beside them, not far from the middle of the table, a newspaper folded double; to the extreme right, two or three issues of a greasy magazine and a book with black binding and gold lettering that seems to be made of the same substance as the flame; and, hidden by the shadow of the mirror, slightly above the tabletop as though hovering in midair, a half-finished cigarette. The smoke somehow finds its way to the lamp and pours, bluish, through the chimney.

A hand approaches the flame.

TRAVEL SCENES (I)

[2]

Holding his breath, his face turned toward the door, the man listens. Something tells him that the people in the adjoining room are awake and only pretending to be asleep. He waits for sleep to overcome them. He has the feeling that by being awake so close to him (between him and them there is only a flimsy door with a big crack along the bottom) they can influence him by the flow of their thoughts. For, especially on quiet nights like this, just before one falls asleep, thought becomes so concentrated as to crackle almost visibly in the air like static electricity or the heat over a red-hot stove.

From the other side of the door, however, no breathing can be heard. Or if anything can be heard in the tremulous silence, it is their breathing, the silence of their thoughts and their sleep.

Now his back is turned to the table. His long shadow, blurred and trembling, cuts diagonally across the room. The shapeless, deformed shadow of his head breaks against the side of the wooden chest. Treading on his shadow like a sleepwalker, the man makes for the corner of the room. Hidden by his body, his hand gropes for an invisible object that he caught sight of while walking toward the corner or when entering the room. Under his fingers he feels the rounded edges of the cardboard schoolbag and the cold surface of a brass lock. Now he holds in his hand the strapless bag (the straps have probably been removed, for there are still shiny rivets on the back) with rounded wooden sides and an imitation pigskin flap. He lifts the flap and holds it up with his chin. Under thin notebooks he feels a square bottle. The bottle is cold and smooth, like an ice cube. He holds it in the palm of his hand and, still with his back to the light, unscrews the top. He raises the neck to his nose, taking care not to let it touch, and breathes in the smell of ink. He closes the bottle and shakes it a little, turning it toward the light. The wavering flame of the lamp trembles on the polished corners of the little bottle and licks the purple ink on its inner walls. The man begins again to rummage in the schoolbag, holding the flap open with his chin. Under the notebooks he finds a thin, spindle-shaped penholder, picks it up with three fingers, and traces an arabesque in the air. He presses the tip of the pen against his thumbnail, making a sound like the buzzing of an insect.

Now he is at the table again, motionless for a moment. From the inside pocket of his coat he takes long sheets of quadrille paper and lays them on the newspaper. The paper is folded lengthwise like an official document, but not pressed flat. At first the small squares are visible, but then little by little the lines recede, merge, and disappear, and a moment later the illumined edges of the paper vanish as well. All that remains in their place is the source of pale-yellow light. If he did not have in his pocket, folded in two, the draft written a few days before (in some anonymous restaurant, beside a red-hot stove, on a table covered with greasy oilcloth; in a dark little room behind an embroidery shop, on an old card table, by the light of a gas lamp; in the compartment of an express train, likewise at night, by the bright light of a mercury lamp; but also half asleep in this same room); if, in short, he had not put so much work into this draft, he might drop the whole thing. But the draft fascinates him despite an intense desire to feed it to the flame and go to bed. No, now that he has taken the first step and saved these few pages from destruction, he can't bear to throw them into the fire. Despite his momentary dejection and doubt, he dimly suspects that this minute segment of family history, this brief chronicle, bears within it the force of those documents which, when they come to light after long years or even millennia, become witnesses to the times (and then it makes no difference what individual they concern), comparable to the scroll fragments found by the Dead Sea or in the ruins of temples, or the writing on the walls of prisons.

So, from his inside pocket he takes the draft written in pencil on identical quadrille paper, and looks it over.

The draft is right next to the lamp. The wick burns fitfully. The flame bursts from its violet center, veers from red to pale yellow. The lamp chimney blackens and a fine silvery film forms around the soot. And, almost inaudible in the silence: the hissing of the flame. The sound of time.

For a moment, the man puts his pen aside. The newsprint acts as blotting paper. Over a printed story about carrier pigeons* the opening words of a letter appear as in a mirror, as in Hebrew.

* When pigeons are dropped from a plane, they take some time to get their bearings. An experienced pigeon lets itself drop like a stone until it is free of the air currents created by the plane. A beginner, on the other hand, tries to fly at once. The wind flings it in all directions like a fishing boat in a storm, and it flies in circles, until it gets its bearings.

[*3*]

The man looks at the pointed flame, which trembles
in the icy draft blowing from the invisible window across
from him. Then he looks down at the glass reservoir of
the lamp. The reservoir narrows in the middle, and the
neck is encircled by a rusty metal ring. The ring does
not form a perfect circle, but consists of two symmetrical
semicircles separated in the front by a gap of one or
two centimeters. From the metal ring protrude two
parallel wires that connect at the top to form a triangle
with rounded sides, which serves as a holder for a
round, half-blind mirror corroded at the edges. The
mirror engenders two twin flames, two jagged flames
one facing the other, identical despite the fact that one
of them, the one in the mirror, the one that is reflected,
owes its existence to an illusion and to the other flame.
The reservoir is brown inside like an aquarium full of
stagnant water and, it would seem, slimy with barely
visible algae and lichen. The man peers at the reservoir,
looking for the line indicating the level of the oil, but
it is blurred by the dirty greenish-brown of the glass.
First he looks for it below the metal ring, examining all
the tiny protuberances on the semicircular reservoir,
half obscured by a film of oil mixed with soot and dust.
Not finding the line (and too lazy to attempt the
complicated and risky maneuver of tilting the lamp in
such a way as to disclose the oil level), he glances at the
rusty metal ring around the waist of the reservoir, and
just as he is thinking that the line must be somewhere
in that vicinity, he discovers at the base of the saturated
wick (which is as white and sluggish as a sated tapeworm)
a barely visible narrowing, a slight deformation, as when

a stick is refracted in water. He realizes, not without
alarm, that there is barely a finger's breadth of oil in
the reservoir. *The lamp will drink it all up, devour it all.* As
though frightened at the thought that the lamp would
go out, he hastens to start writing again, to continue
what he has begun and win his race with darkness.

[*4*]

Legs apart, leaning slightly forward, the man stands
at the window. A blanket is thrown over his shoulders.
The blanket smells of horses and urine. The man is
wearing galoshes that reflect the light shining in through
the low, square window. All he can see from that height
is the whirling snowflakes on the other side of the
windowpane and, from time to time, the blurred outline
of a tree. The snow piles up on the windowsill, creating
a rolling, snowy hill. Under the impact of the wind, the
angle of the hill's slopes, the curve of its horizon change.
At one moment there are two gently rolling hills of
almost equal height, then suddenly the wind redraws
the wavy line, joining the two hills into one; or it creates
a sharp peak where there was a valley a moment before.
When the snow lets up a little, the man has the impression that the distance from window to tree is no more
than ten meters, but when the wind starts driving large
flakes, the tree recedes imperceptibly, like a boat pushed
away from the shore. This space with its deceptive
contours is also covered by snow, and the undulating
surface—it, too, changing—is littered with footprints,
perhaps from last night, perhaps from today, perhaps
from only a few hours ago. The window trembles under

the wind squalls and snow crystals can be heard scratching lightly against the panes. The man raises his head and listens. For a moment, he seems to hear the barking of a dog in the distance. But the sound stops, lost in the howling of the wind, and he is no longer sure whether he has heard the barking of a dog or only the raging of the storm. How long has he been standing at this window with a blanket over his shoulders? Perhaps all day, perhaps an hour or two, perhaps only ten minutes.

Now he is pressed against the window, darkening the whole room. He tries to look beyond the tree, through the hazy light to the wire fence, whose mesh is filled in with snow. Suddenly he hears the crystalline sound of sleigh bells from not far off. At almost the same time, he sees the misty outlines of horses' heads, and a moment later the people in the sleigh: the coachman wearing a fur hat sprinkled with snow, and a woman, who is just getting out of the sleigh. She, too, is wearing a fur hat or a leather cap, unless it is her hair gathered in a high bun that is covered with snow. The woman takes something from the seat, then holds out her hand to the coachman. The man sees the woman with a small suitcase in hand approach the gate, shake snow from the grating as she opens it, and plod through the deep snow, heading directly toward him. Abruptly he leaves the window and goes quickly to the door. He hears knocking. Eyeing the lengthwise crack in the door, he sees a shadow moving, then he hears steps receding, scraping in the snow. He looks through the crack. At first he sees nothing, then only whirling snowflakes. Again he hears steps approaching, scraping through the snow. Now he sees the woman, the same woman as before. She shakes the snow off her head and he clearly sees her abundant curly hair gathered in a high bun, on which snowflakes settle. She is wrapped in a black knitted shawl, from which she takes a blue envelope. The man suddenly raises his head and sees a triangle above the door, the corner of the envelope, moist with fingerprints. Again he looks through the long crack, but the woman is gone. Moving away from the door, the man looks at the envelope but does not touch it. He probably thinks that the woman who has brought the letter is hiding somewhere and is watching the blue envelope, the greater part of which has remained outside, stuck in the slit above the door.

[5]

The man is lying on the bed, or, rather, he is sitting up, leaning against a large pillow. He is covered with a gray blanket, from which only his head and arms emerge. He is holding a thin book or magazine. The title page shows advertising photos of rubber tires of different sizes and with different types of treads; above them, large, stylized letters, indicating the brand name, no doubt. The title is printed on a slant, in larger letters, on the upper third of the page, against a grayish-green background. The pages are spotted with grease and many are turned down at the corners, possibly at random and possibly for reference. The man thumbs through the pages, stirring up a breeze that twists the flame of the oil lamp on the marble top of the bedside table. Along with the flame, the numerous sleighs on the wallpaper start to tremble. They are arranged symmetrically at a distance of some ten centimeters from one another. (Because of this symmetry and the endlessly repeated gray design, the sleighs—including the people in them—reduce themselves to a single sleigh; but in spite of the repetition, or perhaps because of it, the scene, instead of seeming static, comes to life.) It is an old-fashioned sleigh with high curved runners that make it look like an ark. It is drawn by two horses that have stopped moving or are about to stop moving. A coachman with long mustaches, wearing a snow-covered leather cap, is tugging at the reins.

The horses' heads are held high and turned to one side, no doubt because of the pull on the reins. A woman alights from the sleigh; in her left hand she holds a muff, or maybe it is a small suitcase, while with her right hand she grasps the curved bar at the side of the seat. An improbably small foot in a pointed shoe emerges from under her fur coat and her ankle-length dress. The foot stops in midair between the seat of the sleigh and the undulating surface of the snow. The closed shutters of a stately mansion with a large vaulted gate can be seen to the right of the sleigh, on a level with the horses' heads. The woman seems to have arrived unexpectedly, since the window shutters are closed; the heavy Gothic gate is closed, too—and undoubtedly bolted as well. The flame has come to rest, and the woman's foot, suspended in midair, is now quite motionless. The horses' heads are motionless, too. Their forelegs, bent sharply at the knee, are suspended in midair. After casting a glance at the volume he has just shut, the man puts it down on the marble top of the bedside table. In addition to the volume he has just put down, there are also, beside the lamp on the marble tabletop, a tin ashtray and an open pack of cigarettes. The lamp is white porcelain with a shade of thin, transparent glass decorated with big purple irises. Before blowing out the lamp, the man turns down the wick. Now nothing can be seen in the room but the marble tabletop, which looks like a block of ice. The coachman has whipped up the horses. The sleigh glides through the darkness. The bells can no longer be heard. Nothing can be heard. Only the howling of the storm beyond the window and the darkness. The woman in the fur coat has stopped briefly outside the gate, then the gate swallows her up, and a moment later the gate itself is engulfed in darkness. At one window, behind half-open wooden shutters, a streak of light glints through the cracks. The man looks at the streak of light just across from him, shining through the crack in the invisible door. The streak of light moves, as though someone on the other side of the door were repositioning its source, or raising or lowering the flame of the lamp, or merely shielding it from the wind with his hand. Not a step, not a voice to be heard, only the howling of the storm on the other side of the window and the darkness. The streak of light grows wider, tracing one side of a luminous triangle on the floor, and long shadows begin to trace semicircles around the objects in the room. The marble top of the bedside table emerges into the light along with the lamp, the magazine, the enameled tin ashtray, and the open pack of cigarettes. The widening streak of light from the door reveals a lamp, or rather, it reveals only a glass

lampshade shining in its own light. The wick seems to
have been turned down, so that neither the other parts
of the lamp nor the hand holding it can be seen. Only
the purple flowers, probably irises, on the lampshade
of thin, transparent glass are discernible. The luminous
lampshade with the irises hovers for a moment in midair,
swaying just a little; then an invisible hand turns up the
wick. At the same time, the lamp and the hand holding
it begin to move forward and the flame dances in the
draft from the open door and the half-open shutters.
Soundlessly a woman crosses the room, holding the
lamp at eye level, at some distance in front of her. Her
face is utterly expressionless, as though cast in wax; her
eyes seem to be closed. Her hair, gathered into a high
bun, is black or graying. She is wearing a long, transparent nightgown, which comes down to the ground,
falling in thick folds around her invisible or barely
visible ankles. The nightgown is pink or flesh-colored,
or perhaps these two colors mingle and merge in the
lamplight. No more than an arm's length behind her,
another woman glides soundlessly, wearing an identical
floor-length nightgown. Her hair, too, is gathered into
a high bun, her face as though cast in wax, her eyes
apparently closed. This second woman is not carrying
a lamp, but she holds out her hands as though wishing
to take the lamp from the first woman. This makes her
look more like the first woman's shadow than her twin,
like her reflection in a side mirror, in the open door of
a cupboard, or in the polished surface of some piece of
furniture.

[6]

The storm has died down for a moment, only a few stray snowflakes are floating through the air. The man is standing outside the door. He is wearing a gray hat; a long, ragged coat hangs down to the mouse-colored spats that have been slipped over his shiny galoshes. With one hand, he hugs a greasy pigskin briefcase to his chest; in the other, he holds a cane. The man is on his way somewhere. To his left, two or three meters from the snow-covered path, there is a veranda. Muffled laughter and indistinct voices can be heard from behind the glass door leading into the house with the veranda. As the man nears the door, the laughter suddenly becomes shrill. Evidently, someone has opened the door. The man looks in that direction. A table has been placed lengthwise across from the door, and he sees it considerably foreshortened. The place at the head of the table is empty (wasn't the person who opened the door sitting there a moment ago?); a porcelain plate and a half-empty glass of wine are still there. At the foot (unless it's the head) of the table is seated a woman with a high bun, wearing a black dress. On either side of the table, at about the same distance from the observer, two persons are seen in profile: two women in black dresses, perhaps somewhat younger than the first; and across from them sit a man with a sallow face and another person who cannot be seen clearly. In the light coming from the opposite side (small confetti-like snowflakes are blowing through the half-open window curtains), symmetrically arranged porcelain plates, platters, and glasses are plainly visible. A suckling pig has been set down lengthwise in the exact center of the table, slightly upraised. The man sees it foreshortened: short ears and curly tail on a browned, plump, glistening body. The snout is turned toward him; between the blackened teeth, he sees a green apple. The hand of the man with the sallow face has stopped, along with his glass, halfway between the table and the blackened teeth. This happens at the moment when he catches sight, through the open door, of the man with the cane.

[7]

The man is sitting on a boulder by the roadside. The boulder is round and crudely carved, and clearly shows the effects of time and erosion; it is porous and spongy, spotted with lichen and rustlike specks. Obviously, this stone did not get here, at the edge of this precipice, by chance; it was put here by a human hand, which gave it its definitive (if anything can be called definitive) shape. In the upper part of the boulder, there is a small, saddle-shaped hollow, belonging to a darker-gray stratum, undoubtedly of a different geological age and composition from the cretaceous base. A groove as wide as a thumb and some twenty centimeters long runs along the outer edge of the hollow, at right angles to the axis of the boulder. Its straightness proves that it, too, is the work of human hands. The spiral incisions are undoubtedly the traces of a pneumatic drill or of the spike used to bore a hole for the dynamite (unless the boulder was detached from the bedrock by mechanical means). The man turns around. On the level top of the rocky slope on the other side of the road, he discovers a vertical cleft which might well correspond to the groove in the saddle-shaped hollow, all the more so since two different strata can be clearly distinguished in the steep cleft: an upper, darker one and a lower, lighter, more friable one. A rocky massif traversed by deep wrinkles, clefts, and crevasses extends to the jagged summits on the horizon. Some twenty meters below the boulder where the man is sitting, there are reddish and rust-red spots of lichen which in places become as white as if the steep cliffs had been splattered with whitewash or with bird droppings. Near the boulder on which he sits, tufted wormwood leaves, dusty and slightly withered, protrude from deep cracks along the road. The man smells their aroma, which rises up along with the heat reflected by the hot stones. The pale-green leaves of the few bushes scattered roundabout contrast sharply with the light-gray stone and the whitewash-like spots of lichen. On the distant gray slope extending to the horizon, a white road is discernible, descending in ribbons cut out of the rock. The road grows narrower at every hairpin bend; no wider than a goatherd's path as it approaches the green belt, it traces in its twistings a capital M, resembling the three prominent lines in the palm of a hand. Along the curving, broken line dividing land and sea, there are deep fjords and bays, with jagged mountain peaks between them. The sun, perfectly round and red, barely touches the highest peak. The long shadows of the mountains transform the blue of the sea into dark green and draw a clear line between the blue and the green, as between two colors that do not mix, or at least not as readily and completely as the blue of the sky and the blue of the water on the distant horizon.

Schematic clusters of houses, white walls and red roofs, appear amid the greenery on the broken line where earth and sky meet. To the left, a little beyond the bunched houses, at the foot of a tall chimney from which a black thread of smoke rises vertically, the reflection of the setting sun gleams fiery-red on the glass front of a factory. At the end of the short jetty, there is a stone lighthouse. A light sparkles at the top of it. The man cannot tell whether the sparkling is the reflection of the sun or the light of an acetylene lamp. There are bollards on both sides of the jetty. The man is sitting on one of them, not far from the middle of the pier, his face turned toward the sea. A single boat is tied up at the pier, a fishing cutter with one mast. There's no one on board. A rope lies coiled like a snake on the platform at the bow end of the deck. This platform is made of boards that were once painted green; the paint now is faded and caked, or maybe it is just riddled with hairline cracks like old canvas. The hull of the boat is also of boards; these are curved like the staves of a big barrel. The outside is painted black and the spaces between boards are caulked with shiny black tar that blisters like coagulated blood. The gunwales are made of thicker planks; these too, as well as the bow, are painted green; the bow end of the keel is reinforced with a metal plate. Along the sides of the boat hang two worn-out automobile tires, completely smooth, without a trace of zigzagging grooves or bulges, but showing letters on the side, the brand name, no doubt. Between the tire on one side of the boat and the stone jetty a curved line of green water is discernible. The bow of the boat is turned toward the sea, at some distance from the jetty. The sea around the boat is dead calm, dark green, and transparent; thus, the hull, the slanting rudder, and the little propeller shaped like a figure eight are clearly visible. Deeper down one sees the shadow of the boat, shimmering with dots of sunlight reflected from a dead fish, a broken mirror, an empty shell, or a tin can.

Suddenly the shadow of the boat begins to tremble, disintegrate, and disappear. The reflections die away, the green surface of the sea sparkles and undulates. The water can be heard sloshing against the jetty, and against the sides of the boat; the rope twined around the bollard scrapes. The boats in the harbor bump together gently. A boat approaches the pier in a narrow curve. Its soft chugging is heard only after the engine has stopped, for imperceptibly the sound has invaded the silence. The stirred-up water reveals green velvet seaweed and black shells on the stone wall of the jetty. The seaweed and the garbage that have been floating almost motionlessly begin suddenly to move, tossing this way and that: a melon rind, a tomato, a half-eaten apple, bloated cigarette butts, a dead fish, crusts of bread, a dead rat, a box of matches, a squeezed half lemon, a rotted branch, a pinecone, a toothpick, a few wisps of straw, fish scales, a rotten orange, a green beer bottle, a piece of wood, a torn blue envelope, a gnawed wooden penholder, a bunch of bird feathers, a corncob, a cork, a battered straw hat, a punched railroad ticket, a pencil with no lead in it, scraps of newspaper, a sheet of quadrille paper, the letters on which are dissolving, a tin can, a walnut, a pail that once had green paint in it, the stub of a money order, the yellowish-green label from a beer bottle, a cracked lamp chimney, a chess

piece (a white pawn with only its head above water); a
king of diamonds, dog-eared and creased down the
middle but still in one piece, his two symmetrical faces
clearly distinguishable; a picture postcard showing in
the foreground the blue sea and the jetty with lighthouse, alongside the jetty a fishing cutter tied to a stone
bollard, while another boat approaches, cutting through
the water in a gentle arc; in the background, behind
green palms, little white houses with red roofs; in the
far distance, high mountains with a narrow road twining
around them; and, overhead, a blue sky with two or
three pink clouds in it. Somewhere near the middle of
the jetty, a man is sitting on a bollard. The man is
slightly stooped. He is wearing a straw hat tilted back,
and between his knees he is holding a cane, or possibly
a fishing rod. Ten meters away from him, there is a
woman with a five- or six-year-old boy and a little girl
who is somewhat older. All are looking toward the
horizon, at the sunset, no doubt. They are in the center
of a curve, in the place where the road widens into a
kind of observation terrace. A little farther on, at the
foot of a wall built from crudely cut stone blocks, a car
has stopped. Its black paint is covered with a thick layer
of dust. Its square windows are lowered and its doors
are wide open. The red glow of the sunset is reflected
in the large round headlights. Steam pours from the
nickel-plated hood over the honeycomb radiator. The
whole front part of the car trembles in the heat, which
is as visible to the eye as the heat above a red-hot stove.
The wide mudguards make one think of a hansom cab.
Wavy grooves or bulges are barely distinguishable on the
smooth tires; dusty letters can be made out on the sides:

the brand name. A man in a checked cap and big rubber goggles, his arms folded over his chest, is leaning on one mudguard. He is turned toward the persons whom he has driven to that place, the man sitting on the stone ten meters below the bend and the group leaning on the wall not far from him. Then he, too, looks toward the horizon, at the sunset, no doubt. The woman also looks toward the man who is sitting on the stone a little farther down. But he doesn't seem to notice the others. He is looking into the distance, at the sunset, no doubt.

Now he is looking toward the bend. Steps and the crunching of gravel are heard from that direction. Soon a donkey appears, loaded with brushwood. Head bent and ears dangling, the beast plods down the slope. The load of brushwood, roped to an invisible packsaddle, hangs over the donkey's dusty flanks. The knotty branches show fresh oblique notches. The blade of a square-handled sickle sticks out of the brushwood. A sloshing of liquid—wine, milk, or water—is heard from the soft brown wineskins at the bottom of the donkey's load. Two or three steps behind the donkey, a woman in a faded black dress and an equally faded headscarf is bowed under a load no smaller than the donkey's. The man follows them with his eyes until they vanish around the sharp bend. A little later, he sees them again on the next bend, some twenty meters farther down. Then they vanish for a time, only to reappear on the next bend. The sloshing of the wineskin and the crunching of the gravel under their feet can no longer be heard. The man gets up from the stone, climbs the steep road with the help of his cane, and sits down beside the chauffeur.

NOTES OF A MADMAN (I)

[8]

It is hard to lift up your own misfortune. To be at once the viewer and the viewed. To be both above and below. The one below is a spot, a shadow . . . To consider your own person in the light of eternity (read: in the light of death). To rise into the air. The world from a bird's-eye view.

The idea of my flying machine is as old as mankind. It is simply an elaboration on Icarus' invention. I, too, got my idea from watching birds. You don't even need the strength of an oarsman. I am no oarsman myself, nor can I boast of exceptional strength. My biceps are hardly bigger than a woman's. Try to visualize the scene. Dressed for the occasion, wearing a bow tie with polka dots, I slip my arms through the straps and fly away like a pigeon. I let myself fall like a stone from the tenth floor, catch myself with a single flap of the wings, and rise above the crowds in a high arc. I abandon myself to the whims of the air currents and land in a meadow not far from my native village (*Natio borgo selvaggio*, wild native hole in the ground). Then I fold up my wings, put them in my briefcase, and enter my village unnoticed, anonymous if you like.

Seen through your eyes, even if you are on the terrace of a skyscraper, I look first like a crane, then like a swallow, then like a bat, then like a butterfly (or a bow tie), then like a bumblebee, then like a bee, then like a fly, and lastly like a flyspeck. I have vanished from your field of vision, vanished completely. I have flown up to heaven, my dear sir. Yes, to the heaven of pure abstraction.

[9]

If a man endowed with a dog's hearing were to put his ear to the ground at the right moment, he would hear a soft, barely audible gurgling, as when water is poured from one pitcher to another or when sand sifts through an hourglass, that's what he might hear, that's what you're likely to hear if you lay your head on the ground, press your ear to the earth, and let your thoughts bore into the depths of the earth, through geological strata to the Mesozoic and Paleozoic, through layers of sand and dense clay, boring like the roots of some giant tree through layers of mud and rock, through layers of quartz and gypsum, layers of snails and empty shells, layers of peat and fish bones and fish scales, through the bones of turtles and starfish, of sea horses and sea monsters, through layers of amber and fine sand, layers of seaweed and humus, dense layers of algae and nacreous shells, dense deposits of lime, layers of coal, layers of salt and lignite, tin and copper, layers of human skeletons and animal skeletons, layers of skulls and shoulder blades, layers of silver and gold, layers of zinc and pyrites, because somewhere down there, at a depth of a few hundred meters, lies the corpse of the Pannonian Sea, not quite dead yet, just smothered, crushed beneath ever-new layers of earth and rock, clay and muck, animal corpses and human corpses, corpses of human beings and human works, just immobilized, that's all, for it is still breathing, has been for thousands of years, through the stalks of waving wheat fields, through swamp reeds, through the roots of potatoes, not entirely dead, just crushed by the Mesozoic and Paleozoic strata, yes indeed, it has been breathing now for several hours, several minutes (in terms of earth time), breathing heavily, asthmatically, like a miner wedged in by beams and struts and great blocks of sweating coal. If you lay your head on the earth, if you glue your ear to the moist clay, especially on these quiet nights, you'll hear its breathing, its long death rattle.

[*10*]

If everything happens in accordance with the strict determinist laws of God-nature, in accordance with the general principle of causality, then, objectively speaking, there is no such thing as accident, either on a universal plane or even in the most trifling chance event, as for example when someone leaves (forgets?) his book on the train, in a first-class compartment (as though Divine Providence had put it there, or as though it had flown from some unknown, faraway place, like an angel with wings half unfolded, landing on a green plush seat in a first-class car, seat no. 26 to be exact, the window seat reserved for him at the station in the provincial town of Šid), and someone else (by predestination?) sits down in the same place and there finds a book bound in black leather (*Tractatus theologico-politicus*), which will exert a deep and lasting influence on that second person.

[11]

Proposition

For undisturbed mental effort, total solitude is essential; otherwise, the mind will succumb to the dangerous influence of another mind, sometimes without even being aware of it.

Demonstration

If my wife had not been sleeping in the next room, it is certain that the thought of *Montenegrin villages* would not have come to me, but some other comparison, for in my draft there was not so much as a mention of Montenegrin or any other villages, because at that time (when I wrote the draft) my mind was not yet under the influence of hers but (as follows from the foregoing) of some other emanation. Q.E.D.

Corollary

Perfect solitude is unattainable, because to achieve it would be to achieve perfection, which is nothing other than pure idea, or God.

[12]

On the one hand, the black market can bring large profits (at great risk, it goes without saying), but on the other hand, it involves great danger of contagion. The sale of dead or diseased animals; mass poisoning from spoiled meat (recently in the newspapers). A certain kind of worm, an intestinal parasite transmitted from

pork to the human organism: sausage made from wild
boar; not wormy sausage but worm sausage.

[*13*]

Spices probably perform a prophylactic and disinfec-
tant function. They have certain mimetic qualities, which
enable them to exert an exceptional effect on the
olfactory organs of sensitive purchasers of spoiled sausages. As a result of military operations and naval
blockades, etc., spices gradually acquire the value and
price of precious metals, or, rather, they recover the
value and price they had in the Middle Ages, their
faded aureole of rarity.

WERTHEIM & CO. safe. Bank draft, check, owner's
signature, verification, stamp. Well oiled, the heavy door
opens without a sound. The smell of spices pours in
waves from the safe. This no doubt is because of their
specific weight. Invisible particles of pepper hover in
midair: sneezing and coughing; bank draft canceled,
bags of cloves and cinnamon. At your service, sir. One
last look to make sure the leather pouch is secure.
Armed escort and armored car outside the emergency
exit. When the door of the armored car opens, the
captive fragrance of far continents is set free. The soul
of Columbus, of Vasco da Gama.

[*14*]

Repair the roof, replace the beams, the rafters; put
in new gutter tiles; replace the rotten window frames
and widen the windows; scrape the mortar and the

crumbling mold; replaster and whitewash the whole
place; dig a pit a meter or a meter and a half deep
(depending on the depth to which the clay has absorbed
the horse's urine); fill in the hole with earth, cover it
with planks; make the room a meter or two larger, that
is, move the wall dividing it from the shed; clean out
the storeroom and put it to some use; throw out all
useless junk—old bicycles, boxes, trunks, harnesses, etc.,
and oh yes, this too, her geraniums: into the garbage
with them.

[*15*]

When you come right down to it, milk is food.
Mother's milk, for instance. Mammals' milk. Jesus
sucked the teat of a cow. Or a ewe. Or a she-camel.
Instead of the lily-white breast of the Virgin Mary. Mary
is a mammal, too. Her breasts, too, once secreted white
milky juice. For Jehovah in His wisdom gave a thought
to children, to the young of man and beast. Let there
be glands, and there were glands. Let milk flow, and
the milk flowed through the pimply little mouth of the
breast. Mouth-to-mouth resuscitation. A kind of field
ration, enriched by a special process, with all the ingredients necessary to the organism (thus facilitating transportation and alleviating the problem of nutrition). Fat,
protein, carbohydrates, enzymes, vitamins, in short,
everything that the guests at the Paschal (Lucullan)
banquet introduced into their organism, in solid state
and without limit. All those things are contained in
milk, in the form of tiny, microscopic particles. Maddened cows came running and, before you knew it,

devoured everything that was on the table, the roast suckling pig, the chicken, the ham, the cakes, the fruit, the nuts, everything, but without any particular order or etiquette, or, rather, in accordance with some bovine etiquette; right after the cakes they slurped the chicken soup, and last of all, for dessert, they gobbled up the batiste tablecloth, soaked in grease, wine, and sherbet. Then the factory in their bowels converted, crushed, cooked, fermented, refined, filtered, pasteurized, marinated, churned all that, filtered it again, and finally mixed it with caseine, albumen, and lactose. The whole preparation ended up in the cows' udders and then in tin mugs in the hands of my children, three times in a row, as in some fairy tale.

CRIMINAL INVESTIGATION (I)

[16]

Did E.S. postdate his letter?

After the name of his village he wrote the next day's date. His justification was that, according to his Longines watch, only sixteen minutes were left of the day, and consequently not only the anticipated end but even the beginning of the letter would fall on the following day. And it's true that this whole letter, begun at the end of one day, related to the next day, the following dawn, the daybreak to come.

Had he ever postdated a document before?

During the school year 1905–6, he postdated a doctor's certificate, thus extending his vacation by approximately a week; in 1912, he postdated a free second-class ticket on the Kameral Moravice–Zagreb express, extending its validity by almost four months; in 1924, he repeated this exploit, having (apparently) learned no lesson from his previous fine (of 1912), which he had apparently forgotten, and again postdated a train ticket, on this occasion first-class, reduced-fare ticket no. 755363, with a view to traveling free of charge on the Vrbovsko–Novi Sad and Novi Sad–Budapest (via Subotica) line, prolonging its validity by ten days in all, that is, from the first to the eleventh of November; in 1932, he once again postdated a document, medical certificate no. 2249, declaring him provisionally capable of taking care of himself, on condition that he submit every six months to a thorough medical examination— this document was postdated by a whole year (from

1932 to 1933); in 1934, he postdated several documents
relating to the Subotica Brush Factory, of which he was
part owner and a stockholder, etc.

Was he prosecuted for any of these offenses?

Twice. In 1912 (Kameral Moravice–Zagreb), he was
fined ten crowns; in 1934 (Brush Factory), he lost his
lawsuit against Mr. Weiss, his partner, who was unable
to prove that E.S. had falsified documents yet convinced
the jury of his guilt; there were numerous other proofs
that he had been negligent in his work.

Did E.S. preserve among his papers any evidence of
his offenses?

Among his papers, in a file labeled *Railroad Documents*,
he preserved the decision of the chief inspector of the
Royal Hungarian Railways (Magyar Királyi Államvasútak), dated 1912, registration number 1042, whereas he
destroyed all documents relating to the Weiss affair.

Cite the complete text of the decision in question.

Mr. E.S., clerk in the traffic section at Kameral Moravice (care of the station office). It has been established
that on February 23 of this year you traveled on the
Kameral Moravice–Zagreb line, making use of a free
second-class ticket on express no. 1091, issued on November 4 of last year under serial number 95463. You
tried to conceal the invalidity of your ticket by changing
the date from the 4th to the 24th. For this offense I
fine you ten crowns, deductible in two installments from
your pay. At the same time I warn you against conduct
unbefitting a future civil servant. Traffic Inspector I.
Šušnjić.

Did he show this judgment to anyone?

He showed it two years ago to Mr. Gavanski as an

indication of the conscientiousness then prevailing in the administration of the railroads (in contrast to the present day), and also by way of boasting that he had been a real "rascal" in his youth, prepared for any "rascality," however dangerous.

Whom did E.S. invoke at the beginning of his letter?

His youngest sister, Olga.

Did he have other brothers and sisters?

Four sisters (not counting Olga) and one brother; in other words, he had five sisters (including Olga) and one brother.

To whom else, apart from her, could he have written a letter of this kind?

Without expecting a much better result, he could have appealed to his old and, in a manner of speaking only, friend Mr. Gavanski (8 Station Street, Novi Sad), to his brother Dolfi-Adalbert (11 Via Lazzaretto Vecchio, Trieste), to President Roosevelt, Prime Minister Churchill, Chancellor Adolf Hitler, Admiral Horthy, the Transportation Minister, the Minister of Justice, the International Red Cross, the League of Nations, the Society for the Defense of the Rights of Man, the International Zionist Organization, the Society for the Prevention of Cruelty to Animals, to God the Father Zebaoth.

Why, then, did he not appeal to any of these persons or institutions?

To Gavanski, because he did not wish to compromise him in case the police monitored his correspondence; nor to his brother Dolfi, because of their strained relations and the international situation; to the others, because he had no confidence in any of them except the last, with whom he was in constant communication anyway.

How would you characterize the relationship between the sender and the addressee of the letter?

As one of indebtedness, because the former sender, now addressee, had written a short letter some days before to the sender, or former addressee.

What was that letter about?

About atmospheric conditions (cold, snow), health (influenza, cough, rheumatism, headache, nervousness, constipation); about medicines and medicinal herbs (aspirin, sage, camomile, boric-acid compresses, camphorated oil); the rising price of oil and coal (from 240 to 320, from 350 to 380); about the poor condition of the roads (covered with snow); about men's winter clothing, especially a gray suit; about blankets; about lemons (now unobtainable); about ham; about Hanukkah nuts; about the all-seeing and all-powerful God; about socks; about forest fires; about potash.

What was not mentioned in this letter that he would have liked to hear about?

A certain pair of men's shoes and a certain shaving brush.

[*17*]

What did his own frozen fingers make him think of?

Of Mr. Hordós the butcher's short, pudgy, bloodstained fingers.

What was E.S. afraid of?

He was afraid Mr. Hordós might mistake his bloodstained fingers for sausages, cut off one of them, and wrap it up along with the sausages. After that, he stopped buying blood sausages.

What did the undecided customer see?

He saw Mr. Hordós take a piece of pork off the hook, put his sausage-like finger through a slit in the meat, lay a big chunk on the palm of his hand, and pat it; saw the meat slip down over the sides of the basin, twisting like an eel.

What was the undecided customer thinking at the time?

That he mustn't let the look on his face, or any gesture or word, show that he had only five pengö and twenty-eight fillér in his pocket, for fear the butcher might serve him scraps or spoiled meat.

Did he notice any indications that might have led him to conclude that Mr. Hordós the butcher saw through him all the same?

Yes. He watched the butcher, faced with his indecision, take a big pan from under the counter, tilt it, then return it to a level position so as to show the undecided customer a break in the aspic, revealing whitish cartilage and a bit of hairy skin (an ear?).

When did E.S. realize that Mr. Hordós had definitely seen through him?

At the moment when he began to take offal from under the counter: brick-red liver that looked like fermented, coagulated blood, a long, slippery spleen, a foamy, rubbery chunk of lung, lacy, fibrous tripe, two kidneys that looked like twin fetuses, a heart horribly wounded by the butcher's knife.

How did E.S. mentally translate the unspoken question that appeared for a moment in Mr. Hordós's eyes?

You don't really eat pork, do you, sir?

And how did E.S. answer, also with his eyes?

Yes, sir, if it hasn't gone bad.

What image came to rest on the yellow spot of his memory?

His own fingers fiddling with the brass lock of his briefcase, trying to open it.

What sensation?

The sensation, on the palm of his hand, of a quantity of meat wrapped in newspaper; the smell of meat mixed with the smell of newsprint; and a quick but clear look at the layout of the pages.

What does E.S. try to do?

He tries to remember the movement he made in putting the meat into his briefcase. He makes the movement with obsessive obstinacy, analyzing for the hundredth time (in his memory) each of his movements, mentally gauging the weight of each piece of meat.

Did he have any proof that he really had put the meat into his briefcase that day at the butcher's?

There is (was) an irrefutable corpus delicti, a piece of bloody newspaper and a sliver of heart weighing a gram or two.

How did E.S. try to shake off the images that burst in on his memory and the remorse they provoked?

By a lyrical leap forward; he wanted, in remembering, to skip from the butcher's shop to the café and from the café to the village, but in this he was only partly successful, because a spot remained in his memory, in his consciousness, as when an image falls on the blind spot of the retina.

Exactly what question did he ask himself and find no answer to?

Can an image escape from the memory in the same

way that by a deliberate twist of the eyeball one can make an image fall on the blind spot of the retina?

What effect was produced by deliberately turning the eyeball of the mind?

Thoughts, images, sounds were deformed and dispersed, but that nightmarish memory was watched over by the fair-haired angel of dreams, an angel with red cheeks, a big bosom, and hands red and swollen from washing glasses. (Ah, proprietress's hands, fateful hands!)

Did he see the dogs?

No, but he was able to judge by the sound of their barking and the barely discernible shadows on the white snow that he had probably strayed into a dog sabbath, a ghoulish canine carnival, a cannibalistic canine feast, the ritual victim of which was to be himself, E.S., and no one else.

What else did he hear?

The howling of the storm, which modulated, deformed, muffled the sound of the dogs' barking, mingling its howl with theirs, harmonizing its howl with theirs.

How did E.S. see himself?

Through the eyes of a dog, as through a biconvex lens or a curved mirror; the tip of his cane is elongated in perspective as far as the head-sized fist at the other end of the cane. In the same distorted perspective, the head-sized fist tapers into a long thin arm, which at shoulder level is thinner than the cane. Following this long, deformed arm from below, the eye perceives a tiny head, no larger than a fist.

What else does he see through the eyes of a dog?

In the foreground, galoshes with grooved soles and a faded black briefcase containing, invisibly present, a little more than a kilo of pork, a slice of leg (70 grams), chops (200 grams), lard (200 grams), offal (250 grams), all wrapped in invisible newspaper.

How did man and dogs perceive one another?

They by smell, hearing, and sight; he by hearing alone.

What thought did fear inspire in him?

The thought not only of possible mimicry but also of identification; that, by changing the prescription of his glasses, he could become a dog.

What did his well-known instinct for promotion make him think of?

It is within your power to become at will a dog, a cat, a horse, or a bird. Buy E.S.-brand magic glasses. You will be able to see the world through the eyes of the animal of your choice.

What advertisement did he mentally formulate?

Would you like to see your faithful watchdog or your pet cat as they see you, through their eyes? Would you like to go hunting with the eyes of a dog? Or see the public at the races through the eyes of a horse? Become a horse, a dog, or a cat for only ten pengö. The wings of a bird you cannot buy, but you can see the world through an eagle's eye, thanks to the most recent optical, psychological, biological, ophthalmological research. E.S. Optics supplies its illustrated catalogue free of charge.

What did the dogs do?

No longer satisfied with the pieces of meat he threw as far away as possible into the snow (a lure to drive them off), and conscious of their numerical and tactical superiority, they flung themselves on the raw meat, aware no doubt of something else as well (his own secret thought); namely, that their enemy was drunk and dazed, and that, in spite of his theoretical and tactical experience, he was in no condition to fight for long in that Siberian temperature.

What did E.S. do then?

He kept pulling out meat along with newspaper, grabbing big chunks of bloody, frozen meat at random, tearing it with his nails and teeth and throwing it far away, trying with this flimsy, transparent trick to shake off his pursuers.

What did E.S. hear and sense?

The dogs flinging themselves on the chunks of meat, yelping and growling nervously, with heads upraised and hair bristling as though on the hunt, pursuing the fragrant meat that came flying through the air, describing an invisible but perfect arc in obedience to the laws of Euclidian physics but also to those of Marić's crazy son-in-law,* and also to the wind, the storm, and the devil himself; and that the dogs followed this fragrant, bloody trajectory by their sense of smell, heads upraised, the hair on their backs and necks bristling, all turned in the same direction but guided by his (E.S.'s) hand, by the swing of his arm, which was the beginning of everything.

How did the ballistic trajectory of the hurled meat end?

The bloody piece of meat, torn apart by his hands,

* Albert Einstein, whose first wife was Mileva Marić of Novi Sad. [Trans.]

his nails, his teeth, did not complete its trajectory, but was suddenly intercepted a meter or two above the ground, where the starved, frantic dogs ripped it violently and prematurely with their fangs.

What did the dogs do when they caught on to this pathetic human tactic (*divide ut regnes*)?

They organized; prompted no doubt by the law of their remote ancestors, the German shepherds (in whom the memory was still fresh) guided the monstrous horde in a new strategy. While some stayed near E.S., besieging the fortress, sparing only the territory within reach of his cane and obliging him to fling chunks of meat more and more quickly, the rest of the pack, now well organized, followed the trajectory of the hurled pieces and caught them adroitly, avoiding internecine clashes and the earlier confusion.

Conscious of his defeat, what did E.S. do?

He fell on his knees, heard the panting of the dogs and smelled the breath of the dogs—like the taste of raw meat in his mouth.

How did he see himself (metaphorically, so to speak)?

He grabbed his liver and the eagle-dogs tore it to pieces; he plucked out his twin kidneys, and the dogs gobbled them up; he nibbled little pieces of his heart and spat them far from him, and his paternal heart fell a prey to the hungry dogs.

How, in his bed the next day, did he try to interpret his nightmare?

The chase was the sexual act (the medium being Madame Clara, the proprietress of the café). The gaping jaws as well as the briefcase were the bleeding uterus that we long for, that we long to return to, to curl up in again like a fetus; but they were also the woman's bleeding womb, the vagina, the *vulva vulgaris,* vulture, volute, vortex, volcano, void, etc.

How did he account for the presence of dogs in his dream?

Undoubtedly, the dogs came from the pages of *Selection* magazine, which he was reading that night before going to sleep.

What further explanation did he have of the symbolism of his dream?

The snow is the placenta, the heart the uterus, the liver the clitoris, the kidneys the testicles; the bile is the sperm, the chops are the Oedipus complex; the fangs of the dogs are sexual aggression; their tail is the penis, the briefcase the vagina, vulva, etc. Thus, everything in this dream—the heart, the liver, the chops, the kidneys: the fetus—follows from the utero-vaginal briefcase.

How did he try to convince himself of the correctness of his interpretation?

He reached out to the chair beside his bed (where his torn, wet suit was hanging) and took out a copy of *Selection.* It was open to page 36, where there was an article entitled "The Effect of War on Dogs," translated from the London *World Review.*

Quote said article in toto.

"At the very beginning of the War it became evident in England that dogs were taking the offensive on all fronts and massacring one another. In any case, the animal clinics noted an increasing number of dog fights. In September 1941, for example, the London Centre for Animal Care listed 198 cases of wounded dogs, and in October, 410 cases. Mr. Gowent, a technical expert at that institution, has an explanation for this phenomenon. Dogs, he tells us, are extremely sensitive to the moods of their masters. If you are nervous, your dog will be nervous. Reading about air raids makes you angry, and when your dog goes out into the street, he attacks your neighbor's dog or your neighbor himself. He does not know why, he has no 'war aims,' so to speak. His master is angry and nervous, and that's enough for him, because dogs identify with their masters. Another factor is that, because of the blackouts or because their masters are absent for one reason or another, many dogs are deprived of proper care and exercise. The main reason why some dogs have become aggressive or even bloodthirsty, however, is that they have been infected by their masters' war psychosis. If your dog is with you when you read about air raids or about the unsatisfactory outcome of military operations, and if you are overcome with rage at the enemy, your rage infects your dog and puts him in a warlike mood. All preconceived notions to the contrary, a dog is no less sensitive than a human being, no less bloodthirsty."

What thought was suggested by a second reading of this article?

The thought that Freud, in writing his dream book, did not take sufficient account of bedtime reading.

Seized with doubt, what did he do a moment later?

He threw off his comforter and left his bed with a resolute step in spite of his hangover and headache.

What did he find on the kitchen table next to the wooden chest?

His briefcase, whose brass lock was not closed. Holding the flap open with his chin, he felt inside, then suddenly withdrew his hand as if he had cut or burned himself.

What was he holding between his fingers?

A piece of bloody newspaper.

Turning abruptly to his wife, what did he ask her?

Whether she had taken any meat out of the briefcase.

Did he expect her to answer?

No, because her horrified look told him the whole story.

What did he tell her, finally?

That meat had been wrapped in the newspaper, a piece of which he was holding: a kilo of pork (slightly more), a piece of leg, some chops, some lard, and about two hundred grams of offal.

After pouncing again on his briefcase, sniffing it and feeling inside, what did he finally take out?

Between his fingers he held a tiny sliver of pig's heart with the imprint of his teeth in the raw meat: corpus delicti.

Doubting his senses, what did E.S. do then?

He rushed back into the bedroom, glanced at his copy of *Selection*, and on page 36 found an article entitled "The Effect of War on Dogs," which began as follows: "At the very beginning of the War it became evident in England that dogs were taking the offensive on all fronts, etc., etc."

[*18*]

How were the travelers seated in the sleigh?

The letter writer's wife and children were in the back seat; the letter writer, the leader of the exodus, the captain of the ship, the exile, was in front, next to the coachman.

What did the travelers have to keep them warm?

Those in the back seat had two blankets, a light cotton one, and a heavier, goat's-hair one; those in front had wrapped their legs in goat's-hair blankets.

What did the blankets smell of?

Horses and urine.

What did E.S., the captain, and the chief helmsman, Martin by name, talk about?

The weather, the Eastern front, the impressive success of the Hungarian regiments in the most recent operations, breeds of horses, hot peppers, goulash, peach brandy, the shortage of certain indispensable articles, such as gas, butter, tallow candles, razor blades, shoes, etc.

What remark did E.S. make?

He remarked that a large hooked nose is not necessarily a Jewish characteristic, that there are numerous striking exceptions.

What was helmsman Martin's reaction to this remark?

One of suspicion, incredulity, and irritation.

What evidence did the helmsman adduce in support of his belief that the Jews had murdered the Saviour?

The snow-covered crucified Saviour by the roadside, with sky-blue eyes, his bloody palms covered with a salve of frozen snowflakes, and a crown of thorns that looked like a forlorn and empty nest; the crucified Saviour on the outskirts of the village, frozen, and forgotten by all.

On what points were the captain (and Saviour killer) and the helmsman (killer of the Saviour killer) in total agreement?

On garlic as an effective means of warming the blood and regulating the circulation, the high cost of living, and the shortage of certain indispensable articles. Above all, they were agreed that peach brandy warms the blood, improves the digestion, rejuvenates, clears the head, refreshes, inspires, and gives off the finest aroma in this world.

When they had drained the captain's screw-top flask and the helmsman's brandy bottle (with the corncob stopper), what did they do to keep warm?

Within sight of the harbor, their destination, they stopped at Madame Clara's café in Baksa and ordered five deciliters of apricot brandy, for which, as custom and good breeding dictated, the captain paid.

What was the last thing the travelers saw before parting company with the coachman?

The roselike anus of the trotting horse dropping dark-green turds into the snow.

Why didn't the travelers ride all the way to their destination?

Because E.S. could not come to terms with the coachman. The coachman asked to be paid for the return trip, arguing that, because it was late and the horses were tired, he would not be able to get back to Lenti that day. This struck E.S. as extortion, because there had been no mention of it at the start.

What does justice want?

Justice wants to follow its truth to the end; the letter writer's thoughts therefore return to the place where he parted company with the coachman, where he caught the coachman's attention at the last moment, when already the coachman was tugging at the reins and raising his whip, while he himself stood frozen, as though turned to stone.

What did E.S. say to the coachman?

He lowered his briefcase, which he had been pressing to his chest until then, and, without a word, pointed, in the vicinity of his mediastinum, to the Star of David, clearly visible in the wintry darkness.

NOTES OF A MADMAN (II)

[*19*]

Sholet at the New York Restaurant in Budapest (1924, 1925, 1930, etc.); oysters at the Imperial Hotel in Trieste (1921?); sturgeon and pike in Fiume (several times in the year 1931); fish soup at the Fisherman in Novi Sad; Wiener schnitzel at the Silver Lion in Subotica; shish kebab in Skoplje (1935); smoked lamb with beets in Cetinje (1939); steak tartare in the Old City of Zagreb; roast pork and gravy in the dining car of the Orient Express (1921); paella valenciana in Trieste (1931). All this washed down generously with *žilavka*, burgundy, and Traminac.

[*20*]

Paella valenciana, that Spanish, Moorish, Jewish mélange of flora and fauna, was served to me in a flat, round casserole, and as I plied my spoon, it occurred to me that they had dragged this casserole along the sand at the bottom of the sea, thus catching all these blessings, all this flora and fauna, as in a huge net or, better still, a wooden sieve of the sort used for panning gold. In the white, well-washed rice there were a few grains of sand, a few little pebbles, left there, no doubt, to make it seem more natural (unless the grains were sea salt, for they melted on the tongue), but also algae, lichen, and spices, bay leaf, saffron, capers, and marjoram; but also flatfish and sardines, small crabs and shellfish (cockles and mussels and prawns); but also lobsters, cuttlefish, morays, and squid; but also chicken wing, hare's leg, and shoulder of veal. All this buried in rice as though in sea sand, covered over with risotto, and it was only when I dug into this rice and the red mustache of a crayfish, a chicken wing, the crunchy spotted claw of a lobster, the open shell of a mussel, the striped shell of a sea snail, the bottom shell of an oyster came to light that I realized: this was not a meal in the usual sense of the word, it was something mythical, food for the gods, not prepared in the kitchen like other dishes, but culled from the sea in that copper pan, fished up at random, along with seawater and salt and sand and little pebbles; undoubtedly, that pan was dragged through the depths of the sea, then along the shore and upon the shore, plunged into the water over and over again, then dragged through the bushes on the shore, through the dense shrubbery of the green banks—which accounts for the three bay leaves peering out of the pilaf, for the black olive, for the saffron and the marjoram, for the thin slice of lemon on the edge of the pan, shining like the small Mediterranean sun that lights up some distant mythical landscape.

[21]

Treatise on the Potato. The time has come when we must think about ourselves from the standpoint of life and death, not as self-seeking individuals, but as representatives of our entire race, that divine weed scattered over all the continents of the earth, just like the lowly potato (*Solanum tuberosum*), whose origins, like our own, reach back to the dark depths of history and the earth, but whose existence will not, like ours, be called into question as long as the earth endures and there are hungry mouths to feed. This humble potato, *Kartoffel*, *pomme de terre*, this bread of the poor which, slightly disguised, mashed, with gravy, moistened with milk, cream, or meat sauce, also graces the tables of the rich, this vulgar potato, this earthly-heavenly manna, this subterranean growth, this earthly tumor, this hard hernia, this lumpy tuber, has never in all its long history attained the perfect roundness of the apple or the tomato (*Paradiesapfel*, that other heavenly fruit), but has remained imperfect and asymmetrical like man, covered with knots and bumps, bulges and excrescences, holes and cracks, without kernel, center, or anything else that might bear witness to the presence of the Creator and His wisdom. It has thus become a perfect symbol of the earth and of earth-made man, all flesh and skin, without heart or essence, a regular *homunculus* (*homo-homulus-humus*), just like a man, a man without a soul, a man from whom God has been banished.

Do you remember, sister, how, when we peeled sprouted potatoes in the pantry, we found those little potato-men with tiny heads and atrophied, misshapen limbs, little homunculi that we played with as if with dolls, until their heads fell off, until they shriveled and withered like old people?

And today, you see, when I ask for a potato, I can't help thinking about the amazing resemblance between potato and man, and, at the same time, begging your pardon, between potato and Jew. Our origins, as I've said before, go back to the same dark history. But why, gentlemen, is the potato longer-lived than we? Is it

because we are, because man is, more perfect? I don't
believe so. Speaking of us, I am convinced that the
potato is longer-lived and more perfect than we, than
you, and that it will survive us; that it will survive the
great cataclysm. When the dove returns with the olive
branch in its beak, when the ark touches dry land again,
its keel will dig up a potato plant from the ravaged,
exhausted, flooded earth of some new Ararat. And, if
only because of my fondness for images and flights of
fancy, I am beginning to believe in earnest that the
potato (*Kartoffel, pomme de terre*) is the only thing on
earth—may God forgive me—that was not created by
the will of God and the hand of the Creator, but is the
work of some insane, sterile-fertile shaman, the fruit of
some sterile alchemy (of which Paracelsus does not take
sufficient account in his *De generatione rerum naturalium*).
This may explain its youth and hardiness. It is only five
hundred years old, it was not brought to Europe until
the sixteenth century, and then only as a decorative
shrub. And do you know to what country? To Spain,
gentlemen. This, I believe, speaks for itself with regard
to my apt comparison between the Jew and the potato,
for it was undoubtedly in Spain, where the *Ewige Jude*
was selected for further wanderings, that there occurred
the fateful meeting between man and potato, between
the hooked Sephardic nose and the imperfect bumpy
tuber; whence they went out into the world together,
and one day toward the end of the eighteenth century
landed—the potato, that is—on the table of the French
kings, from there spreading over the entire earth and,
through cross-breeding and under the influence of
divergent climates and soils, acquiring the most varied

forms and appellations, such as mealy, quarantine, alate, Irish, sweet, and finally, as the highest mark of quality, *magnum bonum*, white.

[22]

The pig is the least fastidious of animals. This was undoubtedly known to Mohammed as well as the Jewish prophet-hygienists. One day young Mohammed saw a pig eating something truly disgusting, ripping up a cadaver or eating a rotten potato that looked like a human turd. Mohammed, who had just filled his belly with roast pork, then remembered that what he had eaten was pig meat, and began to vomit. He stuck his finger down his throat as drunkards do and vomited into the sand by the seashore. Then he hurried home, picked up the book of laws which he was writing at the time and which he would later call the Koran, and added the words: Don't eat pork, for it will make you vomit. The same with kashruth: some fanatical prophet ate spoiled meat and converted his personal mishap into a sacred ordinance, a law, a divine commandment. In the last analysis, the history of religions (prohibitions, taboos, kashruth, etc.) is the product of individual experience. *De gustibus*: this brand of aestheticized democracy is not recognized by fanatics. They vaunt their own experience as the only possible and acceptable, canonical experience. The same with the prohibition of alcohol. A saint got drunk one day and threw up. He began to talk nonsense and his tongue got hopelessly twisted when he tried to proclaim the prophesies that came to him from on high. By order of the council of sages, he forswore liquor. But the faithful went right on drinking, because beasts are beasts. The saint foamed at the mouth, and the foam ran down his saintly beard. So he retired to his hut and dreamed that God commanded him to carry the following message to mankind: Wine is sin. Pour it into the sea, and throw the drunkards into the waves along with the wine barrels. So be it. Fortunately, no prophet remembered the taste of mother's milk. If they had . . .

[23]

I am inclined to believe that Newton owed his discovery of the law of gravity to shit. One evening, as the first stars were coming out, he squatted down in the grass under an apple tree, secure from indiscreet eyes, for the darkness was dense enough to hide him, the stars were not bright enough to highlight him, and the moon was still behind the horizon. In that moment of silence, when the first frogs begin to croak and lazy bowels respond to the lyrical emotion aroused by the beauty of nature and of God's creation—because the sympathetic nervous system conveys intellectual impulses to the intestines and influences the metabolism—in that seat of all the emotions, Newton sensed the oncoming of his discovery, so simple yet fundamental for the future of science. Still squatting under the apple tree and looking up at the stars (he saw no apples in the darkness, the tree was studded with stars and the apples had been picked two days before under his own supervision, so there was no danger of his being hit by an apple while he was squatting under this new tree of knowledge; if there had been, he wouldn't have squatted under it but would have found a safer place), Newton felt the shit slithering easily and effortlessly out of his agitated intestines despite his chronic constipation brought on by long hours poring over books. And along with his joy at the discovery that suddenly flared up in his mind—namely, that the attraction of the earth gives all falling bodies, including shit, an acceleration of 9.832 m/sec^2, decreasing in proportion to the square of the distance between the body and the center of the earth— and his awareness, brought on by a further emptying of his bowels, of the far-reaching significance of said discovery, he experienced a humiliating realization; to wit, that he owed his discovery of this law, so vital and far-reaching for the history of humankind, to the free fall of his own shit as he was squatting one evening under an apple tree . . . That realization undoubtedly made him blush for shame and led him to wonder whether it was advisable to divulge this essentially humiliating discovery, in which the devil surely had a hand, to mankind. But then, still squatting under the apple tree of knowledge, now once more constipated, Newton thought up his great historical lie and substituted an apple for his shit, so that mankind would never learn the whole truth. He shifted responsibility for his discovery, for the apple was already well known, thanks to its role in the Garden of Eden and its mythological past dating to the Judgment of Paris—of which Newton was also well aware. Since then, apples have fallen in accordance with Newton's new law, while shit has plopped in profoundest anonymity, outside the law, as it were, as though unaffected by the laws of gravity and the acceleration of 9.832 m/sec^2.

[24]

Oh, the painful labor of the hyperactive uterus, spawning its eggs like a sturgeon month after month for forty years, prepared at all times for new birth, ready month after month to embrace the seed of death, to nurture and cradle it.

[25]

I admit it: my heart menstruates. The late, painful menstruation of my Jewishness . . . The man you see before you, esteemed ladies and gentlemen, this quinquagenarian in a gray suit, with steel-rimmed glasses, a cane, and a yellow star (which, however, you do not see because he is hiding it behind his briefcase), well, this man menstruates. That's right. Yes, your honors, my heart menstruates. A biological deviation, a manifestation of the Jewish, feminine principle. An item for the sensationalist press: gray-haired gentleman afflicted with menstrual pains! The most interesting part of it is that he is physically in perfect health (apart from a slight cold), nothing wrong with his glands or his hormonal functions. Male menstruation? No. Feminine principle carried to its ultimate consequence. Menstruation of the heart. Seed of death. *Weltschmerz.*

[26]

If you write about your bleeding heart or if your heart menstruates, your ink is bound to turn red, and not because of the angle at which the light of the oil lamp falls on your manuscript. It would be a childish, poetic extravagance to emphasize this fact by pricking your fingertip with your steel pen, as when a nurse takes a blood sample.

[27]

Strange as it may sound, the man who has written you this letter (madame) is pregnant. Analysis of his urine makes this clear. And equally clear that he is a male. That's all. Since you say he is your brother, advise him to make ready. He is pregnant, madame. The seed of death is in him. My sympathies, dear madame.

[28]

Pannonian Winter's Tale. Outside, white feathers were falling, as though big, fat Pannonian geese were being plucked in the sky. And all the people began to gather them in large burlap sacks: the Jewish shopkeepers and their wives, the shopkeepers' assistants and their sisters, the children of the Jewish shopkeepers and the children of the shopkeepers' assistants. For in their dreams that night Jehovah had whispered in their ears that white feathers would fall from heaven and that no one but they, the elect, would know it. Then, when their sacks were full, they suddenly saw the finest down falling from heaven, descending in dense, light flakes, but they had nothing to put it in, for all their sacks were full, and so were all their feather beds, all their pillowcases, all their pots and tubs, all their hats and caps. Greedy for this gift from heaven, they took the advice of a wise old man, threw out all they had gathered up until then,

and began with greater zeal than ever to collect the
down, which they took for manna from heaven, because
the price of goose down had risen that winter by one silver piece a measure. In the morning, when they had
locked up their treasure in their barns and were preparing at last to rest, some of them went to look at the down
and make sure by the light of day that it hadn't all been a
dream. The sacks and feather beds, the pillowcases, pots
and tubs, the hats and caps were all full of wet, icy snow.
In a rage they went looking for the wise old man to pun-
ish him, to stone him, but the old man had vanished into
thin air. Then the boldest and most pious among the
people looked heavenward and heard the voice of God:
Let this be a lesson to you. Don't ask more of heaven than
it can give you. And let me tell you this: The first fall
really was feathers, and you threw them to the winds.
Run after them and you'll find them . . .

[29]

The brain of Dr. Freud, the surgeon.* A chunk of
frozen, gelatinous pulp, perfectly intact, looking like a
lamb's brain served whole (at the Danubius Restaurant
in Vienna, 1930). The snow, trampled all about by
heavy soldier's boots, seemed only slightly melted
around the brain, whose convolutions, comparable to
those of a walnut, and network of fine capillaries were
clearly visible. The brain lay in the snow at the corner

* A well-known surgeon in Novi Sad, murdered by Hungarian Fascists in January 1942. In this massacre, mentioned several
times in the present book, thousands of Jews and Serbs living in
Hungarian-occupied Vojvodina were killed. [Trans.]

of Miletić Street and Greek School Street, and I heard
someone say to whom, that is, to whose skull, it had
belonged. So this was the brain of Dr. Freud, the
surgeon: a small snowy island between paths trampled
into the snow, an intelligence torn from its cranial husk
as a mollusc is torn from its emerald shell, a trembling,
throbbing mass, lying in the snow as in a refrigerator.
But (seeing as I knew whom it belonged to) it was
nothing like the brain of an idiot in a glass container;
it was the brain of a genius, preserved and protected in
nature's incubator, so that inside (the incubator), freed
from its corporeal shackles, a dark pearl might develop,
the pearl of thought at last materialized, crystallized.

[*30*]

My cigarette has burned down to my fingernails, from
it has fallen a worm of grayish-white ash, resembling
(a) toothpaste squeezed from the tube, (b) a hazel catkin
that has begun to rot, (c) the charred fossil of a worm.
The backbone of my cigarette suddenly snapped at the
frontier of sleep, at the frontier between movement and
breath, and it is not quite certain whether the porous
little column of ash broke up, disintegrated into *dust
and ashes*, at the moment when I wrenched myself out
of my lethargy, my tired brooding, or whether it was
the other way around; namely, that I wrenched myself
out of my lethargic half sleep with its mad whirl of
thoughts, images, and intimations at the very moment
when the porous column of cigarette ash fell with a
barely audible sound, as of (d) pigeon shit falling on
the thin membrane of quadrille paper lying on the table

before me. In that moment I was seized with a violent feeling of transience, as though this little column of ash (still recognizable as a *column*, though already crushed and splintered, the broken backbone of time), as though this ruined column of time represented transience itself, a painful and only too eloquent symbol of transience, comparable to what a man dimly feels when the minute hand of the clock (the big electric clock at the railroad station in Subotica, Novi Sad, Trieste, or Budapest) advances, for this occurs not gradually and imperceptibly but abruptly, with a dull, thudding blow, and the metal hand trembles awhile under the sudden shock, it, too, wrenched out of drowsy timelessness, as though it had remembered its duty at the very last moment, or had been admonished, awakened, wrenched out of its tranquil existence by some superclock, some king of clocks, some stern and incorruptible alarm clock, an alarm-clock God, Chronos-Jehovah, who with his rhythmic heartbeat awakens all lesser clocks, calls them to order, and prevents time from standing still.

[*31*]

Prolegomena to All History. The sweaty, unwashed, ragged mass of the urban poor: emboldened mob, warming themselves by the idea of divine and human justice; heartrending scenes of mothers with starving children in their arms, asking for bread; faith in God, in goodness, in justice, in heaven; cries of despair, of vengeance; rabble-rousers and provocateurs climbing up on improvised rostrums; weeping children who understand nothing; the terrible clamor of history.

But what is going on meanwhile on the other side, *extra muros?*

The cries of the starving mob travel through barely moving curtains of red velvet embroidered with gold, through windows and screens as through blotting paper, as though rising almost inaudibly from the bottom of the sea; the flickering of the candles in the vast golden candelabra, the reflection of the candles in the Venetian mirror, in the open door of a cupboard, or in the gleaming surface of some piece of furniture. Only the dog and the pages, the horses and servants hear the voice of the mob clearly; to them, the pages and servants, it even sounds like the voice of their own kith and kin, like a reproach or a threat . . .

And behold, the Queen rises white-armed from the foam of her fragrant pillows, wide-eyed with wonderment, for she has never heard such an uproar. Just a little shaken, she dresses with the help of her ladies, covers her eyes with a black, transparent veil, dons a black hunting cap, for she is in mourning, God knows for what or for whom, unless it's a mere caprice of fashion—the mob doesn't know, the mob cannot know. And there she stands in the brilliance of her raiment, "as mighty as a regiment under arms," with queenly rings on her snow-white hands, with eyes as blue as the lake in the castle park, holding a fan in her slender fingers. On the fan, as if in a mirror, is depicted a scene in which the Queen stands on her balcony waving her left hand at her adored and adoring people, holding a fan in her right hand, and on the other side (is it the back or the front?), on the side that cannot be seen and with which she hides her divine and queenly bosom, on the side of the fan that is unfolded like (a) a deck of tarot cards (*tarots de Marseille*) or (b) the tail of an exotic bird or of the peacock in her garden, the poet has written a melancholy sonnet—

The bitch, she should have her teeth knocked out, cry the enraged rabble.

—and she raises her snow-white hand, a greeting to bestow upon her beloved people who (still) love her so. Suddenly the people fall silent and the voices of the rabble-rousers and demagogues rise from out of the sudden silence, demanding (not for themselves, but for the people) Bread and Justice. This is beyond the Queen's understanding, it's contrary to custom and protocol, and those are no longer cries of adoration and fealty, but of outlandish rebellion.

What do these people want, for heaven's sake?

Bread, madame.

Bread? Oh, Elvira, have they no bread to break?

No, madame.

Whereupon the Queen: *Why then, my dear Elvira, don't they eat cake? Ladies and gentlemen, why don't they eat cake?* At these words her bosom swells, her queenly bosom, to which she presses her closed fan, which suddenly opens, as resplendent and luxuriant as a peacock's tail, as though the Queen were about to play her trump card.

CRIMINAL INVESTIGATION (II)

Draft a newspaper story about the tragic fate of the letter writer had he turned down the shameful offer to have his wheat ground without authorization at the mill of a certain Rosenberg.

Mr. E.S., retired railroad inspector, and several members of his family were found dead yesterday at their home in Kerkabarabás. According to the police report and the evidence of the medical examiner, they had been dead for five days. Cause of death: cold and hunger. The victims—father (53), mother (40), two children (9 and 7)—died after a long agony two steps from the home of their wealthy relative, the widow of Ignác Boroska, a local businessman. In a statement to the police, Mrs. Boroska declared that the death of said family had come as no surprise to her, because he, the late E.S., that is, had not been in his right mind. In support of this contention, she cited the fact that the late E.S. had rejected the help they had offered him under extremely favorable conditions (*sic!*); that is, two hundredweight of wheat, priced at only forty pengö a hundredweight.

How would the report have read if the letter writer had accepted the shady offer to have his wheat ground without authorization by a certain Mr. Rosenberg, owner of a steam mill at Baksa?

As we learn from our correspondent, a group of Jewish businessmen have appeared before the special court in Subotica, charged with tax evasion, illicit business transactions, bribery, and war profiteering. The principal defendant, the retired railroad inspector E.S., has confessed that in connivance with, and under pressure from, Mr. Gyula Boroska, known as George, he bought wheat from the peasants at the miserly and usurious price of twenty pengö a hundredweight and entrusted this wheat to a Mr. Rosenberg, owner of a steam mill in Baksa, who ground it without authorization, so assuring the defendant of a considerable profit at the expense of our hardworking and long-suffering peasants.

What would the article have said about a certain Madame Rebecca?

Madame Maria, formerly Rebecca—the principal defendant's niece, whom he referred to as Marie Antoinette—declared in court that she did not consider herself responsible for the death of her relative and his family. Appearing in a black hat and a black veil and holding a fan, Madame Rebecca was able to convince neither the judge nor the jury that her grief was sincere.

[*33*]

What attracts attention in the part of the draft manuscript that is written in pencil?

The effect of the seismic tremors of the Lenti–Novi Sad express.

What do the photographs in the first-class compartment show?

1. Over his seat: a Pannonian landscape. A snow-covered plain as far as the eye can see. Black rectangular fields peering out from the snow. In the foreground,

in the lower right-hand corner, a bare, knotty tree full
of frozen black crows. On the left, outside the landscape
as it were, six or seven telegraph wires weighed down
with snow and linked by white pear-shaped insulators,
which are partly obscured by the wooden frame on the
left edge of the picture. This foreground (wires and
white porcelain insulators) is worn and blurred, the
objects in it are almost transparent, with the result that
the viewer disregarded it at first and concentrated his
gaze on the winter landscape in the background.

2. Across from the traveler sprawled in his plush seat:
a city panorama with a cathedral in the distance; in the
foreground, railroad tracks and a few shanties. In the
background a plain, and in the distance a well. On
the left, still in the background, a pit and something
that looks like a brickworks beside a wide, sluggish river
which cuts across the whole right-hand part of the
picture and empties into the lower left-hand corner,
under the frame.

3. To the left of the traveler's seat, the left rear: in
the foreground, the sea and a jetty with a lighthouse;
alongside the jetty, a boat moored to a stone bollard,
while on the other side an identical boat approaches
the jetty, cutting through the water in a gentle arc. In
the background, behind palms, there are houses, with
roofs of rounded tiles, and in the distance, high gray
mountains around which twines a narrow road; above
them, a luminous sky with two or three clouds in it.
Near the middle of the jetty, the back of a man sitting
on a bollard. He is slightly stooped and leaning forward.
He is wearing a straw hat, pushed back over his head,
and between his spread knees he is holding a stick,
probably a fishing rod.

4. To the left of the traveler's seat, the left front: again a city panorama with a cathedral. Possibly the same city and the same cathedral as directly across from him, but seen from a different angle. On the right of this picture, the cathedral with its lacelike rose window over the vaulted portal is clearly visible. The portal is wide open, a silhouette can be made out in its shadow. It is hard to say whether it is a man or a woman. The hands of the clock over the high Gothic portal point to 3, most likely 3 p.m. The streets are deserted. Apart from the silhouette in the shadow of the portal, there is only one person to be seen, probably a street sweeper, for the implement he is holding seems to be a shovel, with which he has just been clearing away the snow and shoveling it into the pile beside him. The sky is overcast and a black cloud hovers over the Gothic buildings clearly discernible in the background; their arched windows and doors are closed at the moment, and so are the shutters. On the square in the foreground, some pigeons can be seen pecking in the snow. They seem to sense no danger. Perhaps they realize that the dog limping along after a wagon loaded with furniture won't even bother to look at them. The wagon passes the closed portal of a Gothic building. Two men riding in it—one wearing a hat; the other, the driver no doubt, a fur cap. It is hard to say what sort of furniture the wagon is carrying. Only curved surfaces are discernible. Whatever it is is tied with rope but not covered. At the moment, the wagon is near a statue, the horses' heads are hidden by its body, just behind which they turn left in the direction of the cathedral. The monument is seen obliquely. On the marble pedestal stands a man who is striding forward vigorously with his right leg, while the

weight of his body rests on his left leg. His right hand is upraised in a dramatic gesture, one finger pointing at the church steeple or the sky. He is wearing a caftan or a cloak or some sort of military overcoat. The cape thrown over the overcoat flutters in bronze folds, which accompany the fanlike motion of his arm. There is fresh snow on the man's shoulders and on the pedestal. Or else a pigeon, which in the picture might be confused with a lump of snow, has settled on a corner of the pedestal. On the other side of the square, blurred and in totally distorted perspective, advertising posters display the words ASTRA, ROYAL, фото; others are lost in the fog.

Turning back two weeks in time and two hundred kilometers in space from the point where the letter writer is at present, how does he see himself?

He sees himself with trembling hands gathering up his papers from the folding table at seat no. 26 by the window of the first-class carriage, stuffing them into his briefcase along with the bottled beer and smoked-herring sandwiches wrapped in quadrille paper, then in newspaper, put there by his sister Berta, and fiddling with the brass lock in an unsuccessful attempt to close it.

Who was standing beside him at that moment?

A young blond conductor, who was aiming his nickel-plated ticket punch like a revolver at the star on his chest.

Who, apart from himself and the conductor, watched him trying (and seeing himself trying) to close his briefcase?

A lady in black hat and veil (aged about thirty)

clutching a sleeping girl child as though some appalling bloodthirsty crime were about to be committed in this first-class compartment of an express train, the kind of thing that happens in novels; a young man with black pomaded hair (about twenty-five), a student or spy, who was trying from behind an illustrated magazine to catch a glimpse of white flesh under the black skirt of the lady in black; a thickset gentleman (about fifty), probably a black marketeer, with a watch on a gold chain, who at that moment was studying his gold watch patiently and at length, as though to appraise its value; an old lady (about sixty) holding a prayer book encrusted with mother-of-pearl; and a dozing officer (about thirty) with jangling spurs.

To which of the above-mentioned persons did E.S. pay the most attention?

To the widow with the white thighs.

How had she become a widow?

Her husband was killed somewhere on the Eastern front while trying to relieve himself.

What was the wording of the official report of her husband's death, as imagined by the letter writer?

You are hereby notified that your spouse, Reserve Captain First Class in the glorious First Hungarian Regiment of Hussars, has heroically laid down his life for the Fatherland in performance of his sacred duty.

How did she take this news?

She immediately consulted a fashion magazine and chose a black dress in the latest style (winter 1941–42), with broad shoulders, gathered waist, low neckline, medium (calf) length, a black petticoat trimmed with black lace and in all likelihood black panties edged with lace, a hat with hat pin, a black veil, and black elbow-length gloves.

What did the curious observer notice?

That the lady in black had applied a small amount of rouge to her pale face.

What provoked the glint in the eyes of the lady with the white thighs? Was it tears, was it grief?

The glint in her eyes was provoked by the prospect of an adventure, perhaps not ending in marriage with a rich man but leading at least to a series of affairs with young lovers, whom she would initiate into the arts of love free of charge, to their satisfaction and her own.

Whom did E.S. suspect of being the first possible lover of the lady in black, hence his first potential rival?

The young man with the pomaded hair, peering out from behind his illustrated magazine and evincing a keen interest in her (black) silk stockings.

What words was E.S., covertly reading in the young man's magazine, able to make out?

German ambassador Jagow with his wife and Okubo Tashitaka, the Japanese consul general, likewise with wife, were watching the parade · · · CLOSING AROUND THE TRAP WAS

What photograph did he see?

A white-bearded man in a fur hat and a military overcoat, holding out an icon to a beardless soldier (about thirty), who smiles happily under his helmet.

What did the icon represent?

The Blessed Virgin and the child Jesus, both with big halos.

What thoughts passed through his head as he was leaving the first-class compartment? (Syncopes.)

I'm awfully nervous. Scrumptious body of a female.
Élan vital. Alcohol, alcohol! Holland cheese and Holland
gin. Now this blockhead'll be free to goose the you-
know. Widow of the white thighs. I suspect she caught
the meaning of my bow. Wow, that smile. Lace, black
lace . . . Goodbye, goodbye forever, fair lady!

What did E.S. do before leaving the compartment?

He cast a quick glance through the window.

What did he see?

An endless snow-covered plain, black rectangular
fields peering out from the snow, and a bare, knotty
tree with frozen black crows in it.

What did he notice upon entering the second-class
compartment?

At first, smells.

What kind?

Dirty feet, wet poultry, military overcoats, damp
leather, damp cloth, soaked shoes, onions, tobacco,
intestinal vapors.

What kind of people did he see?

Soldiers, peasants, clerks, foresters, railroad workers,
shopkeepers, black marketeers.

What objects?

Uniforms, wooden trunks, wicker baskets, guns, bayonets (sheathed), army boots, puttees, straps, poultry,
cards, knives.

What colors?

Dirty gray, olive green, duck-shit green, screaming
red, dirty white, rust brown, steel gray.

What showed him that his arrival had not gone
unnoticed?

A peasant's curved knife stopping halfway between a

chunk of paprika bacon and the peasant's greasy mustache.

Who eyed him with extreme curiosity?

A goose whose long neck protruded from her basket and who, inclining her head now to one side, now to the other, gazed at him out of her red eyes.

What did E.S. gape at no sooner had he sat down?

An enormous plaster foot dangling from the wooden baggage rack some eight to ten centimeters from his nose. On it were inked: nymphs, female and male sex organs, swastikas and arrow crosses,* a heart pierced with an arrow, and below it the names of the owner's girlfriends.

List the names.

Marica, Anna, Fanika, Ursula, Dorottya, Roszika, Gretchen, Juliska, Pandora, Ilonka, Lili, Lulu, Hajnalka, Milena, Grazia, Melanija, Píroska, Margita, Katia, Anita, Lana, Helena, Romi, Ingrid, Cora, Bella, Erzsébet, Tatyana.

What did the traveler see as the train pulled into the station?

Guard post no. 2, a repair shop, piles of coal, a locomotive hangar with turntable, a water pump, a storage shed, administration buildings, the yellowish-gray station building, baskets of flowers, the station restaurant.

Was any locomotive taking on water while the train was pulling in?

No, but one must have done so a few minutes before, because water was still dripping from the nozzle, form-

* Emblem of the Hungarian Fascists. [Trans.]

ing a thin layer of ice on the straw that covered the
cast-iron casing of the pump.

What did this remind the traveler of?

It made him think, not without sadness, of the cruel,
gloomy winter and the unattainable remoteness of the
beautiful, blessed summertime.

In what verses did he express this?

> *Gloomy, madame, beyond measure.*
> *Is the present time of year.*

To whom were these lines addressed?

Undoubtedly to the widow of the white thighs, whose
sturdy white legs (encased in silk stockings) were at that
moment descending from the decrepit running board
of the first-class carriage, hardly a step away from him.

Who had come to meet the widow of the white thighs?

Contrary to E.S.'s malicious prediction, the widow
was met by an old lady, also in mourning. Squeezing
the child between them, the two women fell silently into
each other's arms.

Who had come to meet E.S.?

No one had been informed of his arrival.

Did he catch sight of a soldier with a plaster foot
among the passengers?

It seemed to him for a moment that a plaster foot
was hobbling along among the people hurrying toward
the exit.

Did our traveler stop at the station restaurant?

No, because, looking out of the train window, he had
seen cock feathers fluttering ominously on the black
hats of policemen, and the dull sheen of their mounted
bayonets. He therefore thought it wise to remove him-

self with all possible haste from the dangerous station area, where, in addition to the police, he caught sight of an armed and helmeted military patrol and of several civilians whom he easily recognized as secret agents.

What enabled him to recognize them?

His intuition and experience. Also their assumed air of innocence.

How were these agents dressed?

They were wearing long winter coats of mouse-gray gabardine, broad-brimmed hats, black earmuffs, and sturdy black shoes with double soles.

Did they ask for his papers?

At the station exit he had to stand in line with the other new arrivals and show the agents his papers.

Did they give him any trouble?

One of the agents looked at him, compared his face with the photograph on his identity card, and then returned it without a word.

Did the agent check his railroad pass?

No, though E.S. held it out, wanting to show how exalted a position he had occupied before being pensioned, and confident that the agent would be as much impressed as the trainmen had been.

If the agents had chanced to look into his briefcase, what would they have found?

Three smoked-herring sandwiches wrapped first in quadrille paper, then in greasy newspaper; four hard-boiled eggs, also wrapped in newspaper; an empty bottle of Ormai-brand beer; two Kaiser shirts, one white, one ocher; four celluloid collars; four Breiner pastel-colored ties, one black mohair tie with a Rapayić label; a sheet of quadrille paper (29.3 × 20.8 cm.), most of it covered with pencil writing; a greasy copy of the 1941 issue of *Selection* magazine, put out by the Bata publishing company; two pairs of gray socks, darned in several colors; a checked linen handkerchief, unused; an empty bottle with a patent cap; two soft packs of twenty-five Symphonia cigarettes; a faded pink bath towel rumpled and still damp; a pair of blue linen Tivar pajamas, size 39; a used cake of household soap in a celluloid holder; a brass razor; two Tabula Rasa-brand blades; a grubby shaving brush; a cork smelling of wine; a tin shirt button.

[*34*]

Once outside the station, where did the traveler go?

He rushed to the cab stand, for there were only two cabs left. The third, looking like a huge black gondola with its lighted side lamp, had just sailed off, carrying away from him, perhaps forever, hidden beneath its black leather roof, the widow of the white thighs, the Madonna of the Sleeping Cars, the Dark Lady of Shakespeare's sonnets, the source and object of his brief reveries, to whom he had inwardly addressed two or three lines of verse and to whom, at the moment when she climbed into her cab, he gallantly lifted his hat—a gesture which she failed to or pretended not to notice.

Where were the cabs standing?

To the left of the station exit, in a small square bordered on one side by a wall and on the other by an iron bar that supported the porters' hand trucks. In a square paved with neither macadam nor asphalt but with big slabs of stone, on which horses' hooves struck sparks and horses' urine splashed, foaming like beer, melting the freshly fallen snow, filling the cracks between slabs, and at length draining off into a gutter that led to a rectangular sewer opening.

What feelings were at war within him when his cab drove off?

Satisfaction, relief, anxiety.

Satisfaction?

Because in the cab he was again free to surrender to sweet dreams of another meeting with a female person, possibly the same lady. Also because cabs, like first-class compartments in trains, were his natural ambience, and he felt very much at home in this cab.

Relief?

Because the business with his papers had gone off without a hitch, which proved that his élan vital and intuition had not yet forsaken him.

Anxiety?

Because both his intuition and his experience told him that his next step might be the exact opposite of the last, since human life is governed by the principle of alternation—a crest is followed by a trough, success by failure, ascent by descent—yet man, despite his empirical knowledge, is still incapable of plotting the course of events, of computing the length of the wave, for, if he were, he would be able to forecast events down to the slightest detail.

What happened along the way?

Lulled by the clatter of the horses' hooves, he dozed off for a moment.

What did he dream?

He was swimming in deep water, in total darkness,

but throughout his dream he knew for sure that he was saved, like Noah, and that all those who had been with him only a short time before had been drowned, that he alone had survived the catastrophe. And in his dream this knowledge filled him with a vague pride, for he owed his salvation not only to God's mercy but also to his own merit, his ability to cope with the difficult situations of life.

When did he wake up?

At the moment when the timbers of his dream ship, his ark, shuddered as it struck dry land. But he was not able to look at the new continent, for the cab had turned onto the paving stones of German Street (now Bem Street).

How much did he tip the driver?

The driver asked for three pengö twenty filler, but E.S. rounded it out to four pengö, because he connected his miraculous rescue (in his dream) with his fortunate arrival (in reality) at his first destination.

What decision did he arrive at outside no. 21 Bem (formerly German) Street?

He suddenly changed his mind and told the driver to wait for him, saying he would be right back.

What made him change his mind in this way?

He probably decided against calling on his landlady (Mrs. Mészáros), because his train had been delayed and he realized that it was too late for a visit.

What had he wanted to do on German (Bem) Street?

His intention had been to pay his debts (two months' rent) and to persuade his landlady to keep his belongings until the day after tomorrow, when he would be moving out for good.

Did he nevertheless alight from the cab-ship?

After turning up his coat collar because of the wind, he let himself fall with all his weight on the squeaky running board, then went to the window of his former lodging. But since blue wrapping paper had been pasted over it on the inside, he was not able to see a thing, not even whether his belongings were still inside.

How long did he stay at the window?

A minute or two. Then he went quickly back to the cab and drove to 8 Station Street.

How did Mr. Gavanski receive him?

For a while, Mr. Gavanski watched him in silence through the peephole, as though unable to believe his eyes. Then, breathing asthmatically, he put on his dressing gown.

What did the unexpected guest and his host do then?

After cordially shaking hands and exchanging a few friendly words in the hallway, they hastened, at the guest's suggestion, to listen to the eight o'clock (Greenwich Time) news.

What did the guest think about while, warmed by a glass of Traminac, he developed his impressive Dutch defense? (1 Nf3 f5 2 g3 Nf6 etc.)

He recalled how (in 1937) he and his brother, on meeting after a separation of almost twenty years, had by the end of ten minutes exhausted every topic of conversation, how they had then sat silent for a long while and finally resorted to the chessboard.

What did the host complain of to the guest and the guest to the host?

The host complained of his daughter, who was planning to marry an adventurer, of his more and more painful gastritis, of pains in the back, asthma, increasing nearsightedness, toothache, insomnia (which he combated with liquor or, when none was available, with aspirin), of baldness, loss of virility, failing memory, claustrophobia, cancerophobia, gluttony, and an infantile craving for sweets. The guest observed that he shared most of the host's ailments (pains in the back, increasing nearsightedness, insomnia, which he found no way of relieving), and added the following: fear of the night, fear of the morrow, fear of persons in uniform, fear of old age and impotence, fear of dogs (cynophobia), fear of God, fear of death, and fear of the devil.

Did the guest conceal anything from the host?

In consideration of the host's well-known tolerance in matters of faith, he concealed the fact that he had been put out of the first-class compartment; he also neglected to mention his meeting in the train with a lady, probably a war widow, who had been sitting across from him until he was asked to leave the first-class compartment, a patch of whose firm white flesh he had managed to glimpse above her black silk stockings, to whom he had later addressed two or three lines of verse, and whom, when their paths crossed, he had greeted with an eloquent gesture, impossible to misinterpret: the lifting of his hat.

Did the host conceal anything from his guest?

He concealed the fact that, though bearing the typically Hungarian name of Fekete, the adventurer who was running after his daughter, a traveling salesman by profession, was actually the son of a certain Rachel.

What acquaintances had the two men in common?

Mr. Dragutin Floriani, court clerk, who in a game of simultaneous chess against nine opponents (in 1924) had beaten the celebrated Otto Titusz Bláthy of Budapest; Mr. Richárd Engel, merchant and sufferer from claustrophobia, who had thrown himself under the wheels of an express train in 1938, leaving behind a widow and two daughters; Mr. Tihomir Petrović, an official at the Finance Ministry, who in 1920 or thereabouts had returned from Paris with luxuriant black hair, claiming that a hormone treatment had restored not only his hair but his virility as well; Mr. Adrián Fehér, known as Fedya, whose intolerable headaches had led him to hang himself three years before; Dr. Maxim Freud, surgeon, who had been shot on January 24, 1942, and whose brain, blown out of his skull, had lain all day in the wet snow on the corner of Miletić Street and Greek School Street; one Sándor (surname unknown), who was able to drink three liters of red wine at one swallow; Mr. Jovan Gondja, gravedigger, who was murdered in the cemetery along with his child; Helmár Béla, the town knacker, with whom the two friends had taken a drink now and then at Weinhebbel's, near Catholic Gate, and who had recently sawed a woman in two before throwing her into the Danube; A. Ziegler, merchant, who had suffered a paralytic stroke; Mr. Béla Sternberg, railroad inspector, who in December 1941 had thrown himself under a freight train at the entrance to a tunnel, explaining in his farewell letter that he had been driven to this step by the "general chaos"; Mr. Miksa Kohn, wholesaler, who had been shot along with his family (wife and three children); Mr. Žarko Uzelac, baker, whose mustache and ears had been

cut off, but who had survived; Mr. Paja Schwarz, known
as Herz Schwarz, whose skull had been split with an ax
and who had then been shoved under the ice in the
Danube; Mrs. König, teacher, whom Hungarian soldiers
had first raped, then bayoneted; Mr. Scheinberger,
known as Sanyi, who in a fit of madness had shot himself
in the mouth with a hunting rifle; Mr. Djordje Stanković,
typographer, who had disappeared mysteriously a year
before, after going out to buy beer at Ziegler's grocery
store; Mr. Dezsö Guttmann, engineer, who had pulled
the emergency brake on the Novi Sad–Budapest express
three years before, on the pretext that the wind had
carried away his silk handkerchief, a treasured me-
mento; Mrs. Fischer, a widow, who from sheer terror
had contracted diabetes and acute insomnia; Mr. Anton
Buarov, tax collector, who for unknown reasons had
ended up in the insane asylum; Mr. Gyula Berecz,
notary, who had been married five times, four of them
to widows; Mr. Aladár Sichermann, clerk, who had
jumped into a well when they came to take him to his
wedding; Marko Kapamadžija, who had been killed in
his home along with six members of his family while
working on a homemade bomb; Mr. Žarko Blagotić,
physician, who had jumped out of the prison window
while awaiting trial; Mr. Josip Kostić, railroad worker,
who wrote decasyllabic verse about the impending destruction of the world; Mr. Adolf Singer, physician,
whose legs had been amputated in prison without
anesthetic; Mr. Márton Böszörményi, who had shot
himself in the head with a revolver; Mr. Arpád Kertel,
lawyer, who had jumped from a burning barge in a
convoy and drowned in the Begej; Mr. Bulat, engineer

and prestidigitator, who instead of showing a pass at
the entrance to the station had produced his third-
grade report card, the only document he had been able
to find after his home was ransacked, and who, thanks
to his psychological acumen, had managed on the
strength of this third-grade report to reach America,
and had notified his parents in Novi Sad of his arrival;
Mr. Dezsö Bálint, judge, who was growing breasts in
consequence of some hormonal disorder; Mr. Fülöp
Uhlmann, optician, who, supposing himself to be a mad
dog, had recently left his family and gone to live in an
abandoned kennel; Mr. Ádám Mándi, who had cut
open his abdomen with his saber in an attempt to
commit hara-kiri, but had failed and died of an infection; Mr. Ivan Popov, café owner, whose wife in a fit of
madness had served him an unplucked chicken, from
which she had removed only the eyes with a knitting
needle, and who had been so terrified that he had tried
to eat the chicken, feathers and all, and choked to death;
Mr. Dezsö Bleier, who had lost the power of speech
after witnessing certain events between 7 and 10 a.m.
on January 12, 1942; Mr. Marko Mudrinski, physio-
therapist, who had taken to injecting himself with drugs;
Miss Hollós, cashier, who had married a Jew for love
six months before; Mr. Vladeta Marković, geographer,
who was a bigamist, as had been discovered only recently, on the occasion of an identity check: one wife
lived in Bečej, the other in Subotica; the widow Horgós,
a baker, who had been married two months before (for
the third time) to a Hungarian sergeant; Mr. János
Kovács, who had bathed every year in the frozen Danube
after cutting a hole in the ice not far from the green

fence on the bathing beach and who had been killed only recently in an automobile accident; Mr. Karlo Štajner* from Zagreb, who in 1937 had disappeared without trace in the Soviet Union; Mr. Živan Pavkov, shoemaker, who had received a fabulous fortune from America three days after dying half-blind and in poverty; Mr. Andrija Laufer, functionary, who for love was converted to Mohammedanism; Mr. Márton Fuchs, who had died of a bee sting; Count M. L. Poltaratsky, with whom the two friends had played chemin-de-fer several times and who, as recently reported in the papers, had died peacefully in New York; Mr. Djordje Ivković, printer, for whom they had both worked in 1936, 1937, and 1938, and of whom nothing had been heard in the last two years; Mr. Jovan Šengili, furrier from Bečej, who treated asthma with herbal medicines; Dr. Komáromi from Budapest, who treated all ailments with acupuncture; Dr. Šafarik, who treated hernia and operated on prostate; Mr. Osip Nezmečić, scissors grinder, who had become a priest; Mr. Popović, grocer, who had triplets (two boys and a girl); Mr. Lujo Letringer, machinist, who had become a pilot and, just before the war, had dropped leaflets on his own house while performing dangerous loop-the-loops; Mr. Emil Tumpić, accountant, who, imagining himself to be a high-ranking German officer, had sewn stripes on his overcoat; Mr. Alexandar Vukčević, professor of history, who was suffering from tertiary syphilis; Mr. Arnold Wenzel, employee of the Danube Lloyd's Insurance Company, who in 1928 had married a Russian countess, but had

* Yugoslav revolutionary arrested in 1937 during the Stalinist purges, author of *Seven Thousand Days in Siberia*. [Trans.]

later brutalized her in public; Mr. Johann Krohn, headwaiter, who was a mathematical genius capable of raising multidigital figures to the tenth power in his head and who had ended up performing in a circus; Mr. David Baumann, who had come home from Canada in 1937, because of the deplorable climate in that country; Miss Darinka Mrazovac, waitress, whom both friends had courted somewhere around 1925, and who had recently eloped with an adventurer, leaving behind her four children and a sick (paralyzed) husband, a retired professor; Miss Julianna Farkas, clerk in an insurance company, from whom they had both caught gonorrhea in 1920; Miss Magdalena Ivanović, hairdresser, who in 1939 had suffered a miscarriage at the railroad workers' New Year's Ball; Miss Mariska Kenyeres, prostitute, born in Pécs, who had poisoned herself with caustic soda in 1922, two days after marrying a wealthy man; Mr. Moshe Altarac, who in 1934 had gone to America, where he became joint owner of a soda-water plant; Mr. Albert Einstein, Marić's son-in-law, who despite his eccentricity had become a famous scientist; Mr. Stanislav Simonović, switchman, who had been severely injured; Mr. Ilija Marinković, railroad inspector, who had come down with delirium tremens two years before; Mr. Márton Barabás, a former football coach, who had stopped stuttering when his son was born.

On what pretext did the guest decline the offer of dinner?

On the pretext that, like Nasr-Ed-Din's donkey, he was used to going hungry, but that hunger would not kill him as it had the donkey, because his organism harbored vast reserves of energy, which he occasionally supplemented with alcohol.

In what direction did this remark steer the conversation?

Toward lofty, heavenly things; the host marveled at the perfection of living beings, man in particular, all fashioned by the Creator according to some higher plan, and perfectly adapted to their environment and function.

What example of this perfection did he adduce?

The camel, whose stomach holds such enormous quantities of liquid that thirsty travelers in the desert have often slaughtered their camels and extracted several gallons of fresh cold water from their intricate stomachs.

Did the guest take this observation at face value?

Though agreeing in the main with his host's view that the Creator had devised living beings perfectly adapted to their environment and function, he firmly rejected his camel lore, citing an article in *Selection* to the effect that Dr. Alfred Brehm, in the course of his travels in Egypt, had caused the stomach of a camel to be opened but had found no trace of any drinkable liquid, although the camel had imbibed large quantities of fresh water the day before.

At the end of the six games they had just played, what was the score in the marathon chess tournament they had been carrying on for the last three years?

According to the guest, 85½ to 62½; according to the host, 85½ to 79½—both in the guest's favor.

How did the guest and the host back up their divergent contentions?

The host invoked the greasy notebook in which he recorded the results of all their games; the guest invoked his phenomenal memory.

What political topics did the two of them discuss in an undertone, over a bottle of Banat Riesling?

The economic power of the Soviet Union, with special reference to its heavy industry, electrification, rearmament, oil production, and transportation; the strategic importance of the Russian frontiers; the economic power and military potential of the United States; Japanese fanaticism, with special reference to Prince Konoe; Daladier and Gamelin; German military tactics; anti-Semitism and racism in the light of the most recent political events; the responsibility of Grassy and the Hungarian government for the Novi Sad massacre; the defeat of France, with special reference to the Maginot Line, and France's role in both world wars; the Soviet–Finnish peace treaty; the battle of Narvik; Chamberlain and Churchill; the Allied evacuation of Dunkirk; Franco–Italian relations in the light of the new situation; the Italian capitulation in Ethiopia; Antonescu and his government; the flight of the Yugoslavian government and king and the Yugoslavian gold reserves; the negotiations between the Polish government-in-exile and the Soviet government; the British armed forces in Libya; the Atlantic Pact; the invasion of Holland; the German–Italian invasion of Libya; the capitulation of Singapore; the landing of American troops in Northern Ireland; guerrilla warfare in Yugoslavia; the partisans and Chetniks;* the NDH;† Singapore and the British retreat.

What pessimistic remarks did the guest make?

He expressed the fear that, once Germany was de-

* Serbian royalists who fought against Tito's partisans. [Trans.]
† Independent Croatian State, a puppet state set up by the Germans and the Italians in 1941. [Trans.]

feated, the Soviet Union would make war on the United States; that the East would reject the democratic institutions of the West; that the German secret weapon would prolong the war by ten years; that the victor powers would again enslave and exploit the rest of the world; that human stupidity would remain unchanged; that there would never be an end to injustice and massacres; that after the war a rapid increase in the population would endanger the human race; that democracy would be threatened by new sects and parties; that religious and political fanaticism would claim new victims; that in the postwar world (surviving) members of his generation would be looked upon as relics of an antediluvian age.

What considerations did the host invoke in an attempt to refute the guest's eloquent and in part convincing arguments?

Progress, evolution, democracy, and humanism.

What authorities did they cite in support of their views?

The guest: Spinoza, Churchill, Fritz Sternberg, Bruce Bliven, Nostradamus, Einstein, Moses, King David, Ecclesiastes, the late Count M. L. Poltaratsky, Adolf Singer, Osip Nezmečić, and his own late mother, Regina. The host: the Apostles Paul, James, and John; Vladimir Ilyich, Churchill, Daladier, Dr. Slobodan Jovanović, King Peter I, Vasa Pelagić, Svetozar Miletić, his own late stepfather, his wife, and the reserve captain, first class, Mr. Marinković.

What recipes did the host and his guest exchange?

The guest gave the host a recipe for a mixture of sorrel and nettles with or without margarine, while the host informed the guest of a magic formula for making an alcoholic beverage out of potatoes and other available ingredients.

How did they do this?

The host read his recipe from his greasy notebook, while the guest again relied on his memory. In the course of this exchange, he remarked ironically that fat was not as unavailable to his host as he supposed, for he had only to put his copybook in the frying pan— this would yield enough fat for a whole meal and would present the additional advantage of burning his chess records, which were glaringly at variance with the truth.

How did the host react to this observation?

He offered to destroy the scores he had kept for the last three years and to start all over from scratch.

What medicinal pointers did the two men give each other?

The host recommended gentian (a small glass on an empty stomach) to stimulate circulation and appetite, and camomile tea to combat nausea and vomiting; the guest recommended boric-acid compresses for swollen legs and, as a specific for hardening of the arteries and high blood pressure, an infusion of hawthorn blossoms (*Crataegus monogyna*), garlic, horsetail (*Equisetum*), and mistletoe (*Viscum album*), one cupful morning and evening before meals.

At what time did the host and his guest separate?

At 3:20 a.m. (Central European Time).

Did the guest accept the host's invitation to stay the night?

When the host pointed out that the curfew had begun long before and would remain in force until 6 a.m., the guest gratefully accepted his invitation and lost no time in throwing himself down on the soft couch in the room fronting on the railroad line.

What lulled him to sleep?

Apart from the wine coursing through his veins, warming his blood and stimulating his brain, he was lulled by the howling of the wind, the ticking of the alarm clock in an adjacent room, the rumbling of train wheels, and the whistling of locomotives.

What prevented him from sleeping?

His ice-cold feet, which he tried to warm by rubbing one against the other.

Did he forget to say a prayer of thanks to Jehovah?

Before sleep overpowered him, he turned his face toward His Face and with parched lips muttered a few prayers.

What hindered him from giving God his full attention?

Realizing that he had forgotten to ask his host to leave a bottle of water on the bedside table, he feared that he would soon be tormented by thirst.

What did he not forget to do?

To wind his watch.

What did he forget to do?

To urinate again, for, by the time he went to bed, a good fifteen minutes had passed since his last urination; he had employed them in such trivial activities as brushing his teeth, looking for his glasses, undressing, putting on his pajamas, and so on.

Whither did the light wings of sleep carry him?

As though confusing the wings of sleep with the angel's wings (symbol of the railroad) which unfold at both ends of the axles and spread over the heavy iron wheels, and which were engraved on the lid of his watch, he suddenly found himself in an unidentified railroad station, which resembled those of Šid, Mala Krsna, Lenti, and Kameral Moravice, but was actually none of these.

What problem was on his mind?

The problem of how to empty his bladder.

What prevented him from doing so?

The crowd, unusually large for so small a station, mostly soldiers and gypsies, all besieging the toilet, the wobbly door of which he reached with great difficulty.

What then met his eye?

The outhouse was full of excrement, a stinking sludge that overflowed the funnel-shaped bowl and covered the whole concrete block. Thick fingers had daubed the flaking whitewashed walls with more excrement. Abandoning the project of emptying his bladder, E.S. started back through the sweating, stinking crowd.

What deterred him from relieving himself against the whitewashed fence behind the station?

A man, whose face he could not make out in the half darkness, but whose sparkling teeth he could see clearly; the man was laughing.

Had he ever seen this man before?

To judge by the sparkling white teeth and swarthy face, it was the man who had protested vigorously a moment before when someone had tried to make him pay for the use of the toilet.

While E.S.'s phantom self was standing there irresolutely, what had been happening inside the station?

Amid a muffled sound of flutes, cymbals, violins, and

drums, the crowd had first rushed into the station, then massed outside. To his own surprise, E.S. could not make out what was going on; at that moment a train pulled in as silently as a ghost.

What did the dreamer try to ascertain while watching the tumultuous crowd?

Where, when, and why? What station? What train? But to none of these questions did he find an answer. His agitation was noticed only by the swarthy man with the white teeth, who looked at him with a malicious smile.

What did the observed observer do then?

He went over to the crowd, who had formed a circle around a stretcher that had been put down in an open field behind the stone station building. On it lay a young soldier; his eyes were closed and he was deathly pale. The people were revolving around the lifeless body like pilgrims performing some ritual act.

What else did the dreamer notice?

He noticed that the cymbals and drums had fallen silent and all was deathly still.

What happened then?

Suddenly the young man moved and rose to his feet, then staggered as though about to fall. Cries of consternation went up from the crowd.

And then?

Four powerful men in long raincoats, their hats pulled down over their foreheads, went over to the young man and tried to lay him on the stretcher. They were unsuccessful, for, every time they approached, the young man managed to fling one of them into the grass and to keep going.

Whom did the resurrected one, staggering like a small child, approach?

The crowd made way for him and a moment later he was face to face with E.S.

What did the resurrected one say to E.S. in a dank, fetid voice?

He begged E.S. to do something about the degrading, pain-inflicting commerce in human bones; he personally, he said, had no objection to being killed, but was it not utterly inhuman to treat a man as they were treating him: to take out his bones, leaving his body as empty as an empty sack? To prove his point, he called attention to his gait, which was not only halting but phantomatic. That was what the thieves had done to him.

What else did the mutilated victim of the bone thieves confide to E.S.?

That his daytime temperature fluctuated dramatically between -56 and $+1,100$ Celsius (*sic!*), which gave his young body terrible pain, and for this reason he begged E.S. to intercede for him and his fellow sufferers and divulge to all the world the sad truth about the international organization of bone thieves.

What had happened in the meantime?

Plainclothesmen and bone-thieving doctors (wearing white smocks and armed with big syringes) had overpowered two newly wounded men, who had managed to get up off their stretchers, and tied them to the stretchers with ropes; now they were loading them into the train.

What valuable information did the first resurrected one provide?

He declared that if the bone thieves had overpowered those two, it was only because at that moment their temperature had fallen to -56 degrees Celsius, for if their temperature had been the same as his was then (namely, $+1,100$ degrees Celsius), the plainclothesmen and doctors would have been helpless, just as they were still unable to get the better of him, a state of affairs that unfortunately would not last long, for his temperature was now (toward evening) falling fast; in a few minutes it would attain its low point, -56, and he would then have to get back on his stretcher.

What did the young man finally do (before his temperature dropped)?

He kissed E.S. on the cheek, and E.S. heard someone in the crowd say that this was the kiss of death.

Who saved E.S. from trembling in a humiliating way?

A lady in black, who pushed the dying man away and, in lieu of explanation, embraced E.S. tenderly and passionately, pressing her hot lips to his, and inserted her hand into his fly, skillfully fingering the buttons and touching his hot, swollen member.

Who was quick to step in as a savior and consoler?

No longer the lady in black, but a young girl in a black school smock, who whispered obscenities while holding his burning member in her trembling fingers.

Why, despite his extreme excitement, did he not ejaculate?

Because the crowd was watching disapprovingly and making threatening gestures. He was therefore obliged to push the girl's hand away and go back to his compartment.

What did he do there?

He sank into the soft plush seat and began to read a pamphlet about whales.

Did he, when he awoke, remember any of the pamphlet he had read in his dream?

He was able to recite the last chapter almost word for word; the gist was that, though whales live in water, they often die of thirst; while looking for the mouths of rivers or for springs of sweet water, they run aground; their bodies shrink like deflated balloons and they die an agonizing death.

How did E.S. interpret the nightmarish part of his dream?

He attributed a certain exaggeration to the influence of alcohol (physiology), to the fatigue and agitation of the day (psychology), and to the unfamiliar bed (habit).

What dream did the host impart to his guest, wishing to requite the confidence he had shown the host in telling him the cetalogical part of his dream?

The host told the guest that he had been wading all night in shit up to his knees. This the guest interpreted as a good sign: increased pension, winning ticket in the national lottery, unexpected money order, inheritance, discovery of a well-filled purse or of a bit of money in the pocket of an old pair of trousers that had fallen behind a cupboard.

What proofs did he adduce in support of this contention?

He cited his own experience: in 1911, he had found a purse containing twenty-five crowns and no identification papers outside the Kameral Moravice railroad station; in 1925, he had won ten times the price of a ticket in the national lottery; in 1928, he had won

twenty-five dinars in the tombola at the railroad workers'
ball in Subotica; again in 1928, he had received a money
order for a hundred lire from his brother Dolfi in
Trieste; and each time he had had the same dream the
night before: he had dreamed of wading through shit
or of sinking into excrement and suffocating.

What did E.S. like about dreams?

Their similarity to life and their dissimilarity; their
salutary effect on body and soul; their unrestricted
choice and arrangement of themes and contents; their
bottomless depths and eerie heights; their eroticism;
their freedom; their openness to guidance by will and
suggestion (a perfumed handkerchief under one's pillow, soft music on the radio or gramophone, etc.); their
resemblance to death and their power to confer intimations of eternity; their resemblance to madness without the consequences of madness; their cruelty and
their gentleness; their power to pry the deepest secrets
out of us; their blissful silence, to which cries are not
unknown; their telepathic and spiritist faculty of communication with those dead or far away; their coded
language, which we manage to understand and translate; their ability to condense the mythical figures of
Icarus, Ahasuerus, Jonah, Noah, etc., into images; their
monochrome and polychrome quality; their resemblance to the womb and to the jaws of a shark; their
faculty of transforming unknown places, people, and
landscapes into known ones, and vice versa; their power
to diagnose certain ailments and traumas before it is
too late; the difficulty of determining how long they
last; the fact that they can be mistaken for reality; their
power to preserve images and distant memories; their

disrespect for chronology and the classical unities of time and action.

[*35*]

Why did the letter writer sum up his three-day trip to Novi Sad in two or three sentences?

He felt that certain episodes, such as his visits to Mr. Gavanski and Mrs. Fischer, were without bearing on the subsequent course of events, and that others, such as his visit to the railroad office and the priest, were too sensitive and dangerous to mention in a letter: he regarded the former as a professional secret, the latter as a religious secret.

What did E.S. ask of the priest (and vice versa)?

Secrecy.

Where and when in the past had E.S. spoken with members of the clergy?

In 1903, as a boy of fourteen, he had spoken for about twenty minutes with Rabbi Steinowitz in the school corridor after class, on the subject of biblical miracles; in 1905, he had had a short conversation with the same Steinowitz (in the same place) about the origin of the Hanukkah festival, about the Sabbath laws, and about certain mysteries of the flesh, concerning which the rabbi was either unable or unwilling to enlighten him; in 1912, on the train to Dombóvár, he had (without revealing his identity) discussed dogma with a young Franciscan, taking the position that one can question dogma, in particular the infallibility of the Pope, while continuing to believe in God; in 1929, he had proved to a Jesuit, again on a train, that *The Protocols of the Elders of Zion* were a forgery, a malevolent pastiche of a utopian tract published in Brussels in 1864, entitled *A Dialogue in Hell Between Machiavelli and Montesquieu* and written by one Maurice Joly, a utopian socialist; in 1939, in Cetinje, he and a certain Father Luka had discussed the origin of the common potato, which is known to have been imported to Montenegro from Russia, and the extraordinary skill with which the hands and other remains of saints, whose relics are to be found in monasteries, were embalmed, a skill that seems to be dying out, to judge by numerous bungled embalmings, in particular that of Vladimir Ilyich, characterized by the Viennese press as the work of butchers, tailors, and makeup artists; in 1940, he had conversed on the corner of Public School Street with Rabbi Blahm of Novi Sad, who advised him to give up drink, because a time was coming when he would have to look death soberly in the face, and also advised him to transfer his money as soon as possible to a Swiss bank and to entrust a reliable person with the account number.

What stylistic approach did he choose as the best way of ushering in the Miracle?

Restraint, detachment, and recourse to the tone and contents of common everyday life: on the eve of the Day of Judgment, nothing is heard but the clatter of tin spoons and forks, this idyllic petit-bourgeois clatter providing a counterpoint to the thundering trumpets of the Last Judgment; and on the day when chaos leaves no stone upon stone, the sturdy shapes of Biedermeier cupboards will turn out to have been an optical illusion.

What was left in the apartment after the exodus?

Two cupboards, and in the kitchen a wobbly table with an oilcloth covering scarred by knife cuts.

What was missing?

Two bedside tables with marble tops (sold); a double bed (sold); a bureau with mirror (sold); a kitchen cabinet (sold); four wooden chairs (sold); a wood stove (thrown on the dump); a cast-iron heating stove (sold to a junk dealer); a Singer sewing machine (entrusted to Mrs. Fischer for safekeeping); the frames of family photographs (thrown in the fire).

Describe the cupboards.

Two antique walnut cupboards with single doors, once highly polished, surmounted by a cornice (double arches) with stylized wooden roses centered around spiral-shaped ornaments resembling the scroll of a bass viol.

What was in them?

In one, there were two lumpy bare feather beds; in the other, nothing but old newspapers and a cardboard box full of family photographs.

What was shown in the photograph which, crouching beside the cupboard, he took from the cardboard box?

A young man of eighteen or twenty with short, parted hair, a large mouth, and a straight nose. The lapels of his long coat are lined with shiny black silk; a white celluloid collar makes his long neck look even longer than it is; he is wearing a white bow tie.

What was the subject of the photograph made aware of while contemplating his likeness?

Chancing to see his face in the mirror of the open cupboard, he was made aware of the ravages of time.

Look at the other photos and describe them.

A slender woman with a child in her arms. In the background, a misty view of a city: factory chimneys, a tower, a knotty tree trunk. On the back: *Gabriella e Lully. Trieste* (no date).

In the upper-right-hand corner, a watermark (the sheaf and crown of St. Stephen). E.S. wearing a tie and with hair parted. On the back: *Magyar Királyí Államvasútak. (König. ung. Staatseisenbahnen.* SZEMÉLYAZONOSSÁGI IGAZOLÓJEGY) IDENTITÄTSKARTE. *Vasúton vagy hajón való utazásnál a személyazonosság igazolásáralZum Nachweise der Identität bei Fahrten auf Eisenbahnen und Schiffen. KeltlDatum: Pécs 1920 ápr. 1. A tulajdonos névaláirásalUnterschrift des Inhabers: E.S.*

Three girls between sixteen and twenty, in order of size. The smallest (youngest?) is holding a modest bunch of wildflowers; there is a ribbon in her loose hair. The second (middle) one is wearing a blouse with a lace collar; a small medal hangs from her neck. The third has her hands behind her back. She is wearing a striped dress with a pleated collar and a necklace with many pendants; her hair is worn in bangs. On the back: *Cetinje VIII 1921.* Stamped: *S. Hendler, Wien, III Steingasse 9.*

Two children between three and five, in track suits and rubber boots, their arms around each other's neck, sitting on a light-colored bench.

E.S. wearing steel-framed glasses and a celluloid collar. On the back: *Received 600 (six hundred) dinars, which Hirschl . . . in the form . . .* (the rest illegible).

A little girl of two or three with a ribbon in her hair. She is resting her chin on her hand. Pleated dress. Looking up at the sky. On the back: *PostcardlCarte postale.*

A class picture: eleven boys and twelve girls with the teacher, and to the side another woman, most likely the caretaker or the cleaning woman.

E.S. with a beard, his hair parted on the side. On the back: *1919.*

Two girls and a boy behind a stunted bush. In the background, a white road descending in ribbons cut out of the rock. Along the curving, broken line dividing land and sea, there are deep fjords and bays with jagged mountain peaks between them. On the back: *16. VIII 1939*.

In the foreground, part of a hydrant. Two spindly oleander bushes in square wooden tubs. Beside one oleander stands a bandy-legged child who has apparently just learned to walk; he is crumbling a lump of earth between his fingers. A little girl with a ribbon in her hair is sitting on a low chair between the two bushes. In the background, the shabby back wall of a house, and a wooden door leading to a cellar or storeroom. On the back: *Foto Aleksić, Novi Sad, 1937*.

A long table with one end at the door, seen in foreshortened perspective. A festive dinner or wedding. The place at the head of the table is unoccupied, but a porcelain plate and a half-empty glass of red wine show that someone was there a short while ago. At the other end of the table sits a woman with a high bun, wearing a black dress. Two persons are seen in profile on either side of the table, on one side two women in black dresses, and facing them a man and another person, who cannot be seen clearly. All eyes are turned toward the door. Has the guest of honor at the banquet or wedding just gone off in that direction? Or are the diners looking at the camera? The young woman, who may be the bride, is also looking in that direction. Dark hair, earrings, celluloid comb in her bun. On the back: *Foto Aleksić*, etc.

The same young woman from the waist up. Long

white neck, large dark eyes, dark hair in a high bun, earrings like two drops of jade, celluloid comb. Right arm bent at the elbow. She is holding a white handkerchief or glove. On her fourth finger, two rings: a wedding band and another ring with a stone that looks like an ant. On the back: *Foto Vujović, Cetinje.*

E.S. The sharp point of a carpenter's pencil protrudes from the breast pocket of his coat. Bent over, he appears to be rummaging in some documents, old manuscripts, faded letters, or yellowed photographs. Behind him, two antique cupboards with spiral-shaped ornaments in the center. The rest of the room cannot be seen clearly.

Street snapshot. E.S. and another man the same age, both lifting their hats. In front of them, two boys and three girls. One of the girls is holding a doll, the other a bunch of lilacs. Some ten passersby appear in the picture. In the background, a monument seen in side view. On a marble pedestal, a man striding forward vigorously with his right leg. His right hand is raised in a dramatic gesture; he seems to be pointing at a tower that can be seen on the right edge of the picture. In the foreground, buildings with signs reading ASTRA, ROYAL, FOTO ALEKSIĆ, ФРИЗЕР, GARDEN CAFÉ, and an advertising poster showing a man lifting his hat. On the back: *Foto Aleksić, Novi Sad, 1939.*

What did E.S. do after picking up the photographs and putting them back in the box?

He went into the kitchen, pulled out the drawer of the kitchen table containing the cutlery, and packed it up with the feather beds. He did likewise with some pots and the stout legs of the cupboard, which looked like wooden tenpins.

What address did he write on the cupboards?

With the square carpenter's pencil he wrote the address of Mrs. Agnes Fischer (27 Vitéz Street, Novi Sad), and his own return address on the backs and sides of the cupboards.

What incident might have been interpreted as a hint from God, a first warning?

For some mysterious reason, the only fork that was not tin fell out of the cupboard; it fell on the concrete by the door, buzzed for a moment like a dragonfly, and then hummed like a tuning fork.

As he followed the movers out of the house, what did E.S. turn to look at?

The walls.

What did he see on them?

Squares of dust in the places formerly covered by the family photographs, a reproduction of the Mona Lisa cut out of a newspaper, and a color lithograph entitled *Das Stufenalter des Mannes*, given to him less than a year before by the late Móric; little splotches of liquid on the ceiling suggesting an explosion of antiaircraft shells; a grease spot on the wall where he had leaned his head while lying in bed; traces of green mildew; silhouette cutouts in places where the plaster gapped; designs traced by moisture.

What was he thinking about?

About the possibility of reading the future from spots on the wall, something like a Rorschach test; the patient in his room or cell looks at the spots on the wall and reads them in the presence of his doctors.

For example?

What do you see in that spot? The ocean. And what

else? A ship on the high seas . . . a toad . . . a black
butterfly . . . a vagina . . . the gaping jaws of a dog . . .
a vagina (I said that before). Continue. What do you
see in that spot, Mr. E.S.? A photo of my pelvis at the
moment of conception. Conception? What kind of conception? Intellectual. And what does your intellect con-
ceive? Death, sir.

As he turned around for the last time, when he had
already crossed the threshold and taken a first step,
what did he think he saw, though he could not have
sworn to it?

He thought he saw a gray rat running from one hole
to another in the place where one of the cupboards had
been standing a moment before.

What happened then?

First, a cloud of dust poured from an open window,
the one near the door; it was like the smoke from a
cannon that has just been fired. Then from the next.
Then, at regular intervals, from the other two windows.
A moment later, the unoccupied part of the house (the
part across from the hydrant), with the cellar or storeroom in it, was filled with smoke. And then the wave
of destruction engulfed the roof, carrying away tiles,
beams, and walls.

How long did that go on?

A few minutes or seconds.

What sounds were heard?

A shattering of glass, a smashing of bricks and tiles,
the cracking and bursting of beams as in a fire.

What obituary (newspaper report) did the miracu-
lously escaped E.S. think up as he stood gray with dust
and terror beside the hydrant at the edge of the ruins?

E.S., the founder of muromancy, the science of
reading the spots on walls (a process for which the term
zidomantija, "wall reading," or, perhaps more appropri-
ately, *židomantija*, "Mosaic reading," has been coined in
our Pannonian region), met his death on March 18 of
this year, beneath the ruins of the house in which he
had been cultivating that obscure branch of magic,
which he himself termed a science. The learned *Schwarz-
künstler* can be said to have fallen victim to his own
machinations. The house in Újvidék,* where he had
been living up until then, 21 Bem (formerly German)
Street, which was registered under the name of Mrs.
Mészáros, collapsed just as the author of the obscure
(manuscript) volume *Muromantische Schriften*, was engaged in transcribing certain spots on the wall, on the
basis of which he hoped to demonstrate, *schwarz auf
weiß*, the soundness of his theories. According to the
testimony of Mr. Hanifović, a porter living on the
Danube Embankment, E.S. had spoken at length to him
and his honest fellow worker, Mr. Pupavac, on the
significance of this "science," maintaining that his own
fate and that of his family were charted in those spots
as clearly as in the lines of his hand, "as irrevocably as
in the scroll of the holy Torah" (*sic!*). Both porters
denied the false reports to the effect that E.S. had
claimed to see the day and hour of his own impending
death in one of these "scrolls of the Torah." According
to Mr. Pupavac, porter, and witness to the mysterious
catastrophe, the "Father of Magic" had not said one
word about his own misfortune and was haggling with

* The Hungarian name for Novi Sad. [Trans.]

his porters over the price of moving his furniture when the house caved in.

What was the cause of this cave-in?

At first E.S. was inclined to believe in an earthquake, whose epicenter was far away, or a violent explosion in a munitions warehouse.

Did he come across any news item that might have confirmed this presumption?

Neither that day nor later was there any mention in the newspapers or on the radio of an earthquake in Central Europe or the Balkans; nor was there any news of an explosion in a munitions warehouse—which is understandable, for that would have been a military secret.

Why did he see no connection between the removal of the cupboards and the collapse of the house?

Because the cupboards were not in contact with the walls.

How, then, did E.S., always the positivist, account for the disaster?

He was convinced that a rat had destroyed the house; in the foundations, somewhere at the base of the walls, this rat had located the intersection of forces on which the whole house rested.

What was he not inclined to believe?

That chance had led it (the rat) to the spot.

What would he have liked to know?

Who had given the rat the order to gnaw through that intersection of forces? And why just then? At that particular hour of that particular day?

What else?

In what language was the order given?

Possible answer?

Hebrew.

Why was he not inclined to believe in chance?

Because he preferred to believe in the interdependence of things, in the deterministic laws of God-nature, in the principle of causality.

What did he believe?

He believed that there is no such thing as chance, either on a universal scale or in lesser matters, as for example when someone follows the movers out of his lodgings and turns around to take a last look at the place that has been his home for two years, to embrace it in an all-embracing glance (a nostalgic glance, it must be said, for it was rooted in an awareness of the transience implicit in changes, an awareness of transience and death; yes, nostalgic in spite of the unpleasant experience exuded by the damp walls of those rooms that he was leaving forever, in spite of the treacherous blotches of liquid on the ceiling against which he shattered glasses in moments of rage and despair)—when, in short, someone leaves his lodgings for the last time with a nostalgic glance, and at that moment the house is shaken to its foundations, apparently under the weight of his glance, under the weight of all the misfortunes (his and those of others) that have been condensing in those rooms for years, sustaining the fragile emptiness of those fragile walls, filling the rooms with their dense mass, under the weight of the misfortunes and thoughts that were shut up there as in a vacuum, compressed and ready to explode, which suddenly erupted, spurted in all directions, in a fearful explosion provoked by his contemptuous glance, as though someone had thrown a burning cigarette butt into a pocket of natural gas rising from the Pannonian mud.

What was he thinking then?

He was wondering what might have happened if he had stayed in that apartment a moment longer to carry out the plan dictated by his bladder as well as his mind (or the reverse), if, that is, as he had intended for a moment, he had urinated against the damp walls of his former dwelling. Beams and tiles would have crashed down on his head (as the ice pick had crashed down on the head of Lev Davidovich Bronstein), on the bald spot in the center of his graying head, a bald spot that seemed predestined for the ice pick of avenging fate: *malleus iudeorum*.

What image then came to his mind?

The brain of Dr. Freud, the surgeon.

What sort of lighting?

The fiery reflection of the sun on the glass front of the soap factory in Kotor in 1939, and a cloud seen from celestial heights above the bay.

How did E.S. picture himself?

Lying in the dust; his fly is open, and from his swollen bladder flows warm beer (drunk with the porters at the station buffet): the golden jet is cut off brutally by the scissors of death; the warm stream of urine projected against the wall as though by a horse has dried out, and from his flaccid penis, dangling as inertly as a snapped rubber band, flows a thin stream, no, more like the thread which oozes from one of those pig's bladders that children play with, or which drips from a poorly shut faucet that not even the hand of death can turn off entirely, a trickle that spreads under him and around him and is absorbed by the porous mortar, the thick layers of lime, the cracks of the worm-eaten beams and boards, and the dust that absorbs urine as cigarette ash absorbs ink.

How did E.S. react to this incident?

It was no longer his future, anticipated death, but his past death beneath the ruins of the house in Novi Sad, hence a death that he had already surmounted, a Lethe which he had already crossed, a peaceful *post festum*, when the body is no longer enslaved, when the bladder is already emptied like a pig's bladder, when the blood has already clotted on the shattered skull, when the eyes are already glazed and the soul is set free from its earthly chains.

As he lay there with his eyes closed, what question did he ask himself?

What is the good of everything that exists or does not exist (or might have existed), what is the good of all that if, along with the body, the eyes, and the testicles, the spirit, that cloud, that nucleus of the heart at the heart of the dying heart, dies, too? What is the good of it, if it is not to outlive the perishable dust that is the body and unite in a perfect quintessence past, present, and future, consciousness and intuition, the fine dust and the cloud, the heart and the brain, and all the senses, unite them all in a small eternal cloud, a cloudy vapor, and live on as consciousness and essence.

While his spirit was rising, like a blue cloud, to celestial heights, what were his earthly remains, his residual spirit doing?

Contemplating the earthly consequences of death, contemplating them in the manner of God or of the good old writers—objectively.

His last image (objectively speaking)?

No longer perceiving an earthly landscape—a house, oleanders in wooden tubs, a hydrant—his unsocketed eye, comparable to a camera lens or the torn-out eye of the Cyclops, sees only a ruination: a never-ending moment of raining mortar, of walls collapsing in a cloud of dust, of bricks as red as gums.

Describe in the fewest possible words his state of mind when he saw the house cave in.

Momentary confusion; consternation.

Followed by?

Flight, panic, cries for help.

Who came first to his aid?

The porters came running into the wreckage—protecting their noses and mouths from the dust with dirty handkerchiefs—and began to remove bricks and great chunks of wall.

To what caste do the porters belong?

To the great caste of the companions of death, which also includes firemen, gravediggers, undertakers, doctors, nurses, judges, executioners, policemen, secret agents, bandits, priests, khojas, rabbis, butchers, kosher and otherwise, circus performers, spies, lion tamers, racing drivers, window washers, athletes, pilots, soldiers, officers, generals, railroad workers, fishermen, mariners, divers, miners, bicyclists, motorists, travelers, pedestrians, mountain climbers, scientists, chemists, fakirs, snake charmers, knackers, veterinarians, alcoholics, vegetarians, gourmets, dope addicts, smokers, invalids, neurasthenics, melancholics, hypochondriacs, psychiatrists, prophets, revolutionaries, pharmacists, lunatics, acrobats, electricians, philosophers, plumbers, masons, chimney sweeps, housewives, suicides, lovers, adulterers, clerks, hunters, gamekeepers, tax collectors, customs guards, poachers, foresters, potash burners, night watchmen, elevator repairmen, elevator operators, burglars, jurists, brakemen, stable boys, cab drivers, coachmen, beekeepers, shepherds, peasants, plowmen, prostitutes, old people, bridge painters, builders, caisson workers, gold miners, gamblers, poets, boxers, Olympic champions, dynamiters, sailors, candlemakers, merchants, hired murderers, blacksmiths, glassblowers, headhunters, slaves, slave owners, slave dealers, presidents of republics, emperors, kings, volcanologists, banana pickers, street cleaners, coachmen, nuns, believers, unbelievers, harem guards, pashas, millionaires, beggars, and everyone else.

What do a porter and a gravedigger have in common?

Their activity, which consists in transporting earthly remains from one place to another; their imperturbability and their skill in handling wooden boxes; their use of ropes; physics and metaphysics in the service of daily life.

What sounds could be heard?

The cracking of rotten beams; the crumbling of mortar, prolonged, like the clatter of a cooking pot that has been pushed off the shelf.

What other image appeared to the dying eye?

The faded bluebells of the wallpaper pattern, peering from under chunks of dusty plaster.

An appropriate song (barroom ballad, czardas, gigue)?

Hey, let them when I die
plant bluebells on my grave,

and let the boys and girls
sing, drink, and misbehave.

What sound drowns out the abstract ringing of the bluebells?

Howling ambulance sirens.

What objects come to mind?

Stretcher, white smock, stethoscope, Red Cross armband, leather pouches, shovels, spades, picks, rubber hose.

What onlookers?

Children, neighbors, newspapermen, passersby.

Describe the rescue operations.

The porters lifted a section of the wall with a crowbar; under it they found their (former) employer; they turned him over on his back. Then they washed their hands under the hose that someone had attached to the hydrant to settle the dust raised by the cave-in.

Who then appeared on the scene?

Official persons: doctors, nurses, policemen.

What did the officials note under the heading: DATE, EXACT TIME OF ACCIDENT?

March 18, 1942; 5:12 p.m.

Draw up the official list of the victim's belongings.

Pigskin purse (one); linen handkerchief (one); mechanical pencil (one); yellow carpenter's pencil (one); key ring with keys (three); pack of Symphonia cigarettes (soft pack, opened); box of matches (one); Longines pocket watch (one); small change 2.80 P (two pengö eighty fillér); a bundle of old newspapers; notebook (one); a gray suit (one); black shoes (one pair); shirts (two); underdrawers (one pair); ties (four); celluloid collars (five); a sheet of quadrille paper; socks (three pairs); safety razor (one); tin button (one); wooden clothespins (two).

List the documents found in the victim's wallet.

Identity card no. 225464, issued January 11, 1941, in Novi Sad; railroad worker's card, first class, no. 56666, issued November 8, 1941 (expired); receipt for October, November, and December rent; copies of baptismal certificates issued at the Orthodox Church of the Assumption, Novi Sad, in the names of the members of the victim's family; record of a court-ordered medical examination, issued by the district council of Kovin.

Cite this record in full.

Re the incapacitation of Mr. E.S. of Novi Sad, the Kovin district court takes note of the result of the court-ordered medical examination of March 25, 1940, and delivers the following decision: The district court in Kovin, on the strength of §194, articles 2 and 10, approves the discharge of the recovered patient E.S. from the Kovin mental hospital, on the condition that his lawful spouse, in the capacity of temporary guardian, assumes responsibility for his care and support, and undertakes, in the event of a relapse, to deliver him to the nearest psychiatric hospital. At the same time, it directs the municipal administration of Novi Sad to charge the patient twice twenty-five dinars, or fifty dinars in all, for the above-mentioned medical examination, and remit said sum to this court. Reasons: The patient was examined in the state psychiatric hospital, whose specialists pronounced him incapable of taking proper care of his person and property. However, in view of the fact that his condition has improved appreciably and that he is no longer a danger to himself or to others, he can now be considered harmless and entrusted to the care of his family. The court has delivered this decision on the strength of the aforesaid medical opinion.

Month, day, and year of the victim's birth (continuation of the record).

July 11, 1889.

According to your book of horoscopes, under what sign of the zodiac was he born?

Under the fourth sign, Cancer (*karkata*, the crab), which denotes the summer season presided over by the brilliant star Sirius, which ushers in the summer solstice in the thirty-first zodiacal segment, extending from the summer solstice to the autumnal equinox, when the armies of the day are overcome by the armies of the night.

What planets govern him?

The *Moon*, which determines his sensory ups and downs, his fertility, his feeling, his imagination, his lyricism, his fitful sleep, his digestive euphoria, his laziness, his fatalism, his melancholy wanderings, his manias, hysterias, and anxieties; *Mars*, which determines a certain aggressiveness, taking the form of rebellion against family and religion; *Saturn*, which enters into a dangerous combination with his sign and promotes withdrawal into himself, a crawling back into his shell— hence his introversion, his glacial loneliness, his schizoid aberrations.

What element?

Water, because his soul bathes in a sea of contradictory sensations and his lymphatic constitution fosters an appearance of laziness and immobility, while an intensive nocturnal life goes on under his shell.

The symbolic meaning of the sign?

Conception, sperm, fertility, fruit.

The principle of the symbol?

Depth, abyss, well, ditch, pit, pocket, stomach, vagina, vase, bottle.

General meaning of the sign?

The four aspects of Parabrahman, the first cause; the fourth complementary element of the hidden triangle or triangles.

The sides of the tetragram?

Harmony in private life; dreams without sleep; dreams as thought expressed in images; waking as expression and reflection of thought.

The sides of the triangle?

Intuition (a part of dream); deduction (a part of intelligence); verification (a part of doubt).

Vegetal tripod?

Thirst—hunger—insomnia.

Exposed organs?

Feet, shins, fingers, prostate, pancreas, liver, bladder, sympathetic nerves, glands, skull.

Forms?

Pointed.

Related sign?

Pisces. Conceived in the same element, the crab and the fish have many features in common; they complement each other and sometimes have the same handwriting. They intuitively understand each other and strive for the same ideal of beauty. Their relationship is passionate, profound, and enduring. Enchantment and lucidity.

Tendencies?

Passivity. Narcissism.

Functions?

Seeing, doubting, testing.

Actions?

Creating, multiplying, enduring, waking, flying, writing, sailing, sleeping.

Objects?

Cane, clothes, hat, newspapers, penholder, chair, briefcase.

Places?

Beer hall, dining car, store, bookshop, library, public baths, forest, market, butcher shop, puppet show, circus, processions, religious service, church portal, snack bar, synagogue, auction room, bank, railroad station, cab, bakery, factory, insane asylum.

What did the workers dig up when they were clearing away the rubble of the house at 21 Bem Street?

In the foundations, they found a hermetically sealed container of green glass. In it, they discovered a *document* in calligraphy and a few coins.

Quote the text of the document.

The plans for this house were drawn by Lajos Detzer; it was built by Dezsö Detzer of Budapest, who in the same year built many other dwellings in addition to the district office in Zombor. Franz Joseph was then Emperor. A war was going on in Bosnia and Herzegovina. There was a solar eclipse and a comet was sighted. There was so little water in the Danube that spring that it could be crossed dry-shod at Paksa. In that year, the Jews were persecuted in Russia. The foundations were blessed by the deacon Nikifor Janković. The cornerstone was laid on July 11, 1889.

What private persons sent telegrams of condolence?

His sisters in Kerkabarabás, Szentadorján, Sziget, and Csesztreg; his brother in Trieste; the Drašković, Vujović, and Dragićević families in Cetinje; Dr. Viktor Bugalj, also in Cetinje; the Šicak, Gavanski, Horváth, Schwarz, Baumann, Popov, Rónai, Berecz, Guttmann, Kostić, Böszërményi, Jankov, Mirković, Klein, Konstantinov, Vasiljević, Kesić, Protić, and Krohn families in Novi Sad; the Krauss family in Zombor; the Ziegler family in Subotica; the Mayer family in Porszombat; Dr. Papandopoulos in Kovin; the Rosenberg family in Baksa; the Fischer, Berki, Pap, Lerm, Kiss, Schlang, and Kohn families in Budapest; the Čukljević family in Šid; the A. Okoličanji family in Zagreb; the Koritsanski family in Vienna; Dr. Abravenel in Toronto; M. Margelius in Galicia; L. Perez in Brazil; Aharon Zeitlin in Jerusalem.

What institutions?

The Bereft Yugoslavian Railways, Magyar Arva Vasútak, the Bereaved Nations League, the Distressed Zionist Organization, the International Cheerless Chess Federation, the Mournful PEN Club.

What sort of funeral did he decide on?

He hesitated between a simple ceremony restricted to the immediate family (at the express wish of the deceased) and an elaborate first-class funeral (at government expense, it goes without saying) at which representatives of all religions would be welcomed on an equal footing.

What attracted him to this last variant?

Aesthetic and cosmopolitan considerations: the juxtaposition of rabbinical lamentation (in Hebrew), Catholic counterpoint (in Latin), Orthodox chants (Old Church Slavic), and Mohammedan wailing (in Arabic).

What solution did he favor in the end?

A kind of compromise; in this third variant, his coffin would be followed by a gypsy orchestra, playing mournful gypsy tunes suggestive of love and death.

What could not be dispensed with in this third variant?

A cimbalom, though it would have to be carried by hand like an auxiliary, reserve coffin, or loaded onto a two-wheeled vehicle, as throughout his life cimbaloms had been moved for him from one corner of a restaurant to another, or even out into the street.

In the event of a Jewish funeral, what sort of histrionics were to be expected?

That Gyula (George) would tear his new tweed coat a little too neatly, that is, strictly along the seams, clearly indicating that he had previously cut the threads around the collar and on the sleeves; that Rebecca would squeeze out sounds more like the mooing of an infuriated cow than like sobs; and that Netty would undoubtedly blow her nose in a black-bordered handkerchief, not out of grief but because she had a cold.

What further variant might be considered?

The Subotica railroad workers' band, which won the Central European brass-band competition in Budapest in 1936, might play Mendelssohn's 114th Psalm at the request of the deceased.

Quote in full the text of the funeral oration delivered over the grave of railroad inspector Béla Sternberg, who in December 1941 threw himself under the wheels of a freight train not far from the entrance to a tunnel, published with drastic cuts (of which the author had not been notified) in *The Railroad Herald*, no. 218, of December 20, 1941.

Ladies and gentlemen! Moving people through space

and hence through time is a noble task, deserving of gratitude, for thanks to railroad workers, these companions almost invisible to the traveler, you, ladies and gentlemen, speed across snow-covered plains, through dense forests, over mountain peaks, rivers, and viaducts, through the dark tunnels of night, through rain and snow, at a speed of a hundred to a hundred and twenty kilometers an hour. Eager to embrace your distant dear ones as quickly as possible, you fly on wings of steel (symbol of the railroad), nestled in the soft bed of a *Schlafwagen*, sprawled on comfortable plush seats, or, if the worst comes to the worst, on a wooden bench or a baggage rack in second class, cradled not in the arms of Morpheus but in the warm maternal womb of a train, that marvelous invention of our modern times. Seated on warm plush seats or lying curled up like a fetus in the womb of the iron mother, you move through space and time, as comfortable as in a Russian novel (which you may be reading at this very moment by the bright light of a mercury lamp in a first-class compartment), without a thought to those hardworking, conscientious employees who watch over the telegraph and telephone at the stations, not only in the big cities but also in one-horse towns where God Himself knocks off for the night, without a thought for those who stay awake to service the giant locomotives, who feed them as easily and adroitly as a coachman does his horses . . . Yes, ladies and gentlemen, this man was one of those on whom depended the security and comfort of your journeys, one of those who, like a valiant general, a veteran of many wars, started out almost forty years ago as a common soldier in an almost nameless little station, and

by dint of hard work and selfless devotion to the railroad
rose to the top, to the rank of general, as it were, and
then—after withstanding all the perils, all the splendors
and miseries of the railroader's calling—put an end to
his fruitful and socially useful life by a tragic act. Yes,
meine Damen und Herren, more than once he worked
between dangerous buffers, more than once he came in
contact with murderous wheels, crossed the tracks and
climbed up into locomotives, without ever incurring the
slightest mishap; never did the iron monster kick him
with its iron-shod hooves; it seemed to know him, it was
as though they were friends, as though, how shall I put
it, they were horse and master, an obedient horse and
a benevolent master . . . and now he, the benevolent
master, has met his death, not on *the battlefield*, not in
the line of duty, but tragically, of his own free will,
unable in a moment of crisis to think of dying in any
other way than under the wheels of a train, and now
of all times, in peacetime, as it were, for, despite the
objective state of affairs, despite the international car-
nage, the railroads are, or should be, at peace, extra-
territorial, so to speak, neutral and nonbelligerent like
the Swiss, since they, in spite of everything, continue,
or should continue, to do their duty of providing
international transportation in accordance with their
charter, although certain politicians are trying to corrupt
them, to exploit them for their own vile and murderous
purposes, to exploit the sublime mission and calling of
the railroads, those international organizations for forg-
ing and reinforcing ties among people of good will,
trying to pervert them and cause them to jettison their
moral code until, instead of *bringing people together*, they

divide them and transform rapprochement into estrangement.

You know, ladies and gentlemen, that railroaders, like firemen, must and do stand above the interests of individuals and even of states, because like doctors and priests they are by nature and calling supraindividual and supranational, divine if you will. Yes, fellow mourners, this unfortunate man—as I have said—did not die on *the battlefield*; he was not a victim of a traffic accident; no, of his own free will he embraced the cold steel of the rails, it was the iron wheels of a cattle car which carried out the bloody slaughter that he had chosen for his inglorious end. Nevertheless, ladies and gentlemen, let us show him the military honors he deserves, let the honor guard fire a volley, let the switchmen blow their whistles all together, let the locomotives sound their organs in a long lament. And may he rest in peace.

How might certain famous men have reacted in the press and on the radio to the news of his death?

Everything that is possible happens; only what happens is possible (*Franz Kafka*). Critical of his adversaries, he was uncritical of himself; he thought he had created a philosophy and was unable to transcend it. He will live on in our memory as an alienated man in an alienated society. As an example and a lesson (*Karl Marx*). He was only the embodiment of a dream; his psychological difficulties were related to dreams, and originated in dreams. Thank God that this was so rich a nightmare (*Sigmund Freud*). One way of solving the problem of existence is to come close enough to the things and beings that have struck us as beautiful and mysterious to discover that they are without mystery and without beauty; this is one form of hygiene that we may choose; it may not be very commendable but it gives us a certain peace of mind and makes life easier for us—because it enables us to regret nothing, for it convinces us that we have attained the best possible ends and that this best did not amount to much, and to make our peace with death. Was he one of those who knew this dangerous form of hygiene? I think he was (*Marcel Proust*).

What "causes of the accident" did E.S. suggest in trying to help the insurance agent draw up his report?

Providence, act of God, deus ex machina, gray or common rat, curse.

What possibility did he consider?

That he was the victim of a well-prepared assassination plot. For a single individual (and here, beyond a doubt, several were involved), by aiming the murder-machine of his wishes against another person, can make that person's house collapse on his head or cause him to sicken or die suddenly. He had read about such cases; such curses, or magic, seem to be highly effective among certain primitive peoples (despite the contentions of European positivists).

Did he communicate this idea to anyone?

He told Mr. Gavanski in a bantering tone that Netty and her clique had probably wrecked the house. On the same occasion, he cited several examples from European history: in 1437, a certain Hubert (surname unknown) of Regensburg in Bavaria decided to blind a woman by the name of Ivanka, the widow of Johann Pagani, for having maligned him, and to that end, according to his own confession, stuck two needles into

a portrait of her which he had commissioned, spec-
ifying that it should look as much like her as possible;
in 1640, a certain Magda Muhić, in a suburb of the free
city of Zagreb, killed Mrs. Jelenovačka by pouring milk
into a hole and stirring it with a red-hot poker, while
pronouncing these words: "This spit is now piercing
Jelenovačka's heart," and keeping it up until said Jelenovačka died; in 1327, the French king Charles IV fell
gravely ill and on St. Bartholomew's Day a wax figure
of the king was found in the room of a certain Caroline,
a servant girl at court, pierced through and through
with nails and knitting needles—the good king suffered
as many wounds to his body as there were holes in the
wax figure, and in the end he died; in 1864, a servant
girl in the Nagykanizsa region dispatched her former
masters in a similar way: her victims all died of violent
concussions of the brain.

Had E.S. ever been tempted to avenge himself on
anyone in this way?

Several times he had blown his nose into a newspaper
with the Führer's picture on it.

Was he conscious of the danger he was courting?

Definitely. He always folded the paper as small as
possible before throwing it into dense brambles or the
river, thus doing away with the corpus delicti of his
insane and dangerous act.

Having interpreted his escape from beneath the ruins
as a favorable omen, what did he hope the future would
bring?

A violent Allied counteroffensive, starting with a well-
planned surprise attack (Maccabees), a parachute jump
by night; concurrently, assassination of the Führer and

other Axis leaders, organized by some espionage center in Switzerland; the invention in the Allied camp of a supersecret weapon, a nerve gas or some other poison that would render the enemy armies comatose or delirious for at least twenty-four hours; a pact whereby the Allies would exchange captured officers and soldiers for Jews at a ratio of 1:5 or 1:3 (five Jews for one officer, or three Jews for one private); in return for certain territorial concessions, the Axis powers would authorize the Jews to emigrate to some African country or desert island; sensational kidnapping of the Führer (carried out by some Maccabean lunatic or secret Zionist organization), and in return for sparing his life, the Allies would demand a guarantee that the Jews would be allowed to emigrate to the U.S.A., Canada, Palestine, or some African country; a damaged Allied plane of the Superfortress type would land somewhere near the village, perhaps on the fairgrounds or on the Roman road, and after being repaired during the night, it would take off in the morning carrying him (E.S.) and his family in the direction of some airfield beyond the reach of evil (in Switzerland, for instance); provided with false papers, he would make his way to Montenegro, where his wife had friends and relatives, and at some prearranged spot on the Gulf of Kotor, an English submarine would pick them up; a sign from heaven pointing to some concrete possibility of salvation; a voice in a dream (burning bush) would tell him where the plane would land or where the submarine (Noah's ark) would surface.

What Talmudic injunction did he especially prize for its aesthetic and moral value?

The one bidding the sons of Israel give praise and thanks to Jehovah when breathing the fragrance of an aromatic plant or spice; viz., the heady perfume of the flirtatious lady (about thirty) whom, on the return journey from Novi Sad, he passed in the corridor outside the first-class compartment (paradise lost); the cinnamon-and-vanilla aroma of the still-warm cake which a well-upholstered lady (mother of two children) cut on the collapsible table by the window and offered him, but which, having been expelled from paradise, he politely declined; the scent of the violets that a young gypsy woman held under his nose at the station in Lenti.

How, while contemplating the perfume of the flirtatious lady whom he had met in the corridor outside the first-class compartment (paradise lost), was he able in his mind and soul to reconcile the Talmudic prayer of thanksgiving for sweet scents and the Christian (scholastic) aesthetic?

By believing in the prayer of thanksgiving, which he wordlessly addressed to Jehovah, and at the same time recognizing that St. Bernard was right in saying that perfumes cloud the intelligence (*Odoratus impedit cogitationem*). That perfumed lady, who had appeared for a moment, only to vanish behind the door of the softly cushioned first-class compartment, had with her scent (*odora di femina*) muddled his thoughts and made his exile harder to bear.

Had he ever bought flowers before?

In 1919, in Budapest, he had bought a bouquet of narcissus (a florin apiece) for a certain Fanika and, with his bouquet, waited at least forty-five minutes for her outside the New York Restaurant, after which he had thrown it into a garbage can; in 1928, he had brought a bunch of roses (seven for half a pengö) to the wedding of Countess Artsibashev and one Arnold Wenzel, an employee of the Danube Lloyd's; in 1931, he had personally laid a white rose (one dinar) on the coffin of Miss Maricki; in 1931–32, he had sent, first anonymously, then with a visiting card, seven roses seven times—seven red roses six times, and the seventh time, six red and one white (from half a dinar to one dinar apiece)—to the address of Mrs. Horgós, 8 St. Sava Street, Novi Sad; in 1934, he had brought Mr. Gavanski's sick daughter a bunch of anemones; in 1934, at the Silver Lion Café in Subotica, he had bought an enormous bouquet of carnations (about thirty in all) and presented them to a red-haired cashier who kept her job in that café for only three days; in 1938, at the railroad workers' ball in Novi Sad, he had sent Miss Magdalena, a hairdresser, three tulips (three for two dinars) through the waiter.

With what argument did E.S. try to convince the owner of a two-horse cab that one pengö was a fair price for the trip?

He argued that the one pengö he was offering was quite enough, considering that he, the driver, was going farther in the same direction, and that, as could be demonstrated by elementary arithmetic, an additional weight of seventy-three kilos would not (in spite of the mud, an unknown quantity that need not be taken into consideration) cause two horses, harnessed to so excellent a vehicle, to expend as much energy as they would store up by consuming one pengö's worth of hay or other fodder (oats, corn, or rye).

Was the owner of the two horses convinced?

To convince him fully, E.S. was obliged to adduce the moral weight that a pengö thrown onto the scales would carry on the Day of Judgment: when good deeds come to be weighed against wicked ones on God's scales, a single tin pengö can make all the difference.

What are the advantages of spring (the season of flowering and germination) over winter?

In the spring, man can lie in a sheltered spot, exposing his back to the pleasant and salubrious rays of the sun, and nothing is better for rheumatic pains; the early-morning light in his room makes for pleasant feelings and helps him to wake up; he can read in bed without fear of catching cold; he can sit on the toilet as long as he likes and test his constipation; at any time of day, he can take long walks across the fields, through the woods, or by the river; he can study budding and flowering on the basis of concrete examples which when recorded can serve throughout the year to illustrate the full biological cycle; the chirping of the birds gives the soul a sweetly sorrowful sense of freedom; the problems of heat and clothing lose their urgency; an abundance of wild grasses and other plants rounds out the food supply; women and young girls bare their arms, and their legs to the knee—or even higher.

What is the negative effect of the springtime (the season of growth and flowering) on mankind?

The insane asylums take in an increased number of patients and the suicide rate rises alarmingly.

NOTES OF A MADMAN (III)

[*36*]

(*Draft*) Never fear; I'm not coming for a family visit. Though convinced that you have not yet burned all your bridges, I prefer to believe that you have acted, at least in part, under someone else's influence; that is, contrary to your better knowledge. The reason for my trip: the postcard of March 9. Thank the Lord, I don't need money (so don't worry), and I hope I won't need any in the future, for I mean to do everything in my power to prevent you from selling the house which up to now has been a refuge to those in need, including me. And that is why, if only out of gratitude to the house, I shall do all I can to stop you from selling it. From this it follows clearly: I don't want money, I want my share in the house, and I want that right away. In a word, I want only one thing from you: I want you to sign the enclosed statement and to tell me what has become of Dolfi's share; once you've done that, you've heard the last of me. Otherwise, if you refuse to sign the enclosed statement, I will not stir from the house until you accede to my wish. And if you resist, I will kick up a row that will be heard all over the district, all over the country, in fact. I didn't endure my *Lehrjahre* in order to be threatened and harassed day after day in my own house, by people who have no (real) ties with the house, who take advantage of my goodness. Since you have chosen not to understand my complaints and my embittered letters, since you have not been able or willing to understand the suffering of my wounded

soul, but on the contrary have aggravated it by your
behavior, you will have to pay dearly now. I won't go
into detail about all that has happened to me in the last
few days, all the injustices done me by the members of
my family, I won't speak to you of miraculous signs
(from heaven)—all that is beyond your powers of com-
prehension. Just don't oppose me, don't try to squirm
out of it, that's all I ask of you. Just sign. Because, I
repeat, I must be master in the house where I was born,
I refuse to be harassed in the house for whose sake I
have endured so much privation and suffering. Let me
remind you that time and history are moving ahead
and that both, thank God, are on my side. I implore
you not to force me, with your outrageous behavior, to
take a step the consequences of which would be irre-
vocable. (The business with the forest and the potash
must not be repeated.) I remind you again that time
and history are on my side, that all accounts will be
settled soon, with no mercy shown to anyone. For, as
the Talmud says (*Sanhedrin* 100): by the same measure
as a man judges will he be judged.

[37]

In spite of Marx's critique, I believe that Malthus was
right. And when it comes to demonstrating my thesis,
or rather my speculation, I don't care in the least
whether he, that is, Malthus, was a superficial disciple
or a plagiarizer of other people's ideas. What interests
me is ideas, and in my opinion it matters not at all
whether he copied James Stuart, Townsend, Franklin,
and so on. Be that as it may, the fact remains that the

world's population is growing too fast and that this
population explosion is getting to be our number-one
problem. Economically and existentially, metaphysically,
if you will. People are multiplying like flies; at every
moment of the day and night, several million penises
are in a state of dangerous, menacing erection. The
consequences are clear. This rabid phallus, this prime-
val, mythical symbol, plunges into a woman's bleeding
viscera, humanity pants on sultry nights, and no one
thinks of the consequences. The consequences are catastrophic. The increase in the population brings an
increase in sin. *Perpetuum mobile.* Like the medieval
attempt to harness the force of gravitation. Weights are
distributed evenly on a wheel. The gravitation of the
earth attracts the weight; the weight moves the wheel,
then the next weight enters the gravitational field. And
so on. Something like a waterwheel or a windmill. And
why was this eternal human dream of a perpetually
rotating mechanism dubbed madness? Isn't the dream
of perpetual motion as worthwhile as man's eternal
dream of flying? Were all the Icaruses and suchlike
visionaries really crazy? Certainly not. As for me, I put
an equals sign between those two dreams. Because, in
the last analysis, the wheel is a consequence of the same
sort of dream. And I leave it to you to develop the
parallel to its logical conclusion. I mean, to the airplane
on one hand and the wheel on the other. Why not?
The humming over my head in the quiet country night
(as I write these lines), somewhere high in the sky, those
planes that fly over the village day and night at an
altitude of five to ten thousand meters on a southeast-
northwest axis, that miracle of modern (military) tech-

nology, it, too, is only an offshoot and ultimate consequence of those two wild dreams which obscurantists
and positivists have consistently ridiculed as madness.
Since the Middle Ages, doctors have diagnosed thousands of lunatics on the basis of material proof, or of a
mere confession, that they had harbored the idealistic
desire to become a bird. And don't put this "eternal
dream of flying" down to curiosity or mere thirst for
knowledge, because, I assure you, you would be mistaken. I hold, and I have irrefutable proof (provided
you are willing to accept the lyrical results of a logical
operation as self-evident proof), that the human dream
of flying and its realization are purely and simply the
consequence of flight from sin. For the earth, gentlemen, is a foul breeding place of sin; earth and water,
as the celebrated Sinistario d'Ameno demonstrated, are
two inseparable concepts, and it is therefore no wonder
(I am quoting him from memory, it goes without saying)
that the poets have Venus rising out of the sea, wishing
no doubt with this symbolic image to unite the two
sinful principles, earth and water, these two sticky
elements, from whose mixture man and sin (sin and
man) sprang. Therefore, I say, not only earth, but water
as well, especially water, are breeding places of sin and
vice, and debauchery has its source in moisture. That
is why man strives toward the heights and that is the
eternal meaning of the myth of Icarus . . . Here I have
no intention of citing precise demographic facts, or of
proving the correctness of the Malthusian curves and
formulae (such facts can be found in any encyclopedia).
Nor do I wish, like some provincial rabbi (for that is
what you called me one day), to predict the Apocalypse,
or prove to anyone, to you least of all, that the world is

inevitably doomed to destruction. For that I need no
clearer proofs than those in my possession. And where
are those proofs, you will ask. Here, gentlemen; here,
dear sister, here. Look closely. I am pointing at my
heart.

[38]

Thus, I speak to you as one who knows the secret.
The earth's population has increased dangerously. But
it is not my intention at the present moment to tell you
what our world looks like when seen from a higher
moral vantage point. I shall only say that the population
is increasing at a terrifying rate and that the means by
which mankind is trying to defend itself are neither
adequate nor effective. Forced or voluntary sterilization,
family planning, war as a spontaneous application of
Darwinian principles, natural selection, starvation, eu-
thanasia, and all the rest are futile and laughable efforts.
China with its five hundred million or six hundred
million inhabitants, the long-heralded yellow peril, that
ancient bugbear, is not the only danger to the world.
Don't worry about an invasion of the yellow ants, God's
punishment will not come from the swamps. It will
come from heaven, and there will be no mercy for
anyone. All will suffer alike, poor and rich, and more
than anyone else we the chosen people.

[39]

(*Draft*) Even seen from this distance in space and
time, your swinish behavior loses none of its virulence.
When I think of all you have done to me, of the shame

you have inflicted on me, I get the feeling that it's all a bad dream. But since, sorry to say, I am still capable of distinguishing a dream nightmare from a waking nightmare, I implore you to prevent your daughter and George from harming my family, for I will not countenance any allegation that my family (that is, my wife and children) started the quarrel with you. And, believe me, it had better not come to that. I also beg you, you in particular, to make sure that I find my family alive when I come back; I hope you haven't become heartless enough to let them die of starvation. And don't forget the words of the Midrash: When we do good, we must do it joyfully (*Vayikra rabbah*, 34).

P.S. The poor man does the rich man more good in accepting his gift than the rich man the poor man in doing him a kindness (*Ibid.*).

TRAVEL SCENES (II)

[40]

A tree appears in the midst of the horses' swaying heads, then begins to dance between their ears. Wrenched out of his sleep, the coachman pulls in the reins just before the metal gate. The man sees the grimacing mouths of the horses, twisted slightly upward and to one side (the big teeth, the color of old dominoes, black on the inside), and for a moment he sees white foam on the steel bit. The tree is slightly bent; below the crown he sees a protuberance jutting out horizontally, at almost a right angle to the trunk. The branches are covered with a transparent film of ice, in places as thin as a sheet of cellophane. The trunk, too, is coated with glass, but its wrapping is even thinner, especially on the side exposed to the sun; and on an east-facing bulge the wrinkled bark can be seen clearly. Water drips rhythmically from the branches and the sheet-metal gutters emit a gurgling sound. Now the horses' heads are turned toward the shaft, which is almost on a level with their eyes, for both heads are unnaturally twisted, as though they had suddenly reacted to a senseless, impossible impulse to turn—one to the left, the other to the right—not away from the shaft but toward it, and inevitably collided in that narrow space. The wagon has stopped with a screeching, grinding sound, but seems to be moving slightly backward. Now the man sees two great black horse's eyes behind the loosened blinders. The horses, or so at least it seems to him, are looking somewhere ahead, as though the same inertia that has brought them this far were drawing them on into a vague and uncertain distance, with the result that their eyes, like their heads, are drawn forcibly down and in toward the shaft, and only their eyes (or rather their cross-eyed gaze) seem to be continuing the movement of the stopped wagon. Now the man looks back at the empty wagon, in which a few wisps of very yellow straw glint in the sunlight. Then he looks at the iron rims of the mud-thickened back wheels, and behind them, on both sides, at the parallel wheel tracks in the mud.

[41]

The square of sunlight shining through the little window falls unobstructed on the yellow clay. The man has the impression that the clay is steaming. Or that is only an illusion. His coat, muddied at the elbows, is hung over the back of a chair. His boots and trousers are muddy. His tie is loosened and his shirtsleeves rolled up. He is holding a spade. It is somewhat rusty, but the metal still shines through the rust spots on the blade. The man plants the spade at the edge of the sunlit square and presses with all his strength. The blade penetrates five or six centimeters into the clay and breaks off a lump of hard yellow earth.

[42]

His coat with its muddy elbows has been thrown on a pile of bricks ten meters away. On it he sees the yellow star, deformed not so much by perspective as by the

folds of the coat. The bricks have been thrown on the
pile, some shapeless, others broken in half, still others
only slightly damaged. Their color has faded, as though
the brick had turned to stone with the passage of time,
or seemed to, because of the layer of mortar clinging
to the flesh of the brick and merging with it. The white
skin of his left forearm (his left sleeve is rolled up to
the elbow, while his muddy and rumpled right sleeve
dangles around his wrist) is sprinkled with red freckles,
and the fine red hairs are just visible. He plants the
spade in the hardened ground, puts one foot on the
already deformed upper edge of the blade, and brings
his full weight to bear on it. Crunching as though
cutting through or tearing out a root, the blade penetrates five or six centimeters into the ground; then it
can be heard striking something hard. The man moves
the handle from left to right and right to left; the blade
seems to be wedged between two hard objects. A crunching is heard, as when a tooth cracks between the jaws
of a dentist's forceps. Then a red brick, as red and
moist as a chunk of fresh beef, emerges from the
ground. The man bends down and picks it up. Each
hand is wrapped in a rag, probably a handkerchief, but
neither the color nor the possible lines of the checked
pattern are discernible, for it is encrusted with dried
mud. The rag is tied around the palm of his hand in
such a way that his fingers are cramped and slightly
bent, and the movements of his hand are awkward and
uncertain. He turns the brick over on its side, grasps it
between two fingers as if they were tweezers. It slips
out of his hand and falls back into the mud. The man
turns around; in the red glow of the setting sun, he

sees the sharp point of the bayonet on the guard's rifle.
For a moment he sees nothing more, because the lenses
of his glasses with their muddy fingerprints are flooded
by the red glow. The guard is sitting on a pile of rotten
beams, holding his rifle between his knees. Noticing
that the guard is not looking at him, the man inspects
him for a moment, as though seeing him for the first
time. Before long, he makes out a clear but faceless
silhouette, the guard against the red horizon, his stiff
hat with the cock's plume, which is no longer dark
green but yellow and red like flame. Then the man
lowers his eyes and tries to pick up the brick with his
finger-tweezers, which do not open far enough. In the
end, he succeeds and throws it in the direction of the
pile. The brick falls a meter or two away from him. He
hears the guard say something, a few meaningless
words, maybe an oath, maybe a threat. Frightened, the
man starts abruptly and rushes over to the brick that
has fallen into the mud. He can still hear the guard's
voice. Maybe he is only laughing.

[43]

The square of sunlight at whose edge he began to
dig into the clay has moved. Now there are two squares
of equal size on the floor between the table and the
square window: the one lighter, traced by the sun; the
other yellow, the color of freshly dug clay. Now the sun
has moved, and one of these squares half covers the
other. The second, clay square has been hollowed out
irregularly. The exhumed clay piled beside the hollow
looks like big chips of acacia wood. In places the smooth,

shiny surfaces left by the spade stand out clearly, like the inside of a plaster cast. Slightly stooped, his coat thrown over one shoulder, the man is now sitting at a rickety table with his hands on the tabletop. His right hand is wrapped in some sort of rag, no doubt a handkerchief, but because of the mud the checked pattern is scarcely discernible. He is holding a cigarette between his cramped, dirty, tweezer-like fingers. The smoke rises invisibly; then, swirling like blue mist, it appears in the transparent column of yellow sunlight falling obliquely from the window. The spade is leaning against the wall beside the stove. It is not directly lit by the sun, but a beam of diffused light touches the blade, which glistens now that the rust spots have been rubbed off. Why has the man suddenly stopped digging? Perhaps he is exhausted, perhaps the clay is too hard, perhaps the spade handle has blistered his hand.

[44]

Awkwardly, he picks up the brick in both hands and heaves it onto the pile. The brick rolls, making a sound as of wooden tenpins knocking. In spite of his muddy glasses, the man thinks he can see a bright-red wound on the brick and a pink cloud of brick dust. He turns around and picks up the spade that is lying on the ground in the place where the tracks of his galoshes are still clearly discernible. His gaze is pointed at the blade, as if to dig into the ground with it. His movements are stiff and uncertain, his head bent low. Suddenly a spasm runs through his body, as if he had been startled out of sleep. Has the guard again said some-

thing, or was it the sound of a whistle? The spasm lasts
only a moment. Dragging his spade behind him, the
man goes over to the pile of bricks and picks up his
coat. Then he marches in the column, carrying his
spade over his shoulder.

[45]

Wrapped in a rough blanket that smells of horses,
the man is sitting at the table. The lamp is no longer
on the table, but is hanging from a nail on the wall to
the left of it, slightly higher than his head. The light
from the square window across from him is grayish-
white, more a reflection of the snow than daylight. The
window trembles under the impact of the wind; from
time to time, needle-sharp flakes of snow seem to be
blowing through invisible cracks between the sill and
the window frame. Or perhaps it's just that the blasts
of wind are sending waves of cold air through the
cracks. Bent slightly forward, his hands on the tabletop,
the man is looking toward the window. There is nothing
to be seen but swirling snowflakes and a small sloping
pile of snow that has formed behind the glass at the
bottom of the window frame. Suddenly his fingers stop
moving and for a moment his hands lie motionless
before him. Then he reaches for a volume at the top
of the pile, to his right. He draws it closer, holds it
unopened, and looks at the cover as though seeing it
for the first time. It is a greasy, dog-eared old magazine.
The green title page shows advertising photos of rubber
tires and some large stylized letters, indicating the brand
name, no doubt. The title is printed on a slant, in larger

letters, on the upper third of the page, against a reddish-gray ground: *Selection*. Two columns of words in a large, light-colored rectangle below the title are doubtless the table of contents. The man leafs through the greasy, dog-eared magazine, apparently paying no attention to the rapidly turning pages; then he puts the magazine back on the pile from which he took it. The second volume he picks up seems to be identical with the first: the same photographs of tires with wavy treads, the same slanting strip with the title printed on it, the same light-colored rectangle containing the table of contents in two columns. Only the color of the ground is slightly different. The man puts the magazine back in its place, throws off his blanket, and goes to the window. His hands crossed behind his back, he looks out. Swirling snowflakes and from time to time, between two gusts of wind, the misty outline of a tree.

[*46*]

The man has draped his coat over his shoulders. He has a large yellow flower in his left-hand buttonhole. In places, the forest path is surmounted by a vault of trees. The man whips the nettles beside the path with his knotty stick. Suddenly he stops walking; he has heard the blows of an ax. And then, he thinks, voices. He slips off his coat and throws it over his arm. A moment later he finds himself in the open, dazzled by the sun. Shading his eyes with his hand, he sees, in a clearing some ten paces ahead of him, ax blades flashing like the pieces of a broken mirror. He doesn't see the woodcutters clearly—he barely glimpses them through the foliage at

the edge of the clearing, on the other side of the road—
but already he hears their grunting, which accompanies
the flashing ax blows. High above the flaming thicket,
a green treetop shudders. The flowers and leaves of
the elder across from him are motionless, as are the tall
nettle stalks and the green treetops all around him. For
a moment, he is puzzled. He looks up at the sky above
the swaying treetop. The sky is blue, deep blue. Just
one little white cloud above the swaying treetop. Even
before discovering the muscular torsos of the woodcutters through the curtain of leaves, he realizes that it's
their ax blows that are shaking the treetop. But he
doesn't seem to believe his eyes.

The woodcutters must have noticed him, for they
have suddenly stopped work. Now the man thinks they
are looking at him. He expects them to take flight and
foresees their movements: they will throw down their
axes and run for their shirts, which they have hung on
a bush. Or put them on while running; the cloth will
catch on thorns and tear. Nothing of the kind. Maybe
they haven't noticed him. Or maybe they are pretending
not to notice him. They have set their ax heads on the
ground and are holding the handles like canes. The
sun has clearly traced the outlines of their undershirts
on their torsos, and if it were not for the clumps of hair
on their chests, the man might not have noticed that
they are naked from the waist up. Their necks are dark
and wrinkled like the bark of the tree in front of them.
Two deep notches have been cut into the trunk, one
on either side. A brightness flows from them, as though
a flame were coming out of the tree, or as though there
were a powerful source of light inside it. The top of

the tree has stopped swaying. The woodcutters exchange axes, lift them first with one hand, then with
both hands. They swing them through the air as though
attacking the tree. The man goes straight toward them
through tall grass and hawthorn bushes. He hears one
of the woodcutters, who is still not looking at him, say
something; his ax handle, he says, isn't quite thick
enough, he is used to his own ax and this is his son's
ax or his brother's—something of the kind. The man
realizes that they are only pretending not to notice him
and that they will not run away. They speak to him.
The gentleman has sent for them, they say. What
gentleman, the man asks. "The gentleman." Paying no
further attention to him, they start swinging their axes,
cleaving the air with powerful, rhythmic strokes, accompanied by grunts. He is about to turn around and leave
when one of the woodcutters, raising his ax high above
an imaginary tree, says: "The one with the leg." Bare
to the waist, they stand facing each other (as they had
no doubt been standing before), swinging their sparkling blades in the beam of sunlight which slants down
from the crown of the tree they are felling and which
rises among them like a tall shining column.

[47]

All that can be seen through the square window is
the upper branches of a tree surrounded by swirling
snowflakes and covered by thick layers of snow; the thin
tips of the branches are lost in the storm. The man
stands up and goes to the window. Now he can also see
the tree trunk; it is almost entirely white, at least on the

side facing him. To the left of the tree, he sees the
blind wall of a house; farther off, in the direction of the
tree, a rusty wire fence is barely visible through the
curtain of snow. Its mesh is undoubtedly white by now;
the snow clinging to the wire makes the openings seem
smaller than they are. Or else the mesh is so full of
snow that the fence has been replaced by a white snowy
wall. Somewhere in the distance the barking of a dog
is heard, muffled as though wrapped in cotton. But the
man sees no dog, he sees nothing. Only the whitened
tree trunk and the blind wall. Suddenly, through the
snowflakes, he sees a square black object. It is approaching from the side, from the direction of the blind wall.
At first, the man does not know what it is. Until an
invisible hand turns the object toward him. A moment
later he sees the man. The man is lame, wrapped in a
cinder-gray blanket that looks like his own. The man at
the window thinks he can smell the blanket; it smells of
horses and urine. Snow is falling on the man's shoulders
and his hair. Bent forward, he is pushing a stove ahead
of him. The stove is black, possibly rusted; it moves
slowly through the deep snow, which shortens its legs
by half. Then stove and man disappear. The man at
the window can no longer see their trail in the snow.

[*48*]

(The man with the cane is outside the door, facing a
low blind wall, a stone fence, or the back of a house.
To the left of him, there is another wall; there are
windows in it with closed shutters. To the right, a high,
vaulted doorway. Under the vault, where the snow has

been cleared away, a man is sitting cross-legged, his
back to the wall. He is wearing a shapeless brown hat,
from which, as can be seen from the dark ring on the
crown, a ribbon has been removed. His ankles, above
his muddy shoes, are bare. Beside him there is a narrow
wooden trunk, trimmed with sheets of tin that look like
foil. From a drawer in the wooden trunk he takes a
small gypsy anvil, which he wedges between two of the
stones with which the courtyard is paved. He is holding
a hammer. He picks up one of the pots that are piled
beside him. After wiping the enameled bottom with the
palm of his hand, he raises it to the light. The man asks
him a question. The other shrugs his shoulders and
goes on hammering. The man repeats his question and
the other answers that the lady has company. The man
with the cane says nothing but stands there for a while.
He listens to the crackling of the enamel, and looks on
as lead rivets that look like 6.35 mm. bullets are driven
into old tin pots.)

[49]

The thin, wobbly legs of the stove cross the low
threshold. The black box moves slowly with a rattling
of tin. Something can be heard jiggling inside it; the
layer of mud and fireclay with which the stove is lined
has probably shaken loose. The man who was pushing
the stove has straightened up. For a moment he stands
still, as though blinded. The door behind him is wide
open, admitting the pale light of a winter afternoon.
Apparently, he has just discovered, in the half darkness
beside the window, the man who has been watching

him. While brushing the snow from his shoulders, the
new arrival says something. The other man does not
hear him or pretends not to. Suddenly the man by the
window throws the blanket off his shoulders and goes
to the corner. For a moment the other does not see
him. But only for a moment. Then the first man emerges
from the darkness, holding his stick in front of him.
Without a word, he approaches the stove and the man
who is standing beside it, breathing heavily. He raises
his cane and aims it, slantwise, at the stove. A moment
later a crash is heard. The iron tip of the cane has
pierced the side of the stove. A jangling of metal and
the crumbling of fireclay can be heard. Half the length
of the cane has passed through the rotten metal; the
man has a hard time pulling it out: scraps of rotten
metal fall out, looking like ashes. The man gives the tin
a powerful kick. The stove tips slowly, then pivots on
its axis.

[50]

The man has stopped for a moment. Possibly to
estimate the distance he has already covered. He no
longer hears the crunching of his shoes. From somewhere in the distance the wind carries the long-drawn-
out barking of a dog. Peering into the snowy darkness,
he sees nothing, not a shadow, not a movement. Resum-
ing the stance of a fencer, he listens. An unseen dog is
barking somewhere in the distance; the wind breaks up
and diffuses the sound.

Suddenly a little boy appears out of the falling snow,
just in front of the cane; the cane is pointed at the

child's chest. The man sees the boy open his mouth like a fish, but hears nothing, for the storm has obliterated the child's voice. The boy comes closer, until the iron tip of the man's cane touches his chest. Again he says something, trying to make himself heard above the howling of the wind. Then, realizing that the man cannot hear him, he takes hold of the cane near its tip and, holding the cane, walks on ahead of the man. Each holding an end of the cane, they plod on through the snowstorm.

NOTES OF A MADMAN (IV)

[51]

Aware that I am incapable of killing myself, because my body, death, blood, and all the trappings of death (rope, razor blades, weapons) disgust me, I recently, when on my way to the village after taking my son home, had a sudden inspiration, I thought of a painless way of throwing off all my worries and fears without submitting to any Grand Guignol spectacle: death in the snow, a gentle death without blood or bodily mutilation, without pain or violence.

For I've come full circle. My return to the village is just that, a return to my beginnings, to the earth, the final stage of the great circle that every living creature describes in its headlong race from birth to death, where the two ends meet.

It wasn't really a decision, it was never a decision—decision presupposes will—just a vague intention that I tried to smuggle not only into my body, my animal self, but also into my consciousness; because if I had as much as admitted it to myself, I might have committed suicide.

[52]

Nature rules over all things except the terror it inspires. (*Berakhot* 33B).

[53]

This feeling of being abandoned by my own self, this perception of myself through the eyes of another, this confrontation with myself as a stranger*

while I stood in line on the bank of the Danube.† It was the same feeling: on one side E.S., fifty-three, married, father of two children, who thinks, smokes, works, writes, shaves with a safety razor; and on the other side, next to him, or rather inside him, somewhere in the center of his brain, as though asleep or half asleep, another E.S., who is and is not I, because while the first E.S. is shaving with the precise movements of an untrembling hand, the second, shrunk to the size of an embryo, is doing something entirely different, engaged in unknown and dangerous occupations, and sometimes, just for an instant, I catch him in these forbidden, secret activities, catch him *in flagrante*, doing *something different*, something utterly incomprehensible to me, for it is absolutely unrelated not only to shaving or tying a tie or eating but also to my ideas and thought processes: he is someone else. But what terrifies me most of all is that I cannot tell exactly what horrible thing this other self is doing (while I'm shaving, for instance), because this other self hides from me, and when, in the midst of shaving, I think I've grabbed him by the throat, caught him in the act, he slips away into some part of my own brain, into some diseased fold of

* Incomplete. A line is missing.
† In the massacres of January 1942 the victims stood in line, waiting to be killed and pushed under the river ice. Some were released after waiting for hours. [Trans.]

my own brain, and I never have him entirely in my power, I can never call him to account or even bring him out into the open and, without a word of blame or reproach, get rid of him with God's help. What does this other E.S. do while I am shaving? He wanders off to unknown regions, utters incomprehensible syllables, incomprehensible words and sentences; incomprehensible, not because they are incoherent, but because he says them in a whisper or, if he says them out loud, immediately adds a lot of other sentences or incoherent syllables that make me forget the perfectly clear and unmistakable meaning of the first sentences, that clear meaning which encompasses the significance of the whole text, the whole thought. This other self goes roaming around in regions unknown to me, and when I surprise him for a moment, by pretending to be wholly preoccupied with shaving or with the little hairs lining my nostrils, I sometimes succeed for a moment, but only for a moment, in observing this other self. I see him taking part in a funeral procession, though I can't be sure whether he is in the hearse or just happens to be attending the funeral, and a moment later (or actually in the very same moment) I'm not even sure whether it is a hearse or just a cab that has been painted black and whether this fellow is really he, my other self. And the worst part of this pursuit of the other man, who is and is not I, is the terrifying fact that this other self, who is connected with me like a Siamese twin by the backbone, the brain, and the sympathetic nervous system, that this Siamese twin of mine, who moves independently with untrammeled hands and feet in a different direction, that this twin brother of mine, this

I and not-I of mine, actually *thinks* with my brain, steals the thoughts of my brain, as though our brains were joined or at least situated in one and the same monstrous skull, in two skulls that have grown together, that have become one single monstrous *Wasserkopf* containing two brains side by side, in such a way that the thoughts of one are communicated to the other, but not quite clearly or articulately, because one interferes with the other, as when we listen while half asleep to a conversation behind a wall, behind a thick wall that divides and at the same time connects two rooms. In the other room, a jealous couple may be cutting each other's throat, a cold blade may be digging into living flesh, we hear cries, struggling, groans; but what we hear may just as well be the panting of passionately entangled lovers (one cannot be quite sure through the thick wall), or it may be hysterical laughter or desperate sobs. Thus this other self pursues me, turning up unexpectedly inside me while I am shaving in front of the cracked mirror, peacefully looking at my foam-framed face in the cracked mirror. It's morning, the snowstorm is over, the sun is shining through the square window, cows are mooing at the farm across the road, the bell is ringing in the village belfry. It is warm in here, pinecones are burning in the tin stove, the smoke is spreading, the room smells of resin and forest. At this moment my other self turns up inside me; anguished and trembling, he escapes my brain, because something terrible has just happened to him, a disastrous thought has inflamed his brain, the thought of death, an intense, merciless thought, as when a man wakes up in his grave, but I, E.S., don't know the exact meaning of his thought, I don't even know that it's the thought of death, but I feel the intensity, the weight of the thought, its dangerous pessimism, its killing reality, and I begin to tremble somewhere in the depth of my being. My hands don't tremble, my hands are still holding my razor, my nicotine-stained fingers follow the bony line of my chin, probe the little hairs, but my sympathetic nervous system, my heart, my innermost being, my frightened, worried self tremble. For all my energies are concentrated on trying to clear up this enigma, this riddle, this *ténébreuse affaire* that confronts the other self within me; on clearing up this crime story, in which there is not a single positive element, not a single solid fact, in which nothing is known except that death is involved, the death of some person, or death as such, quite apart from any vital statistics; the trembling inside me, the mad eyes of my other self looking at me from the cracked mirror as I shave, they show that death is involved, some peril, some terrible existential catastrophe—of that, there can be no doubt.

[54]

All that was left in my mind was the impression of a nightmare, all that I could formulate coherently was a single word: BIG, an adjective coupled with some impossible thing, with some concept that I could not identify but that emanated unconscionable horror. Yet this word BIG, which with painful effort I managed to move into the realm of reason, of articulated thought, to hold fast for a moment amid the swift dreamlike procession of concepts and images, this word was totally

adequate, it fitted in quite naturally and logically with
some unknown concept, agreed with it in gender,
number, and case, even though this concept was still
outside the confines of the intelligible, outside the yellow
spot of consciousness. This terrible and terrifying BIG
oppressed me with its enormous, horrifying presence,
and the reason for my horror was the inability of my
mind and consciousness to join a noun to this adjective,
for I knew that such a clarification of concepts would
have made my nightmare more intelligible, would have
given my horror human contours, or at least the di-
mensions of a clear, definable horror. When at length
I attached this neutral (or rather, neuter) adjective to a
noun, or perhaps a verb, my terror, my inner trembling,
was transformed into a waking nightmare, and it occurred to me that what was going on inside me was
simply the continuation of a suddenly interrupted
dream: while a part of my being pursued everyday
(logical) thought processes, another part was sound
asleep, tortured by a nightmare which it was unable to
throw off; fragments of this waking dream, this nightmare (from which that word BIG had slithered), ravaged
my mind and inner being, and in my mind and being
two processes went on side by side, sleep and waking,
nightmare and lucidity, but the two processes were
divided by an impenetrable wall, the nexus between
them had been shattered: my waking personality concentrated all its efforts on trying to catch a word from
the other side of the wall, from the sleeping part of the
brain, for even if I could not see, I wanted at least to
hear what was going on in my own being, now, at this
moment. The word BIG was still the only clearly artic-

ulated, intelligible word, though it may have been mere translation, a mere surrogate for some other word, some other concept, some other condition. What was happening on the other side of my consciousness was happening much too quickly, images were rushing past at an unconscionable speed, and the things that were going on there, in the darkness of my being, the images that were passing through the cortex of my brain, were too horrible to analyze calmly, even if I had been able to capture them: all that happened on the other side of life, in the profound, mythical realms of death, in the dread valley beyond the grave. That other self, my other being, was myself after death: the dead E.S. had come to meet the living one; rising from my dream, the dead E.S. had become flesh and come to live beside the living one.

*

My pitiful split self.

[55]

What are all man's strivings, all that goes by the name of history, compared to his vain and ludicrous attempt to combat the absurdity of universal death, to give death a so-called meaning, as if it were possible to give death a meaning, to give it any other meaning than the one it has. The most cynical philosophers try to console the public by giving meaning, with the help of some higher logic or clever turns of phrase, to the meaninglessness of death. But what remains, to me at least, an inexplicable mystery is this: how has man been able, despite his knowledge of death, to go on living and acting, as though death were something outside him, as though it were a natural phenomenon. The trembling that has taken hold of me in the last few days has enabled me, despite my paroxysms of fear, to understand the nature of my sickness; namely, that from time to time, for reasons quite unknown to me, and with heaven knows what motives, I become *lucid*. Then the knowledge of death rises up in me, of death as such; in such moments of diabolical illumination, death, death *an sich*, assumes its full weight and meaning, which most people (deluding themselves with the help of work and art, whose meaning and *vanitas* they obscure with fine phrases) do not so much as suspect, until it knocks, clearly and unmistakably, at the door, scythe in hand, as in medieval engravings. But what terrifies me (knowledge brings no consolation) and adds to my inner trembling is the consciousness that my madness is in reality lucidity, and that what I need if I am to recover—for this constant trembling is unbearable—is precisely madness, lunacy, forgetfulness; only lunacy can save me, only madness can make me well. If by chance Dr. Papandopoulos were to ask me about the state of my health, about the origin of my traumas, my fears, I would answer clearly and unmistakably: *lucidity*.

A WITNESS INTERROGATED (I)

I received the summons on my return from Porszombat; that is, yesterday.

What were you doing in Porszombat?

Visiting the Mayers.

Who are the Mayers?

Mr. Samuel Mayer is an old friend from business school. We hadn't seen each other for more than thirty years. A few days ago I heard that a certain Mayer, a businessman, was living in Porszombat, and I thought it must be he. So I decided to go and see him.

For what reasons?

Mainly because I wanted to see my old school friend, but also because I hoped he would give me moral and material support.

Who told you that Mayer was living in Porszombat?

I don't remember. Possibly my nephew Gyula, known as George.

How did he happen to mention the Mayers?

By pure chance, if I'm not mistaken. To tell the truth, I'm not on very good terms with George, I mean Gyula; I might even say that we are on the outs.

Then how did he come to mention the Mayers?

In the course of one of our quarrels, I told him—that is, George—that I wasn't interested in any of his shady deals, and he said I was just a bankrupt and a *Luftmensch*, because otherwise I'd live decently like Mayer, the respected merchant in Porszombat, who had told him that we had once been at business school together in

Zalaegerszeg. That gave me the idea of going to see Mayer and, as I said before, asking him for help.

You mean money?

At first I wasn't thinking of money or of anything in particular. I just wanted to win the confidence of a well-to-do businessman who might lend me a little money, flour, or tobacco from time to time. It might have come in handy, especially now that I'm on the outs with George and my sister, with whom I and my family of three are living at the moment.

Did Mayer oblige you?

He lent me forty pengö and promised to send me a certain quantity of flour in a few days.

Free of charge?

I think he meant free of charge, but I pretended to take it as a temporary loan, same as the money he gave me.

Have you repaid the money?

Not yet. The new law has drastically reduced my pension, and the expense of moving and getting settled has been staggering. I expect to repay the money in installments spread over a year. At the most.

With interest?

There was no mention of interest.

Getting back to the Mayers—how many are there in the house?

His wife, who's from Budapest. And one of their three sons, the oldest, who works with his father in the business. It's a retail business, a kind of grocery store, but it doesn't seem to be doing very well just now. I heard that from Mayer himself. He complained of difficulty in getting supplies and unfair competition. He

suspects that many of the local people, his former
customers, are staying away from his shop because of
threatening letters from the local party.

Where are Mr. Mayer's other sons?

The youngest is on the Eastern front. He hasn't
written in more than a month, and they fear the worst.
The middle one, an archaeologist, is somewhere on the
Hungarian–Yugoslav border; he was studying some
Roman–Pannonian excavations, and now he has been
arrested on suspicion of planning to cross the border
and join some illegal organization. They're not really
sure about this news, because it came from a dubious
sort of person who refused to give his name and
demanded a sizable sum of money for the information.
Oh yes. I forgot to tell you that Mayer's mother lives
with them, she's paralyzed and half deaf, and there's
also a kind of handyman who helps in the shop and the
house, a man of about fifty; he chops wood for them,
tends the stoves, and looks after the old lady. If I
remember rightly, his name is Alojz, he's a Slovene
from Muraszombat. He's been working for them for
more than twenty years. That's all, I think.

You say you're not acquainted with Mayer's sons?

That is true.

How, then, do you know that one of them has been
involved in an archaeological dig in the place you
mentioned?

I heard it from Mayer himself. He even showed me
a ceramic figurine belonging to his son; he claims it's
authentic and keeps it in a vitrine.

Describe the figurine.

It's ceramic, pretty well preserved, about twenty centimeters long, it represents a wounded boar. The hind

part is damaged, but the head, the forepart of the body, and the forelegs are intact. The boar seems to be wounded, the forelegs are crumpled as in the grip of death, the head is inclined slightly, and the snout is wide open, revealing the tusks. But the wounded animal's grimace suggests helplessness and death rather than power and blood lust. The eyes show an almost human fear, though you could hardly call the head stylized.

What else is there in the vitrine?

A statue of fine-grained white marble, representing Hermes with little Pluto in his arms. It is some thirty centimeters high. The head is missing, and so are most of the right arm and both legs up to the knees. Hermes is completely naked, except for a sort of chiton that hangs from his left shoulder, drapes over his back, and winds around his left arm. Fragments of his messenger's staff can be seen in the hand in which he is holding Pluto. The weight of his body probably rested on his right leg. Little Pluto is also badly damaged. The head, his chest, his abdomen, and both legs from the knee down are missing. The hands of the divine child and a small remnant of his left leg can be seen against Hermes' chest.

Continue.

The figure of a naked tutelary deity, about seventy centimeters high, also badly damaged. The head and neck, the legs below the knee, and the whole left arm are missing. The long wings are only slightly damaged. The right arm is held across the chest, only the hand is missing. It seems likely that the god was holding a snake in his hand.

Continue.

A few earrings, also Roman, coins from the reign of Hadrian, fragments of sacred urns, some Jewish ritual vessels, a menorah, all this of less value, or so he says.

Did he show you a photograph of his son?

He showed me several photographs of him at different ages. They were in an album, bound in green velvet, with metal fittings.

Have you the impression, on the basis of these photographs, that you have met this man, Mayer's son, somewhere?

I don't believe so.

What does he look like?

Medium height, slight potbelly, prominent lower lip, broad fleshy nose, short bristly hair, metal-rimmed glasses, bushy eyebrows, short arms, rather carelessly dressed.

Gait?

I couldn't say.

Since when have Mr. Mayer and your nephew George known each other?

I don't know. All Mayer told me was that he and George had been exchanging certain commodities for a long time.

What kind of commodities?

I don't know.

Do you know a certain Mrs. Fischer in Novi Sad?

Yes.

When did you see her last?

On the sixteenth or seventeenth of March, a day or two after arriving in Novi Sad.

What brought you to Novi Sad?

I went to get some of my belongings that were still there. Two cupboards full of bedclothes.

What does Mrs. Fischer do?

Until recently, she sold needlepoint canvas, notions, and crochet and embroidery patterns.

Until recently, you say?

Yes. She's sick and nearsighted now. She suffered a nervous shock recently.

What happened?

I don't know. She didn't tell me anything about it. I only heard she'd been ill from the caretaker who let me in.

Describe Mrs. Fischer's shop.

It's a small shop, fronting on the courtyard, three meters by two, with one window that must have been used as a showcase. The vitrine, in which she used to display her wares, now has a handwritten notice in it, offering a sofa, two armchairs, a mirror, a sideboard, and a stove for sale, *on extremely reasonable terms*. Inside, the window is covered with blue wrapping paper and a blanket, so the room was always in half darkness; the only light was provided by a single candle. When I came to see her, Mrs. Fischer lit a gas lamp.

What was there in the room?

In the corner, a silver-plated stove; beside the window, a folding table with scissors, a pincushion, paper patterns, snippets of different-colored cloth, balls of yarn, spools of thread, ribbons, braid, and bits of lace on it; there was also a card table with another lamp, unlit, a worn-out deck of Spanish playing cards, and some cretonne. The walls were covered with embroidery canvas, showing scenes from domestic life drawn with blue lines: for instance, a housewife lifting a pot cover and releasing fragrant steam, while her husband, holding a bunch of roses behind his back, smiles. This design is repeated over and over in almost identical form—it is thumbtacked to the wall, thrown over the back of the chair, over the sewing machine, on the tablecloth.

Did you know her husband?

Yes. He was a traveling salesman for Weiss & Company, brush manufacturers, but along the way he also sold needlepoint and embroideries made by his wife—Mrs. Fischer, that is.

What were your relations with the aforesaid firm?

I was part owner. As a result of Weiss's lawsuit against me, I lost all the capital I had put into the business.

What did you manufacture?

Brushes.

What else?

Nothing else. Only brushes: for masons, for house painters, for artists, hairbrushes, and so on.

What do you mean by "and so on"?

Steel brushes, scrubbing brushes, shaving brushes.

Did you ever discuss the Mayers with Mr. Fischer?

No. I don't remember.

Was there another entrance to the shop in addition to the one you've mentioned?

There is only one door, the one that only opens halfway because of the sofa.

Describe the sofa.

A plain, old-fashioned sofa with a backrest and velvet upholstery which must have been red at one time but is now all frayed and spotted with wax, sperm, and blood. Later Mrs. Fischer spread the embroidery canvases I've mentioned over the backrest and the whole sofa.

Why did she do that?

David Fischer, her husband, killed himself on that same sofa. Until recently, the hole made by the bullet that passed through his head could be seen in the backrest.

Did you see any masculine objects in Mrs. Fischer's apartment?

No, I saw nothing of the kind.

Think again.

One vitrine, covered by a soiled curtain of embroidery canvas showing that same identical scene drawn in blue ink, contained a few objects that might conceivably have been called masculine, not only because they had belonged to Mr. David Fischer, her late husband, but also because their natural gender, so to speak, was masculine: an amber cigarette holder, a silver snuff box, little things like that.

You haven't left anything out?

Some phylacteries, a Torah scroll, and some utensils.

What kind of utensils?

Knives of different sizes, slightly rusty, though I have the impression that Mrs. Fischer takes loving care of them. Whenever she showed them to me (as she did every time I went to see her), she would breathe on the shiny steel blades and wipe them with a piece of dirty embroidery canvas.

How many of these blades were there?

At least ten.

What was the significance and function of these knives?

Her husband, the late David Fischer, was a *shohet*, a kind of religious figure, authorized to slaughter animals for Jewish dinner tables.

Were any of these knives missing?

I couldn't say.

Why did Mrs. Fischer show them to you?

As I've told you, that was part of the regular ceremony whenever I visited her. Whenever trustworthy people and old friends of her husband's came to see her, she would open that vitrine. That brought the conversation around to the late David Fischer. She would put two chairs in front of the vitrine, raise the curtain, and start talking. At certain moments, while studying the amber cigarette holder or the silver snuff box or wiping the knives with the canvas, she would speak to David, in a natural tone of voice, as if he were there: Don't you remember, David? You're quite right, David.

Are you sure she was speaking to him, her late husband?

Perfectly sure.

So you say they are butcher's knives?

Yes.

Didn't you just say that Mr. Fischer was a traveling salesman?

That was a long time ago. Under certain circumstances, the two occupations are not mutually exclusive.

What do you mean by certain circumstances?

I mean exceptional circumstances. It has become very difficult to find anyone capable of ritual slaughtering. Being an experienced butcher is not enough. And to make matters worse, it pays next to nothing. Fewer and fewer people observe the old customs. After Mr. Glessinger's death, the only possible candidate for the job of *shohet* was Mr. Fischer. True, he wasn't a butcher, but he met all the other requirements. He was an

Orthodox Jew, an old synagogue rat, and he knew the
laws by heart (he had learned them mostly from his
father), and, besides, he had stuffed birds, so he knew
something about animal anatomy.

Why didn't you tell me before that Mr. Fischer stuffed
birds?

I did tell you.

You told me he was a traveling salesman.

I didn't think the other was important.

Let me remind you that everything is important.

I only wanted to . . .

Let's get back to your nephew George. You said you
were on the outs with him.

Yes.

Yet you live under the same roof.

Feeling the need for independence, I left my sister's
household of my own free will. Now my family and I
live in the so-called annex, which is simply a former
stable.

Be that as it may, I assume that George's habits are
not unknown to you.

As far as I have been able to observe, he takes no
interest in anything but his shop. I would not say he
has a real head for business; with him, it's all a way of
killing time: his money-grubbing, his double-entry book-
keeping, his mania for rearranging his shelves, his
passion for collecting advertisements for everything
under the sun, especially things he has never sold and
probably never will. Oh yes, and his bicycle. I do think
his bicycle is worth mentioning. It's specially adapted
for his paralyzed left leg. The left pedal has been removed.

Continue.

As far as I know, George has had no affairs, with
women I mean, though once, about ten years ago, there
was some talk of his marrying a certain lady in Donja
Lendava. She was the widow of a local shopkeeper, a
Mr. Bernfeld. My only source of information about this
is a letter my sister, George's mother that is, wrote me
in Novi Sad. But nothing came of it, it wasn't mentioned
in any other letter. As far as I know, George kept going
to Donja Lendava on his bicycle until just before the
war. He regards the bicycle as the modern vehicle that
has replaced the old-fashioned carriages his father used
to ride around in.

Does your nephew hunt?

At the time when I was staying at his house, he left
the shop just once, and they told me he had gone
hunting early that morning. I myself did not see him
go, and I didn't ask him about his luck. Anyway, I had
no intention of eating his game. I personally am no
lover of the hunt. I might even say . . .

Let's get back to your nephew.

That's all, I think.

Where does he keep his gun? And what kind of gun
is it?

I never saw a gun of any kind in the house, and the
only hunting equipment I ever saw—on that same
morning—was a leather cartridge belt, but there wasn't
a single cartridge in it. Later, under the bed, I found
an empty shell case, which had probably fallen on the
floor when George was filling his shell with shot or
putting in caps. As for the gun, I saw it only once, and
then from quite a distance, and not very clearly, what
with my nearsightedness and the atmospheric conditions. While taking my morning walk, I saw George at

the edge of the woods. With his gun at the ready, he was stalking some game, probably a hare. I hid behind an oak tree; I didn't want to meet him, because our relations had been getting worse ever since I arrived. It was snowing hard, so I couldn't see what kind of gun it was. At first I wasn't even sure whether it was a gun or a stick George used to scare away magpies. It wasn't until sometime later, when he passed my hiding place, that I saw it was a shotgun, double-barreled I think, because I heard two shots in quick succession and instantly saw their tragic effect: two innocent crows fell from the tree over my head and landed at my feet, so to speak. I believe he shot those crows just to show me that he thought nothing of firing a gun. I'm sure he had seen me before I hid behind the tree and he wanted to frighten me, or rather to warn me.

What kind of shot did he use?

The shell case I found under the bed that day was empty. But the crows were massacred, literally torn to pieces. It may have been bear or wild-boar shot.

Are you sure it was your nephew George?

Yes, sir, I'm sure.

Are you sure it was he who fired the shots?

Just about.

On what ground?

Because of the time that elapsed between the moment when I caught sight of George and the firing of the two shots in quick succession.

How much time was that?

A minute or two.

Is that sufficient ground for concluding that he fired the shots?

I saw no other hunter, nor any footprints other than

his. They were easy to recognize, because his stiff left leg with its orthopedic shoe leaves a characteristic print, you'd think a flatiron had been plunked down. Besides, the crows had been torn to pieces. That looked just like George to me.

What are your nephew's political views?

Conservative.

What do you mean by that?

Nothing in the world would make him enlarge or modernize his shop, or stock anything more than the standard articles—kerosene, sugar, shoe polish (two colors), shoelaces (two dozen), candles, flypaper, cheap candy, etc. He thinks that to stock anything else, such as fine soap or toilet water, not to mention electric belts, would arouse the suspicions of the peasants and the authorities. He's also afraid the peasants would de-nounce him as a modernist, pornographer, and enemy of the patriarchal way of life. What I think, and I've often told him so, is that he's just expressing his own convictions; it's not the peasants who think that way, it's him.

What are his political convictions? I think you under-stand my question.

When it comes to politics, George is a total ignoramus. In his opinion, politics is something that can't be helped, a kind of natural phenomenon, like thunder or snow-storms. In other words, it doesn't interest him. His logic is simple and terrifying in its simplicity: politics is incomprehensible and intrinsically dangerous, infec-tious, like cholera. If you keep away from it, it will keep away from you. That will reduce the danger of infection to a minimum. Then you just have to wash your hands as often as possible, as hypochondriacs and gynecologists do, and you'll be able to sip your raspberry juice in peace. The one thing he's afraid of today is the Allied planes that fly over the village, not because they might drop their bombs on the village (because he knows that bombs *cost money*, so they won't drop them just anywhere); his worry is that a damaged plane might be forced to jettison its bombs or that they might drop of their own accord, "without the help of any human hand," and, on the whim of chance and providence, destroy his shop and scatter his sugar cubes in all directions. On my first day in the village, I declared categorically that I would not discuss politics with George, because, in my opinion, politics has nothing to do with superstition. I also said that I considered the political opinions of any coachman more plausible and intelligible than George's nonsense about bombs that fall from the sky for the express purpose of destroying his shop and his powdered sugar.

What else does your nephew sell, besides sugar?

I've told you: salt, cheap candy, flypaper, shoe polish, dubbin, shoelaces, axle grease, candles, kerosene, lamp chimneys, toilet soap, gingham, ribbons, lamp wicks, and notions. That's all, I think.

You haven't omitted anything?

At any rate, I've listed his present stock. I may have exaggerated. I said toilet soap, when actually it's common household soap made from animal waste. He bought this soap from a peasant in case someone should ask for soap, someone from the city or some officer or traveler who had lost his way. Actually, I'm inclined to think that his only purpose in buying this stinking soap was to sell it to me. I can't see anyone else in the village buying soap.

Did he carry a wider variety of articles before the war?

For a time he stocked the products of the Mepol Company in Vrbas, Mepol–Šlonski & Strauss. Somewhere around 1925, he wrote me a letter asking me to intercede with this firm to release him from the contractual obligation (whether written or verbal, I don't recall) to carry certain articles that he, that is, George, was unable to sell. George had hoped to sell certain products to the local peasants and rich people, because it was rumored that the whole region would be electrified in the next two or three years. However, as you undoubtedly know, nothing came of it, and the village is still without electricity.

What were these articles?

According to Mr. Glušac, the firm's only official agent, who sent me a written report on the activities of Mepol, it was articles made of celluloid or Bakelite: telephone casings, medicine chests, sugar canisters, electrical switches, insulators of all kinds, tableware, bathroom tiles, combs, safety razors, brushes, mirrors, picture frames, and other cheap goods that did not have the firm name stamped on them and were sold under the counter to gypsies, peddlers, and small village shopkeepers like George. Well, George asked me to intercede with said firm and obtain a new contract that would modify the existing arrangements as follows: they would stop sending him products with the firm name stamped on them, because—with the exception of the sugar canisters—they were no longer in demand, and would continue to furnish only those of the other category; namely, cheap trinkets, combs, mirrors, picture frames, buckles, and celluloid knickknacks.

Is your nephew still doing business with this firm?

According to Mr. Glušac's communication, the firm of Šlonski & Strauss closed its doors in 1929, when Mr. Avigdor Strauss emigrated to Eretz Israel. With his departure, the firm lost its reputation and standing, but for a time continued to sell its remaining stocks of notions. The firm of Mepol had been liquidated, to all intents and purposes, at the time when I interceded for George. It was then that George decided, once and for all, that it was risky and therefore unnecessary to add to his inventory.

What became of Šlonski?

Šlonski also went off to Palestine, as Mr. Glušac informed me. It is uncertain, however, whether our Šlonski is identical with the well-known poet Avraham Shlonsky, author of *Stones of Chaos*. The late Paja Schwarz assured me that they were one and the same person, adducing as proof a letter from one Feuerstein, a relative of his, in which he said that Šlonski had become famous and allegedly had asked for news of various friends in Vrbas and Novi Sad, especially Herz Schwarz, as the late Paja was called.

Who is Feuerstein?

Feuerstein is also a writer, a native of the region. He emigrated to Israel at about the same time as Šlonski, and they are often mentioned together as belonging to the same school. He publishes his books under the name of Avigdor Hameiri. You could have learned more about him from the late Paja Schwarz, who, as I said before, was related to Feuerstein alias Avigdor Hameiri, and corresponded with him in Hungarian and Hebrew, which the late Herz Schwarz had studied and had a fairly good command of.

Did you attend to any other business for George?

About 1939, at the time of my trip to Trieste and then to Kotor and Cetinje, George wrote me, asking for information about the prices of exotic fruits and the possibilities of shipment. He wanted to draw me into some kind of partnership, because the idea of importing exotic fruits originated with me. I, however, had never set myself up as a potential partner, I had merely suggested in a letter that he might sell pomegranates and dried figs and offered to get him a few addresses and recommend him to a few dealers. But in his letter he proposed that I should take care of purchasing and shipping, in return, of course, for a share of the profits, while he concentrated on sales—in other words, that I should incur all the risk. That's why I never answered his letter, because, on the one hand, I had no desire to let myself in for all that, and on the other hand, frankly, I didn't take George's offer very seriously, since the whole idea of selling exotic fruits to peasants was ridiculous. I therefore decided to write, promising to bring him a basket of oranges and dried figs that would last him for two or three seasons, and I even wrote the letter, but in the end I didn't mail it, because George can no more understand a joke than fathom the mysteries of commerce. He is a typical specimen of an old-fashioned Sephardic shopkeeper and I would go so far as to say that he has always regarded even his little grocery store as a great luxury. I sincerely believe that he should have carried a tray with a strap slung around his neck and sold little mirrors and rubber bands at country fairs, or peddled feather beds, like his grandfather.

Are there any indications that he sold a wider variety of articles before the war than he does now?

Labels for rice, pepper, vanilla, bay leaves, cinnamon are still clearly distinguishable on empty drawers and canisters in his shop. Still, I would not swear that those particular drawers contained those particular articles. According to my sister, he also carried nails, wire, thread, pots, pans, knives and forks, paper, tobacco, tax stamps, ink, pens, and penholders.

Did he carry hunting accessories?

Not to my knowledge.

Do your nephew and Mrs. Fischer know each other?

No, they do not.

Did your nephew know Mr. Fischer?

I don't believe so. In any case, he never came up in our conversation. George never mentioned him. Besides, as I've already said, George rarely left his shop; when he did go out, it was almost exclusively on his bicycle, to Muraszombat, Nagykanisza, or Lendava, so there is little likelihood of his going to Novi Sad.

What did you do in Novi Sad apart from visiting the aforementioned Mrs. Fischer?

I've already told you. I shipped my belongings by slow freight: two cupboards full of bedclothes and kitchen utensils, which, incidentally, have not yet arrived. Aside from that, I went to see my old friend Mr. Gavanski.

Who is Gavanski?

We've known each other since I had my first job in Novi Sad. He helped me find an apartment and procure furniture. You see, I couldn't afford new furniture, but thanks to Mr. Gavanski, who was working for an agency, I was able to buy secondhand but well-preserved furniture at a reasonable price. Gavanski vouched for me on that occasion.

Continue.

We had met at the Bosnjak. That was a fairly decent bar near the railroad station, or rather the railroad office; I often went there because I was working part-time for the railroad. One day we got kind of crocked together and then we went to his place in a cab. Gavanski had quite a lot of bottled wine in his cellar.

What did he do?

As I've told you, he worked for an agency. His job was selling real estate.

Does he have a family?

A wife and daughter. But he doesn't seem to be on good terms with them. I know he cooks for himself most of the time, because he claims that his wife's cooking is bad for his blood pressure, and that he doesn't want to change his habits. You see, he's been a vegetarian ever since he can remember; he's been living on fruit and vegetables for years, though it seems to me that he has been untrue to his herbivorous principles lately; he often eats bacon with lots of onions, in secret, as though trying to fool himself.

Tell me about his daughter.

She's twenty-four, engaged to a businessman by the name of Fekete from Csantavér. I've never had occasion to meet him, but I have the impression that Gavanski is not exactly pleased with the engagement.

For what reason?

I couldn't say. He doesn't like to talk about it, so I haven't dared to ask him any questions.

What are the relations between Gavanski and Mrs. Fischer?

To the best of my knowledge, they don't know each other.

Does Gavanski travel much?

I don't think he has set foot out of the house for years. He dreads the slightest exercise, even indoors; he sits in his bergère all day, as if it were a wheelchair. That accounts for his swollen legs and unhealthy fat. I once told him so.

At the time of your visit, were there other persons in the house?

No one but him and his wife.

Where was Miss Gavanski?

They said she was off on a trip with her fiancé.

What kind of trip?

I couldn't say.

You said her fiancé is a businessman?

Yes, a businessman or a traveling salesman. That's what they told me.

What does this Fekete sell?

I don't know. We never talked about it.

Try to remember.

We never talked about it.

When did you leave Gavanski?

I spent the night at his place.

Why?

Gavanski told me it was curfew time and I'd better not go wandering around.

How long were you under his roof?

One night.
Where did you go then?
I took a cab.
Where did you find the cab?
On Louis Barthou Street.
So you went there on foot?
Yes.
Did it take you two hours to walk from Station Street
to Louis Barthou Street?
Yes. I dropped in to see the priest.
What did you want from the priest?
Certificates from the baptismal records for members
of my family.
How much did you pay him for them?
The price of the tax stamps.
We will check your statements.
Two pengö for each certificate.
Did you go into the church?
No.
So the priest gave you the certificates?
Yes.
Did he give them to you in his rooms? Yes or no?
Yes.
Through whom did you get in touch with him?
Through the parish.
Had you known him before?
No.
Who sent you to him?
There was a young secretary at the parish office, I
don't remember his name; he sent me to the priest.
This secretary was extremely cautious. He told me there
had been many requests of this kind lately, that lots of

people were trying to get false papers for members of their family. I assured him that I was not one of those, and that what I wanted was perfectly legal. Then he directed me to the priest.

In an earlier interview, I'll give you the exact date, yes, that's it, March 28, not so long ago, you said the following (I quote verbatim): "My niece Rebecca, now Maria, is studying the catechism under the direction of a young priest. It seems to me that her conversion reflects a leaning toward a kind of spiritual prostitution rather than any conscious conviction."

Yes, that is just what I said.

I quote further: "No religion is so perfect as to justify conversion. The only religion is the belief in God."

Yes, that is what I still think.

If I understand you right, you have no intention of imitating your niece, who is taking catechism lessons.

Exactly.

How do you account for the fact that you went to an Orthodox church and not to the synagogue?

I never went to the synagogue before, and I was not on good terms with the rabbi.

Did you meet anyone other than the persons you have mentioned?

I think I have mentioned all my private calls.

Meaning that you also made business calls?

Aside from my visit to the priest, the term "business call" might apply to my stop at the railroad administration, where I asked about certain business matters.

What business matters?

My pension.

With whom did you discuss that?

With Mr. Laufer. Andrija Laufer.

Who is Laufer?

A clerk in the railroad administration. We once worked together in Šid, in the days when he was still a trainee.

What is his job now?

He never got beyond the rank of dispatcher. Now he has been demoted to clerk or something of the kind. Anyway, he is still working, though he expects to be fired any minute.

Isn't it surprising that he is still entrusted with such responsible work?

It has to be remembered that Mr. Laufer is a Muslim, a convert. His official name is Alija Latifić, but we kept on calling him by his old name, which is Andrija. Somewhere around 1920, he married a Muslim woman from Sarajevo and was converted. I don't believe her parents had to put much pressure on him, I believe he did it out of love. When his wife died, a year or two after her marriage to Andrija, I mean Alija, he became a kind of lay dervish; he learned Arabic and studied the Koran. I think he was secretly preparing for some sort of mission to Mecca or Palestine, but he never summoned up the strength to go. He couldn't bring himself to leave her eternal dwelling place, and he was convinced that the Mohammedan faith was his only hope of being united with his late wife in the other world.

Make it short.

That kind of conversion is an act of faith: love is an emanation of God.

What did you talk about?

Laufer works in an office with two other clerks; he did not wish to discuss personal matters in their presence. At first I thought he didn't recognize me, but then, when I told him my name, I realized that he was only pretending. So I confined myself to my official business and merely asked him if he knew what had become of the complaint I had lodged when my pension was reduced. He told me that the file had come to him and he wrote the registration number on a scrap of paper for me. In the end, he advised me to wait a month and then apply to him *in writing*. He hoped the matter would be settled by then.

Where were the two clerks you mention sitting?

The younger one, in civilian clothes, was sitting directly opposite Andrija. He was writing something, or pretending to. The other, about the same age as Andrija, was sitting to his right, at the same big table— actually, two office desks pushed together and covered with blue wrapping paper. This second clerk had a small bald spot; like Andrija, he was wearing a faded overcoat belonging to a railroader's uniform, the place on the sleeves where the insignia of rank had been removed could still be seen. He was eating a slice of bread spread with lard and paprika. I think he was absorbed in his work and paying no attention to us. I'm not even sure he was aware that I had come into the office. After a while, he turned to one side; after that, he almost had his back to me and I couldn't see his face. I think he looked in a drawer for some paper to wipe his greasy fingers with. For a while, I could hear him smacking his lips and sucking the crumbs from between his teeth.

Could the station be seen from the place where Andrija was sitting?

Andrija's back was turned to the window on the station side. The light came from the window on the right, which looks out on a wall. A warehouse or a silo, I think.

Could the station be seen from the place where you were sitting?

Nothing could be seen but switches, tracks, the metal base of the pump, and, a little farther away, the cattle scales. The pump is wrapped in straw. The station itself is a considerable distance away, about five or six hundred meters to the right.

How do you know how far it was to the station?

I once worked in that station. I covered the distance between the pump and the station several times a day, sometimes on foot and sometimes on an inspection trolley.

Why on a trolley?

I was sometimes urgently needed in the machine shop or the roundhouse and sometimes, early in the morning, I'd go on an inspection tour with the line inspector or the head mechanic.

Who is the head mechanic?

There have been several. The last was Halupka, a Slovak. I don't know who it is now.

Did you draw a plan of the railroad station for your 1938 *Travel Guide*?

No, sir.

Would you have been able to draw one?

Perhaps very roughly from memory, unless something had changed in the meantime.

Were you in the labor brigades?

In spite of a medical certificate attesting to my poor physical and mental condition, they put me to work on the railroad embankment and in the brickworks in January '41.

So you know all about laying tracks.

I worked on the embankment. The tracks must have been laid by other brigades. I don't know. Actually, I don't believe any tracks were laid on those embankments.

What do you mean by that?

Those embankments were built by incompetents, without studies of the terrain and without specifications. I am convinced, in fact, that they no longer exist.

Explain yourself.

There were some engineers in my labor brigade—Ofner, for instance; they told me those embankments would be washed away by the first rains.

Who is Ofner?

An engineer, as I've just told you. I got to know him in the labor brigade.

Do you know his present address?

I heard he was killed.

You said there were other technicians in the brigade.

In addition to Ofner, there were several engineers, Pollak and Herz, for instance, and a number of surveyors and geologists, such as Weiss and one of the Krauss brothers, the older, I think. They, too, were convinced that this embankment wouldn't survive the first rains, and they were right.

Why didn't they bring their expertise to bear?

Because the supervisors didn't give them any say in

the work. Ofner once told the head supervisor that the work was being bungled and that the embankment wouldn't last. The supervisor's answer was to lash him across the face with his whip, on the pretext that he was trying to get out of working. A few more attempts were made to persuade the people in charge to set up a field office to draw up clear and precise plans based on geological studies and accurate calculations, but never with any success. All the technicians—and as I've said, there were quite a few, the aforementioned Ofner, the Krauss brother, and Herz, I mean Paja, Schwarz— would have engaged in this work. They'd have had to draw their plans at home to avoid being suspected of shirking—that way, they could have fulfilled their work quotas on the job. When Schwarz, who has died since, proposed this scheme, the supervisors went at the engineers with sticks and whips, and accused them of wanting to draw plans of railroad stations and military bases, of airfields, firing ranges, and antiaircraft emplacements for the benefit of some foreign intelligence service. That was their last attempt to do anything about those embankments.

Why do you suppose Ofner and the others worried their heads about those embankments?

I believe that it went against their grain as engineers to do useless work. They felt humiliated.

Did you see any of these engineers during your last visit to Novi Sad?

To the best of my knowledge, only Pollak and one of the Krauss brothers are still alive. But I didn't see either of them. Pollak is in jail, and the younger Krauss has been reported missing.

How about the others?

They were killed in or after a fight with the supervisors. And Paja, Schwarz that is, hanged himself in a refrigerator. For a long time everybody, even his wife, thought he had escaped abroad or drowned himself in the Danube, something of the sort, but then he was found in the refrigerator: human meat.

Who gave you that information?

I heard about it the same day he was found in the refrigerator. It was reported in the newspapers later. The *Völkischer Beobachter* had a story about bankruptcy and some crooked business that Schwarz was allegedly implicated in. *Der Stürmer* also ran a sensational article, quoting a statement by a certain Malmos, a veterinarian in Čurug, to the effect that human flesh had been found in Schwarz's sausages. According to the same issue of *Der Stürmer*, the corpus delicti was a sliver of meat found in one of the sausages, which on examination was proved scientifically and irrefutably to be (I quote from memory) "a slice of fingertip including its horny excrescence, measuring so and so many millimeters; it has also been scientifically and irrefutably proved that this horny substance was identical in composition with a human fingernail, in the present instance that of a human child aged between eight and twelve months." Naturally, all this was pure fabrication, based on the profession of Schwarz senior, Paja's father, who was a butcher and sausage maker. Paja, who was unemployed, had taken over his father's shop, as Schwarz senior was totally blind and quite unable to carry on.

Who told you about the other members of the engineers' group?

I heard about Pollak from Mrs. Fischer. She told me he had been taken to the prison hospital unconscious and with mutilated sex organs.

From whom had she heard that?

Before committing suicide, the late Mr. Fischer had been in pre-trial custody with Pollak, first in the Yellow House and later in the so-called Tunnel.

And Krauss?

I heard about him from his wife.

Where and when did you meet her?

Before leaving Novi Sad, that is, sometime at the end of February or the beginning of March. We met at the town hall, where we had been summoned for an identity check. She told me then that her husband, that is, the younger Krauss, had been reported missing.

What else did she tell you about her husband on that occasion?

Just that.

How do you interpret "reported missing"?

I suppose he was drowned in the Danube or deported.

And Ofner?

I've told you: he was killed. The late Béla Sternberg told me. That was just before he, Sternberg, committed suicide.

So, for practical purposes, you are the sole surviving member of the engineers' group?

I was not a member of the group. As I've told you, it was made up exclusively of engineers, geologists, surveyors, and such. I was in the same labor brigade as the so-called engineers' group.

You worked with them?

Yes, I hauled sand and earth for the embankment, I shoveled and carted bricks.

Were you acquainted with their plans?

I don't understand.

Did you see the plans they submitted to the administration of the labor brigade?

There were no such plans. The suggestion that plans should be drawn up, that measurements and computations should be carried out was never accepted by the administration, though for a time they conducted discussions with Ofner and others in the hope of discovering their true intentions, and getting hold of plans that could be construed as hard evidence of espionage and set before the public as such. I believe the members of the engineers' group abandoned their project when they realized what was going on.

Was your nephew Gyula, known as George, in the labor brigades?

As a certified invalid, he was exempt. Besides, to the best of my knowledge, the situation in the villages wasn't at all the same as in the city. I mean, George could have kept out of it even if he hadn't had a doctor's certificate.

Let's get back to the scene in the woods. I assume that you know what I have in mind.

I've told you all I know about it. When I heard steps, I hid behind a tree. Then I heard a shot, or rather two shots in quick succession, and the mangled crows fell at my feet. That's all.

What time did this happen?

About eight in the morning.

Doesn't it strike you as rather unusual that you and your nephew George should both have been in the same part of the forest at eight o'clock in the morning without having made an appointment either directly or through a third party?

I assume that George followed my tracks in the belief that I was a hunter. Or, if he identified me by the prints of my galoshes, he may have followed me on purpose.

What could have aroused his curiosity?

He may have thought I was setting traps for hares; or some such thing.

Had you ever set such traps in the forest?

Long ago. Forty years ago.

So that couldn't have been the real reason for George's curiosity?

I only said it was possible that George followed me out of curiosity. I don't know. As we're not on speaking terms, I couldn't ask him why he was spying on me.

What other reason could he have had for spying on you?

Maybe he just happened to be following my tracks. Or he wanted me to see him holding a gun; that would put him in a position of superiority, because up until then we had met in situations where I was armed and he was barehanded. I'm referring to my iron-tipped cane. This one.

Had you ever met a hunter in the woods on your previous walks?

Once or twice during my stay in the village.

Did you know any of them?

Once, a day or two before said encounter with George, I met some hunters; one of them was a certain Tót from our village. He was with a group of seven or eight men, all unknown to me. I assumed that they came from other villages, possibly from Baksa or Csesztreg.

Who is Tót?

One night he appeared under our window with a

shotgun and threatened to kill us all. I think he was drunk. He fired a few shots into the air. Finally, the mayor and some peasants took him home. And that time I ran into him in the woods, he shouted insults at me and loaded his gun to frighten me.

What kind of insults?

He sicced the dogs and hunters on me. He said, loud enough for me to hear him, that he was going to pump a 9 mm. shell into a hyena (characterized by a particular epithet) and it would be their duty, the other hunters' duty that is, to testify that they had seen him shooting at a hyena. But I know he only meant to scare me, because if he had intended to kill me he wouldn't have talked so much, he would have fired. After that, I avoided places where I'd be likely to meet hunters, insofar as it is possible to avoid such places. I never left the main path and I never ventured deep into the woods. Luckily, the dogs had found a fresh scent; they raced off into the woods, so that day nothing happened to me.

Did you meet anyone else on these walks?

No one.

Firewood thieves, for instance?

No, sir. I never met anyone like that.

Had you ever met George in the woods before?

No. That was the only time.

Did he often go hunting?

As far as I know, that was the first time George went hunting. I was surprised. Usually he spends the whole day in his shop, because he hates to entrust it to anyone, even his own mother.

Did he bring home any game that day?

I don't know. I wasn't very much interested.

Did you notice what time he came home?

Yes, it was about two in the afternoon.

Was he carrying anything?

I don't know. He had the old game bag that had belonged to my grandfather slung over his shoulder, but whether there was anything in it I couldn't say. Even if it was plumped up, I wouldn't swear there was game in it.

What do you mean by that?

I believe George would have been perfectly capable of filling the bag with snow, branches, or God knows what, just to impress me as a champion hunter.

So the bag was full?

It was snowing hard and I couldn't see clearly. George passed the wire fence and then suddenly slipped into the house, so I couldn't see whether his bag was full or not. It was slung over his right shoulder.

How far is it from the wire fence to your window?

About twenty meters. Maybe less.

Did you come across any more fresh tracks in the woods that day?

Only George's. As I've told you, his orthopedic shoe leaves a characteristic mark in the snow, something like a flatiron.

And before that?

I occasionally saw tracks but avoided following them. I mean, I was careful to follow the tracks of animals and birds, but not of people.

What were you afraid of?

Another meeting with Tót or someone like him, and the possibility of some hunter mistaking me for an animal and filling me with buckshot. And I was even more afraid of being torn to pieces by dogs.

Does George know how to handle mechanical devices?

I don't understand.

You told me he sold mechanical devices for the Mepol Company, including telephones.

Just telephone casings, Bakelite shells, and very crudely made, at that. Only idiots and ignoramuses like George bought these Šlonski & Strauss products. To the best of my knowledge, he took five of them and succeeded in selling only one, or, rather, in palming it off on some poor traveling salesman from Pécs, who hasn't unloaded it to this day, I'm ready to bet.

What became of the rest of them?

Somewhere around 1939 or 1940, George returned the other four in a package addressed to the firm from which he had bought them, but the package was never delivered because, as I've told you before, the firm had gone out of existence. After several written inquiries, he was notified that the Mepol Company had been liquidated, but the casings were never returned to him. He wrote me several letters when I was living in Novi Sad; he wanted to be compensated for his loss and asked me to do something about it. I told him he would only be compounding his loss by wasting his time on this business. I even wrote that the stamps on his registered letter were worth more than those casings. At that point, he seems to have given up. At least, he stopped bothering me about it. Whether he went on arguing with the post office or with the ghost of Šlonski & Strauss, I don't know. I don't think so. I think my letter opened his eyes and he realized not only that he had lost those casings once and for all but also that the whole business from beginning to end had been a waste of time and money.

Who was the traveling salesman who took that one box from George?

All I know about him is that he was from Pécs. George himself told me that at the time.

Did you meet him?

I personally never laid eyes on him. In my opinion, the whole thing was a fairy tale; I mean, about this traveling salesman from Pécs buying a telephone casing. I think George made up the whole story in the hope of getting me to think he was less of an idiot than he is. He wanted to prove that these telephone casings weren't as worthless as I claimed, that some people were able and willing to sell them, even knowledgeable types like this traveling salesman from Pécs. The main trouble, *vis major*, came from the government, which reneged on its promise to electrify the whole district. It was just that little detail that stopped him from selling his merchandise.

But we've never found the slightest trace of that one casing.

I am convinced that George returned it to the Mepol Company, along with the four others. He just refuses to admit that he failed to sell a single one. That's why he thought up the story about the traveling salesman.

In your opinion, would it have been possible to install any of these casings?

Maybe certain types of telephone could have been built into them. Only certain models, of course. If they were made of sound material, which I doubt.

What makes you say that?

Everything about the firm of Šlonski & Strauss. They were a bunch of amateurs and poets, driven to business by necessity.

Did you ever have one of those casings in your hands?

I saw them, but I never handled one.

Where did you see them?

When George wrote asking me to intercede with Mepol, I went to the Orion store in Novi Sad and looked among the electrical supplies for articles bearing the Mepol trademark. Telephone casings with that trademark could easily be identified on the shelves by their flimsiness and unwieldiness. The joints and seams were not properly finished. The trademark stamped on them was also the work of poets and told you all about the Šlonski & Strauss team.

What did this trademark consist of?

The dark Bakelite surface has a white vase stamped on it, a vase or an hourglass or a chalice; but then you notice that this vase is an empty space, negative, hence an illusion, and that the only positive, that is, real thing is the two profiles turned toward each other, face to face as in a mirror, which delimit the vase or hourglass. This same emblem, which was probably supposed to represent the perfect symbiosis and equality of the Šlonski & Strauss partners, also figured on their letterhead.

Would you be capable of assembling any of these Mepol Company devices?

Of installing telephones?

You understood me very well.

No, I would not. Everything mechanical . . .

Would you be able to put one of these casings to a different use? A different technological use.

I am without mechanical ability and I dislike that kind of work. I mean, repairing electrical equipment, that kind of thing. And besides, in all probability these casings can barely be used for their intended purpose, as telephone casings, that is, and not for anything else.

All the same, as a former railroader you presumably have a certain technical know-how? You must have learned how to operate the telegraph? Am I right?

Yes, of course.

What kind of telegraph did you operate?

At first, in Šid and in Kameral Moravice, it was a Morse; later, in Novi Sad and Dombóvár, we had a Baudot and a Hughes. They were more complicated than the Morse, so all of us telegraphists and train dispatchers, and even some higher officials, had to take supplementary courses. The Hughes telegraph demands a certain virtuosity, a kind of musical gift: you're sitting at a keyboard with about thirty keys, and the machines operating simultaneously have to harmonize in such a way that on both sides the same letter is over the tape on which the message is being taken down.

Would you be capable today of sending a message on one of those machines? Say, in the event you were recalled to the service in some exceptional situation.

I don't believe so. Anyway, I'd need long practice to get my old skill back. It's like playing the piano or the harmonium. You have to get used to looking at the page above the keyboard and striking the unseen keys with precision. It's easy to forget. Given a certain amount of repetition, playing the piano is all a matter of ear and of talent. But reading music is something else again. Ear and talent aren't enough. Because there are definite mathematical rules, like rhythm, harmony, and so on. That's how it is with Hughes telegraphy.

Do you play the piano?

No. I never learned to play.

You once claimed to be a virtuoso.

I don't know when or where I could have said that.

You said it to your nephew George—recently.

It was a stock joke of mine to speak of my work with the Hughes telegraph as a musical performance. With my friends at the café, when I'd had a few drinks and the conversation came around to music, I used to say how sorry I was that I hadn't *perfected* my piano technique. And I really do regret that I didn't learn to play an instrument when I was young, especially the piano; but actually I was always thinking of the Hughes telegraph, and my friends knew it. And I was consistent about my little joke, I called telegrams scores and transmission a concert, and so on. At school, incidentally, I played the violin for a time, it was compulsory in secondary school back around 1910. But the scraping of the violin soon discourages you, because you realize that it will take a whole lifetime to turn that scraping into more or less tolerable music. It's different with the piano, I think. Anyway, it's only in that context, speaking figuratively, as it were, that I could have said such a thing to George, though it surprises me to hear that I spoke that way to George.

Does anyone you know play the piano?

To the best of my knowledge, no.

Does Mrs. Fischer have a piano in her apartment?

No.

Gavanski?

I saw a piano in Gavanski's guest room, in the corner—more precisely, in the part of the room that juts out in a kind of oriel, which coincides with the towerlike bulge in the façade.

Who plays this piano?

Gavanski's daughter. Her father pays a musician to give her private lessons.

Who is this musician?

A poor devil who came here from Budapest, where no one would employ him because he had had an affair with an underage pupil. It seems the story was in the papers.

How could Gavanski have confidence in him after that?

It seems that this erstwhile Don Juan has grown older and renounced his youthful follies. He's married to a rather dubious lady who is expecting a child by him. Gavanski told me that.

What's his name?

I don't know.

Try to remember.

Something like Zöldes or Zilas. Maybe Zöldesi.

Is that his professional name?

No, I think it's his real name.

In your opinion, would this Zöldesi, or whatever he's called, have been able, as a pianist, to operate a Hughes telegraph?

My comparison between piano technique and the technique involved in operating the Hughes telegraph and similar keyboard telegraphs was metaphoric and devoid of practical significance. Though it may seem to contradict what I said before, I believe that a knowledge of piano technique can only be a disadvantage to anyone trying to learn the principles of Hughes telegraphy; certain routine movements, mental and manual habits, would inevitably make for confusion. A person accustomed to the keyboard of a musical instrument, be it the piano or the harmonium, might even be misled by enthusiasm, habit, fatigue, or absentmindedness into trying to play a chord. The consequences could be catastrophic.

Is what you tell me also applicable to radio telegraphy?

I personally have no knowledge of radio telegraphy, but I do know that it is in regular use on certain European railroads.

Where did you find that out?

I read it in *The Railroad Herald* and recently in *Selection*.

Have any of your acquaintances taken up radio telegraphy as a hobby, as amateurs, that is?

Not to my knowledge.

Possibly Miss Gavanski? Or her fiancé?

Not that I know of.

You said the piano is in the widened part of the room, near the window.

Yes.

Describe the piano.

It is a well-preserved black concert grand, usually under a covering of the same material as the curtains of the big bay window, from which light falls into the room. The legs, shaped like stylized cones, are supported by brass casters. The copper or brass pedals are affixed to a lyre-shaped mechanism. I only once saw that piano open, without the red covering. The lid was raised, supported by a wooden rod. It was then that I first saw the keys, somewhat yellowed as though from nicotine. There was an open score on the music stand.

When was that?

Three or four months ago. Early one morning, after staying out all night, I dropped in on Gavanski for coffee.

Where had you spent the night?

I started at Márton's, then I went to Weinhebbel's at the Catholic Gate; I ended up at the station restaurant. I had drunk quite a lot of bad wine, but I sobered up on the way to Gavanski's.

Who had you been drinking with?

Some workers whose names I don't know. I only remember one, by the name of Sándor. A disabled printer. I remember him because at about midnight he gulped down three liters of red wine on a bet. He seems to have done that every night.

How do you account for the fact that the piano was open and that someone had been practicing so early in the morning?

Gavanski complained to me that he hadn't been able to sleep because his daughter had been giving a party. The living room was a mess, and so were the other rooms. There were empty or half-empty glasses all over the floors and carpets, the cushions on the couch were rumpled, and the kitchen, where I went for a glass of water, was also in disorder: the sink was full of dirty dishes, scraps of food, and empty bottles. I sniffed one: adulterated wine.

Who were the people at the party?

I don't know.

Gavanski didn't mention any names?

No.

How many?

Nothing was said about that.

Did Gavanski himself attend?

He told me he drank half a liter of wine, but in his room. He hadn't wanted to bother the young people.

Were the curtains on the window above the piano open when you went in?

Yes.

What can be seen from the window beside the piano?

On the right, part of the city, including the cathedral; straight ahead, in the foreground, the railroad embankment, tracks, and some huts; in the background, a plain, and far in the distance, a well; on the extreme left, still in the background, some pits, a brickworks, and the Danube. If you stand beside the window in the space between the wall and the concave side of the piano, you see a railroad siding, some artisans' huts, and some wooden sheds at the back of gardens. In the summer, tomatoes, onions, squash, sunflowers, and cucumbers are grown in those gardens. You can see the whitewashed outhouses through the greenery.

Can you see the firing range or the airfield from that window?

I never have.

You mentioned some pits near the brickworks.

Yes. From there, you can barely see those pits with the naked eye. There used to be a brickworks, but it was wiped out by a flood. If you dig down a few feet, you can still find well-preserved bricks in the clay.

With the naked eye, you say. Does that mean that you've observed that landscape through binoculars?

Gavanski told me he had watched us—that is, the labor brigade—through binoculars, but hadn't been able to distinguish one man from another in that human anthill.

What kind of binoculars?

Just a lady's opera glass, encrusted with mother-of-pearl, with a handle about fifteen centimeters long, also encrusted with mother-of-pearl.

Have you ever held that opera glass in your hands? You've looked out the window with it, haven't you?

I once held it to my eyes, but all I could see was a red flickering, like at sunset; it must have been the curtain or the piano covering.

What had you seen before?

Only that red flickering.

I repeat: What had you seen before? Or afterward, it makes no difference.

Some men near the brickworks.

What were they doing?

Probably digging bricks out of the mud and sand and throwing them onto a pile.

Did you recognize any of them?

One couldn't distinguish faces at that distance. Gavanski once told me that. Though his eyesight is better than mine.

At what time of day did you look out the window with the opera glass?

It was in the evening, just before sunset.

What did you see at that time?

On the left, right next to the ruined brickworks, I saw a man picking up bricks. I noticed him because he was some distance away from the others.

Continue.

His hands were wrapped in rags of some kind. Suddenly he stopped working and another man came up to him, probably to help him adjust the bandages on his hands.

Continue.

Then some men ran up to them and hit them with sticks until they fell to the ground.

Continue.

Later I saw them stand up and march off in a column with the others, all carrying spades or shovels over their shoulders.

Continue.

That's all.

To whom does the opera glass belong?

Gavanski bought it for his wife about ten years ago from Mr. Poltaratsky.

Who's Poltaratsky?

A Russian émigré. He came to Novi Sad in about 1925. Before that, I think, he lived in Valjevo and in Belgrade. He was said to have been a count, on intimate terms with the Russian court, and a member of some government, a counterrevolutionary government of course, but he seems to have grown disillusioned with the Whites and gone in for *la dolce vita* after that. At the time, he supported himself by selling his belongings, his own and his wife's or mistress's, I don't know which, and by giving lessons—piano, singing, fencing, riding,

anything. Sofia Nikolaevna took up spiritism, and then
for a while she supported the old count with the money
she made singing in wealthy houses. And oh yes, she
was said to be a nymphomaniac and to cuckold the
count right and left.

Did you know Poltaratsky personally?

Some time between 1925 and 1930, we played chess
and billiards a few times in the reading room of the
guildhall.

What became of him?

I believe he died peacefully just before the war in the
arms of a *mulata* in California.

Who told you that?

I read it in a Vienna newspaper. It said that Poltaratsky was a member of the highest society and associ-
ated with former kings, regents, and counts.

What was the late Poltaratsky's connection with
Trotsky?

Once, in the course of a conversation over the billiards
table, he told me that he was definitely planning to visit
Lev Davidovich at his home in Mexico.

You recently compared your skull with that of Lev
Davidovich Bronstein.

I don't remember.

You said (I quote): "I might have incurred the fate
of Lev Davidovich Bronstein. I was saved by providence." Etc.

Yes. I may have said that.

On what occasion?

I don't remember.

What kind of explosive did you keep in your
apartment?

I don't understand the question.

Witnesses claim to have heard explosions before the house at 21 Bem Street caved in.

Fairy tales.

What terms were you on with Mrs. Mészáros, the owner of the house?

I saw her very seldom.

How many months' rent did you owe?

Three.

What terms were you on with her husband?

I think he kept out of my way.

Why?

I couldn't say. Mutual antipathy, most likely.

You say you disliked Mr. Mészáros?

It would be closer to the truth to say that I was indifferent to him. I simply took no notice of him. That was easy for me, because it was Mrs. Mészáros who attended to financial matters. I had no reason to have any contact with him.

How do you account for the fact that the house caved in just a few moments after you left?

I was saved by providence.

Answer my question.

I'm tired.

What made the house cave in? I repeat: What made the house cave in?

I believe a rat was the cause of the cave-in.

When did you see this rat?

I saw it twice. First when the porters were moving the cupboards out, and then when I turned back before leaving the house. So there may have been two rats.

Where did you see them?

One, as I've said, was in the corner, right next to the wall. It crawled out of a hole in the floor, then scurried away and vanished in the opposite corner into one of the holes at the junction between the rotten floorboards and the spongy, waterlogged wall. The other one, unless it was the same one, ran diagonally across the room and vanished into the big hole in the middle, where the rag rug used to be.

Were there cracks in the wall?

No.

Did the house lean, or was it supported by beams?

As I have already made clear in my written statement, there was no outward indication that the house was about to cave in.

Had you made any repairs in the house?

No. Unless you count replacing a few floorboards.

Who replaced them?

I did.

Where did you get the boards?

Actually, it was four wide laths. I found them near the house one evening. They had probably fallen off a truck. None of them is more than a meter or a meter and a half long.

Did you dig up the ground under the floor?

No. I only removed the rotten boards and put the laths in their place. There was a gap of about ten centimeters between them.

Did you nail the boards?

No. Because the joists under the floor were also completely rotten and waterlogged; it would have been pointless to drive nails into them.

Was the house insured?

Mrs. Mészáros stated in writing that the house was insured with Pannonia Insurance and that her policy was paid up. She said there was an orange plaque on the wall with PANNONIA written on it. But when the workers cleared away the wreckage, they did not find any plaque.

Does this insurance policy entitle you to compensation?

I don't believe so. Anyway, as no property of mine was damaged, I see no reason why . . .

Did you do any digging in the cellar of the house?

The cellar was hopelessly flooded, with groundwater I believe, and it was always locked, probably because of the children. I myself never went down there. I only knew about it from Mrs. Mészáros. When she gave me my keys, she told me she wasn't giving me the key to the cellar because the cellar was useless. I don't remember if she told me about the groundwater at the time.

Where was the entrance to the cellar?

Access to the cellar was by a wooden stairway at the front of the house. You could tell by the big rusty padlock on the door that no one had been down there in a long time.

How do you know that the cellar was flooded and that access was by a wooden stairway?

I found that out when the wreckage was being cleared away. The workers' rubber boots were covered with a thick layer of clay. Besides, there were strange sounds under the floor at night, as if somebody was sloshing around in water. That was the rats. One day I told Dr. Freud about it and he advised me to see a psychiatrist.

Who is Freud?

A surgeon. Someone else I got to know in the labor brigade. I noticed him the very first day. His hands were bandaged. The guards ripped off the bandages and beat him.

Did you meet him again later?

I saw him only once. He was standing in the column near the green shack. After that, I only saw his brain. It was a little island in the snow on the corner of Miletić Street and Greek School Street.

So you maintain that the sounds you heard in the cellar were made by rats?

Yes.

What makes you think that?

The sloshing was usually accompanied by a squeaking, like the sound rats make.

Have you ever fished?

I used to fish with a pole and with a plain hook and line, but that was long ago.

Did you ever fish in the Danube?

No.

Do you own rubber boots?

No.

From the cellar of 21 Bem Street, did you ever hear any other sounds beside the squeaking you mentioned? Coughing, talking, whispering?

Never.

Does your landlord Mr. Mészáros own rubber boots?

I don't know.

Did you ever see anyone fiddling with the padlock on the cellar door?

No.

Describe the padlock.

I'm tired.

Describe the padlock.

I don't remember it.

I repeat: Describe the padlock.

Square, six by six centimeters, steel stirrup spotted with rust. Round lid, diameter eight to ten millimeters, over keyhole. When the lid is pushed aside, the guide pin can be seen; it looks like a thick nail. The lid, too, is so rusty that it can hardly be moved, and then only in one direction (to the left). The letters ELZETT, some ten millimeters in height, can be clearly distinguished on the underside of the lock.

Continue.

That's all.

Describe the underside.

In the middle, at the intersection of the diagonals, there is a slight swelling which marks the end of the guide pin. These diagonals, which stand out in relief, are present on both sides of the lock.

Continue.

I'm tired.

When did you come back from Novi Sad?

Three days ago.

Why didn't you report sooner?

I received the summons on my return from Porszombat, that was yesterday.

What were you doing in Porszombat?

Visiting the Mayers.

Who are the Mayers?

I'm tired.

Who are the Mayers?

Mr. Samuel Mayer is an old friend from business

school. We hadn't seen each other for more than thirty years. A few days ago, I heard that a certain Mayer, a businessman, was living in Porszombat and I thought it must be he. So I decided to go and see him.

For what reasons?

I hoped he would lend me some money.

Who told you that Mayer was living in Porszombat?

George.

What made George mention him?

Once, during a quarrel, George called me a bankrupt and a *Luftmensch* and spoke of Mayer as an example of a successful man.

Continue.

I'm tired.

Continue.

CRIMINAL INVESTIGATION (III)

[57]

What were E.S.'s suppositions with regard to the purpose and significance of the summons he received from Novi Sad?

That he was being reinstated in the service at a lower rank than before being pensioned; that he would be subjected to a medical examination with a view to forced labor; that the police would try to recruit him for undercover work among the railroaders; that prominent persons were being arrested as hostages; that hostages were being shot in reprisal for acts of sabotage on the railroad.

What connection did he perceive between these events and the shipment of all his movable property?

The speed with which his cupboards were moved by rail was directly proportional to the success of the Axis Powers on the battlefields and inversely proportional to the success of the Red Army.

What possibilities did he envisage of raising the sixty pengö needed to redeem his movable property?

Borrowing, stealing, luck.

Borrowing?

As potential lenders he saw Mayer, Gavanski, Rosenberg, and Madame Clara, the proprietress of the café, though he was already indebted to all of them: from Mayer he had twice borrowed about twenty pengö, once by oral agreement and once against a written receipt, which, however, made no mention of a deadline for repayment; to Gavanski he owed fifty-six pengö in all, as he had returned a hundred pengö at an earlier date; from Rosenberg he had not yet borrowed, because Rosenberg, on the occasion of a meeting with him, had adroitly sidestepped the topic toward which E.S. had been trying, with unmistakable allusions to money and loans, to steer the conversation; to Madame Clara he owed some twenty pengö, a sum which he regarded as chickenfeed compared to the vast sums he had spent at her café.

Stealing?

If he had known where George and Netty kept their money, he would have helped himself to a handful, considering that he would merely be collecting payment for the forest, which they had burned and to which he laid claim. Nor did he exclude the possibility of filching the purse of some groggy merchant or black marketeer in the train, after either getting him drunk or holding a handkerchief soaked in anesthetic to his nose.

Luck?

Finding a purse in the corridor of a train, on the street, or in a café; a gift from some unknown benefactor; a money order from the Red Cross or some other charitable institution; an exceptionally favorable revision of his pension, whereby, thanks to a new law, the increase, covering all his years of service, would be made up retroactively; finding a prize-winning lottery ticket that someone had lost; inventing some marvelous secret weapon and selling it to the Americans. And so on.

What did he fear?

That during his absence his relatives and his own children might have concocted a sinister plot against him.

What was E.S.'s reaction upon reading his sister Netty's list of all those who had died a natural death, been killed in accidents, been murdered, or simply disappeared?

He looked quickly through that part of her letter, trying to forget it, and then, supposedly (but not at all) by chance, wiped his nose with just that part of the letter, the end, or more precisely the last two paragraphs, for when he tore the letter up and stuffed it into the right-hand pocket of his coat, he did it in such a way that this scrap would come into his hand first when considerations of hygiene or habit would lead him to wipe his nose on newsprint or writing paper. But being nearsighted, he made sure, before wiping his nose, that he was using those paragraphs that he wished to get rid of first.

Why was he so eager to get rid of them?

Because the names of onetime friends and acquaintances bore clearer testimony than Ecclesiastes or the work of any philosopher to the way of all flesh. Even the gloomiest speculations about death were easier to bear than the sight of its harvest. Not a few of those mentioned by Netty in her letter (the balance sheet of the last two or three years) were his own age or even appreciably younger. *Vanitas vanitatum* . . .

What fantasies did he indulge in?

In a fit of righteous indignation suggesting one of P. Howard's (Rejtö Jenö's) comic thrillers, he plays the role of paterfamilias and leaps at his relatives with a knife. With well-aimed blows in the region of the heart, he puts an end to this intolerable family circus. While the bodies of those who have suffered their just deserts

lie in pools of blood, he, in handcuffs, is led by the
police first to prison, then to an insane asylum; there
would be no difficulty in proving to the court that he is
not responsible for his actions.

What would the press have to say about this triple
murder in a Jewish household in Kerkabarabás?

(*First story*) Yesterday the village of Kerkabarabás,
Baksa township, witnessed a triple crime. Victims of a
family quarrel, Mrs. Netty Boroska (59), widow of the
late I. Boroska, her son Gyula, known as George (39),
merchant, and her daughter Maria (formerly Rebecca),
the widow of István Horváth (36), housewife, were
struck down with a knife. This loathsome crime was
committed in a fit of rage by Mr. E.S., retired chief
railroad inspector, the father of two children. The
criminal surrendered to the police without resistance.
His look of bewilderment revealed his mental state.
(*Second story*) As we learn from our correspondent, the
trial of the triple murderer (see our issue of April 4)
has been postponed *sine die*, the medical commission
having concluded that the criminal committed his hid-
eous crime in a state of dementia. According to the
testimony of Dr. Papandopoulos, who had treated Mr.
E.S. on two occasions, he displayed unmistakable symptoms of aggressivity and was discharged from the Kovin
psychiatric hospital on the condition that his wife assume
responsibility for his care. (*Third story*) With regard to
the triple crime in the village of Kerkabarabás (see our
issues of April 4 and 10), we learn that a Miss Nedomački, salesgirl at the Record Bookstore in Novi Sad,
recognized the criminal from a photograph and informed the police that some days before the crime she

sold him the paper knife with which the crime was committed. Miss Nedomački declares in a sworn statement that Mr. E.S. behaved with the greatest courtesy and looked upon the Japanese paper knife more with the eyes of an aesthete (*sic!*) than those of a criminal. One reason, she declares, why the purchase of the Japanese paper knife by Mr. E.S. did not arouse her suspicions was that he had bought several sheets of quadrille writing paper at the same time, obviously as camouflage.

After all his misfortunes (being shot, being hanged, dying a natural death in bed), and after being resurrected or at least visited with total amnesia (whose partial effects he has already experienced), what would E.S. do?

He would take the poor freckle-faced young girl in the Record Bookstore by the hand and embark on a new life (*Vita Nuova*) with her.

How would he win her?

With wealth (material and spiritual), with bouquets of flowers accompanied by his visiting card; by making lavish purchases in her bookshop—without a word (words only complicate matters)—until he had emptied the last shelf. He could see by her face that she at last understood his noble intentions. Everything—the quadrille paper and the Japanese paper knife—would be a mere pretext, a game. Everything.

Give a brief summary of the short novel that E.S. was planning to write in 1932 in Kovin, for therapeutic purposes, on the suggestion of Dr. Papandopoulos, after Dr. Papandopoulos had perceived extraordinary powers of observation and an astonishing gift of tragic irony in E.S.'s account of his own illness.

Driven by obscure (historic) guilt feelings and fear, a certain Malchus or Kartafil or Johannes Buttadeus (sometimes plain Buttadio) begins at an early age to change not only his name and identity but also his occupation and place of residence. Encountering incomprehension wherever he goes, he ends up bankrupt and is relegated to a mental hospital, where it comes to him in a kind of illumination that he was born to work on the railroad and that travel will cure his anxieties. After all manner of travels and adventures, he becomes first a day laborer, then a regular employee, and finally an inspector of the state railroads, first the Yugoslav JDZ, then the Hungarian MÁV, then of railroads in Bulgaria, Belgium, Italy, Austria, Germany, Czechoslovakia, Poland, and Portugal, at every step changing his name and place of residence. Of course, he takes advantage (in the novel) of the opportunity to describe the people and customs of numerous countries and depict the divers forms of his nightmares. In the end, he experiences another illumination, very much like the first: in his office at a small railroad station, Mr. Joannes Buttadeus (or Buttadio) or João d'Espera em Dios, alias Isaac Laquedem, meets Jesus his executioner. Madness or dream? At this point, the book degenerates into pure delirium.

Give a short review of this novel which treats the protagonist's recent and often incredible experiences with ironic detachment.

Parade in the Harem, which comes to us in the excellent low-priced Tábor edition, is Mr. E.S.'s first novel (as the publisher tells us in a brief note). Behind the deliberate sensationalism of the title, inspired no doubt by the work of P. Howard, the reader discovers with satisfaction a sensitive, talented writer and a highly interesting social and psychological theme. Not wishing to reveal the entire contents of the novel to the reader, as certain bungling spoilsports do, we shall only say that the story does not, as the title might lead one to suppose, unfold in the exotic atmosphere of an Oriental court but in a remote Pannonian village during the present day. After a shattering experience (a police raid in Novi Sad), E.S., an extremely sensitive and, one might say, unbalanced individual, is unable to cope with the commonplace situations of daily life. In the short space of a single night he relives the most important episodes of his life thus far, and comes to certain conclusions. His war with the world is in reality a war with death, whose approach he senses. We warmly recommend this novel to our subscribers and new readers, to all those who are not on the lookout for cheap adventure stories and who agree with us that so-called plot is not the soul and essence of a true literary work.

Cite two versions (but not the last, definitive one) of the acknowledgment drafted by E.S. on April 4, A.D. 1942, with regard to the payment of certain debts.

1) Acknowledgment of 50 (fifty) pengö, which I shall receive from my brother E.S., retired, as soon as he is able to pay them, as remuneration for the board and lodging of himself and family over a period of two weeks. April 4, A.D. 1942.

2) Acknowledgment of 30 (thirty) pengö, received from my brother, the retired railroad employee E.S., in payment for the two weeks' hospitality accorded by me to him and his family. Kerkabarabás, April 4, 1942.

Etc.? (Variations.)

"Herr Inspektor is threatening us with a knife!" "If he had twenty pengö, he'd buy a kitchen stove." "We're sick and tired of his nonsense about the forest." "What forest?" "Grampa arranged it all with him." "He himself authorized us to burn potash in that forest." "He himself recommended that Pollak to us, we've got it in writing." "His lordship wanted to be a potash manufacturer." "Twenty pengö, I ask you!" "Does he even know what twenty pengö are worth nowadays!"

Etc.? (Syncopes.)

"He left at least twice as much with that Clara woman in Baksa." "Baksheesh yes, he always left full measure." "Sure, but could he afford to buy his children books?" "Zooks, he always drank like a fish, but now it's more like a cow." "How he's milked us!" "Doesn't know when it's time to stop." "The cops'll know how to handle him." "Imagine going to court about a stupid heater." "Beat it, George, as fast as you can." "The man is crazy." "He'll kill us all."

How much time passed before E.S. opened the door and hurriedly reached for the blue envelope that had been inserted in the crack above the door?

Exactly twelve minutes by his Longines watch, which he was clutching in the ice-cold palm of his left hand.

Where was his right hand?

In his right hand he was holding his cane, whose iron tip had been thrust into the keyhole.

How did E.S. check the weight of the ham (a gift from his youngest sister)?

First he hefted the fragrant, reddish-brown, sooty stump, then he picked up the greasy paper the ham had been wrapped in and smelled it up close until his mouth watered. Then he put the ham (wrapped in ragged newsprint) under his arm and brought it to Mr. Horváth to weigh.

How was the net weight of the ham (without the newsprint and the greasy paper) established with the help of Mr. Horváth's scales?

Two cast-iron weights marked 1 kg. were put into the left-hand (from the vantage point of the ham's owner) pan, then a third with the same numerical value. The weighted pan sank quickly, and one beak-shaped pointer distinctly passed the other; one of the three 1 kg. weights was then removed and another cast-iron weight marked 0.5 kg. substituted. At this, the pointers moved somewhat closer to each other, and Mr. Horvath tried with his thumb and forefinger to bring the two pointers together; on the third attempt, the iron weight marked 0.5 kg. was replaced by two brass weights, each marked 0.20 kg. At last the pointers were equilibrated, at last the pans were level, balanced in a state of relative equilibrium, equidistance, and equipoise, of weight-meat equivalance.

What two patented inventions (among many others), which E.S. had recently read about in *Selection*, now came to his mind?

The electric blanket and the electric belt for men.

What were the advantages of these articles?

Electric blanket: minimal weight compared to the classic feather bed or duvet filled with feathers or sheep's wool; maximum heat, along with temperature control; easy handling. Electric belt for men: in addition to the classic function of holding up the trousers and thus preventing unpleasant surprises, it warms the abdomen and back, the entire *nox microcosmica*, with the help of a battery activated by a switch disguised as a button, thus increasing potency, preventing prostatitis, curing impotence, regulating the kidneys, liver, endocrine glands, and bladder. It further enables the sleeper to avoid nocturnal pollution (by simply shutting off the battery) and induces, as desired, imposing erections and leisurely ejaculations.

Why, a month ago, did he not accept the shoes (inherited from the late Móric) which his sister Olga, Móric's widow, offered him?

Because he hoped for better days (optimism); because he had no desire to wear a dead man's shoes (superstition); because he disliked them (aestheticism); because they were one size too small (realism).

Describe the shoes.

Antelope skin (imitation), gray, round tips, hard counters, size 45, six pairs of eyelets for round laces, double soles (tanned pigskin and cardboard), decorative perforations shaped like snowflakes and arranged in a semicircle at the toes, the same sort of perforations on both sides of the laces, flat heels, white double stitching along the soles, Bata model for the autumn and winter of 1940–41.

When did he switch from his high-quality Solingen razor to a cheap Tabula Rasa model?

In 1932, in Kovin. He wanted to cut his throat but was prevented by the doctor, or rather by a nurse. Standing two steps away from him, she ordered him in a calm, severe voice to throw "that thing" away, or to give it to her, closed. For a while he went on fiddling with the sharp blade, now cleaving the air with brisk gestures as though cutting up potatoes, now moving it slowly and calmly as though peeling apples. Then with a grimace of disgust he threw the razor into the grass and sat down on a bench. It was springtime. The chestnut blossoms in the hospital park gave off a heavy, repugnant smell.

What did the man, whose shaving brush is today reduced to a wretched stump, with peeling enamel, cracked handle, and scanty bristles, forget to mention in his letter?

The fact that he himself was once part owner of a brush factory (Weiss & Kohn) which turned out some fifty thousand first-class shaving brushes a year and shipped them to every country in the Balkans and Central Europe, and even to Soviet Russia, until about 1930.

How did he console himself when he no longer had even a shaving bowl?

Holding a sliver of soap between his fingers as a priest holds the Host, he consoled himself with the story of the wise desert hermit who discovered in his old age that it was possible to manage without a glass: he had seen a shepherd gathering water from a spring in the palm of his hand.

TRAVEL SCENES (III)

[58]

The man picks up the brick and tries to throw it onto the big pile nearby. His hands are wrapped in rags, handkerchiefs no doubt, for the dark lines of the checked pattern, maybe blue, maybe brown, maybe green, can be seen through the crust of dried mud. Now he has stopped for a moment and is trying to arrange his bandages. Since the rags on both hands have come loose and are twined around the fingers, his movements are awkward and nervous. There is something panicky in his movements that accentuates their awkwardness. Not knowing what to do with his cramped fingers, he seems to be wondering whether to rip off his bandages with his teeth or try to straighten them. His indecision is short-lived. Suddenly two hands as muddy as his own, but free from bandages, appear just in front of his glasses, in the small space framed by his cramped fingers. Helplessly, he surrenders his hands to the other two hands. Only then does he look at the face. A somber, hard face, downcast eyes, wrinkled forehead, muddy hat. Concentration can be read in those features; the mouth twitches strangely, as though it, too, like the fingers, were busy untying knots. The man hears the other's soft breathing. They do not talk. The man feels that all this, the knots being undone with teeth and nails, his hands being bandaged with dirty rags, has been going on for a dreadfully long time. He also feels that the other is probably losing patience, because his movements are becoming more and more frantic. He tries to say something, probably to make his helper abandon his laborious efforts, or to thank him, or to tell him to tear off the bandages and throw them away. But no voice comes out of him, only a kind of gasp, as though he were trying to clear his throat.

The other is still fiddling with the bandages. Having just finished one hand, he takes hold of the other and is trying to find the knot in the dirty handkerchief. At last he finds it, but again he has trouble undoing it. He lifts the surrendered hand to his mouth. For a moment the man sees the other's short, apparently truncated teeth, then he sees only his hat. He looks past the bandager's hand. Through his muddy glasses, he cannot see the railroad embankment or the house with the rounded façade. All he can see, barely a step away from him, is shadows moving on what he knows to be the muddy embankment. He hears the squeaking of the wheelbarrow and the dull thud of colliding bricks which makes him think of tenpins knocking. His face turned toward the sun, he sees only a bright-red flickering above the moving shadows. Suddenly he has the impression that all the shadows have stopped moving and that the squeaking of the wheelbarrow and the thudding of brick against brick have also stopped. He thinks he must be mistaken, or maybe that he is blacking out from exhaustion; the red glow of the setting sun seems to be pouring through his eyes into his brain. But just as it comes to him that he was right (the squeaking of the wheelbarrow has indeed stopped), he realizes that it's too late. For his insight is accompanied by a sharp pain on the crown of his head. He does not lose consciousness. The blow from behind, probably with a rubber trun-

cheon, merely fills the horizon with a strange red glow.
Convulsed, the man falls on his knees, protecting his
head with his hands. He hears the blows rain down, but
some bring no pain, and he realizes that they are falling
on the other man, who was bandaging his hands a
moment ago. He hears the other man's groans, mingled
with the cries of those who are showering the two of
them with blows. A blow on his head loosens a hard
object in his mouth, and he spits it out with surprising
ease, along with blood and saliva. To his horror, he
realizes that he has spat out his denture. Then he hears
(or so it seems to him) the wheelbarrow squeaking again,
but very near him, right next to his head. And he hears
bricks falling on the pile, more quickly, he thinks, than
before. Suddenly he knows that his bandages are in
place again, because his face is touching them. He smells
the dried clay on the bandages. He stays in his cramped
position for another moment, thinking that he will never
be able to get up. The men with the clubs seem to be
shouting something at him, but he is not sure whether
they're shouting at him or the other man. Now on his
hands and knees, he tries to find his teeth and his
glasses. He gropes about in the caked mud with his
fingertips and his bandaged hands. His fingers feel a
hard, slimy object, and even before looking at it he
knows it is his excruciating teeth, his excruciating upper
denture with the big ceramic teeth. He tries clumsily to
pick it up, but he feels a cutting pain in his hand and
he cries out. At the same moment, he sees a heavy
hobnailed boot pressing down on his fingers with all its
weight. He hears a cracking as of glass and sees his
teeth cutting into the palm of his hand.

[59]

His spade over his shoulder, the man limps along in the column. His head is bent low, the bandage on one hand (the one hanging down at his side) has come loose and is wound around his wrist. With his left hand he grips the handle of his spade. The red glow of the sun can still be seen on the roofs of the houses between which he is marching, and on the dome of a tall bell tower in the distance. But this the man does not see. He sees only the muddy shoes of the man ahead of him. And hears the dull impact of his steps.

Now there are only six of them. They turn into a square. The square is empty. In front of them, a cathedral; to the left, in the middle of the square, a monument. On the pedestal stands a man with right hand upraised, pointing at the cathedral or the sky. They turn into a side street on the left. The man is limping, his head bent low. They pass a well (now there are only three or four of them). He hears the water stop flowing as someone lets go of the pump handle. They turn again. (Now he seems to be alone; the other man's steps have died away; he hears the squeaking of a gate.) Now the man is walking alone, first skirting a yellow wall from which bricks protrude, then a wooden fence. He thinks he sees a white, gauzelike curtain moving in one of the windows. Almost at the same time, he hears the iron wheel of the pump turning with a rhythmic squeak and hears a gushing stream of water.

He reaches the wooden gate and drops his spade, blade down. With his right hand, the one with the dangling bandage, he presses the handle and opens the gate a crack, just enough to let him squeeze through, but he cannot prevent the hinge from squeaking. There is already light in the windows to his left. He tiptoes a few feet; now he is directly below the windows. Here at last he evidently feels safe, for his step becomes more assured, though he is still limping. He puts down his spade by the door with the big hinges and the padlock and starts tinkering with the lock. Then for a time he holds it helplessly in his wounded hand, as though wondering what to do with it. He moves the rusty lid of the lock, then takes a bunch of keys out of his pocket and tries to insert one of them into the lock, but is unable to. In despair, he props his head in his hands and stands there awhile. Maybe an hour, maybe two, maybe longer.

A WITNESS INTERROGATED (II)

[60]

Try to remember.

We were building an embankment, I've told you that.

What happened that day?

I stopped work for a moment to straighten the bandages on my hands. They weren't really bandages, just two handkerchiefs. Ofner helped me with them.

Who is Ofner?

An engineer. I met him in the labor brigade.

Did you fulfill your work quota that day?

Yes, I believe I did.

What else happened?

I was blinded by the mud on my glasses.

Continue.

Suddenly it seemed to me that I saw, or sensed, that something was happening. I had the impression that the wheelbarrow wasn't squeaking anymore and that the shadows had stopped moving. I was just beginning to wonder what was going on when something hit me on the head.

Continue.

My head began to swim. Then, under the blows, I realized that Ofner had been knocked down.

Continue.

I fell to my knees, protecting my head with my hands. Then, through the cries of the men who were beating us, I heard the wheelbarrow squeaking again, close to me, not far from my head. I knew my bandages were in place, because my face was touching them. I smelled the clay with which the handkerchiefs were encrusted.

Continue.

That's all.

What did you want that day in the cellar of the house at 21 Bem Street?

I don't remember going into that cellar.

You tried to open the padlock with a skeleton key.

It was just my own keys. I think I wanted to hide. To spend the night there. I didn't want to show myself at home in the condition I was in, without my upper teeth and my glasses.

Why did you choose that particular cellar?

I don't know. An old woman hanged herself in that cellar two years ago.

So you wanted to hang yourself?

I don't know. Maybe.

In your previous statement you said you wanted to kill yourself.

I may have said that.

Why did you change your mind?

Maybe I couldn't get the padlock open. I don't know.

In your previous statement, made in Baksa, you said only Ofner was beaten.

I was referring to a different incident. That other time, Ofner was whipped because of something he had said.

But you were involved in that incident. So why didn't you mention it?

I don't know. Anyway, I want to forget it as soon as possible.

How long did you stay outside the cellar door?

I don't know. Maybe an hour. Maybe two. Maybe longer.

Whom had you gone to see before that?

I couldn't show myself to anybody in that condition.

You once declared (I quote): "The one thing I said to Netty before she went to Budapest was to tell her children to leave us alone, because if any of them lifted a finger . . ." And so on.

Yes, maybe I did say that. I only wanted . . .

Who is Netty?

My sister.

What did she want in Budapest?

Some documents. As far as I know.

What documents?

Proof of her nationality and of her father's and grandfather's; also proof that they, our father and grandfather that is, had paid their local taxes regularly between 1870 and 1880. And maybe, while she was at it, she was interested in certain documents concerning the sale of our father's forest and the affairs of the firm of Weiss & Egell.

Explain.

The late Jakob Weiss arrived in Agram somewhere around 1800 with his wife Franziska, née Pollak, of Nagykanizsa. Thanks largely to the influence of his wife's family, Weiss was able to develop a thriving trade with Kanizsa and its environs.

What did he sell?

At first exotic fruits, raisins, tobacco, and slivovitz. Later, around 1810, he acquired a dry-goods store: SCHNITTWARENHANDLUNG.

Continue.

Thanks to his business acumen and a number of advantageous lawsuits, Weiss was able to extend his commercial network to a large part of Hungary and to diversify his stock; in addition to the articles already mentioned, he now dealt in wine vinegar, honey, and cereals. Around 1850, he signed a contract with Martin Egell, a Zagreb potash manufacturer, and the two of them obtained a license to burn potash in the forests of Hungary. Other partners in this business were a Mr. Schlesinger and Pinkas Pollak, the brother of Weiss's wife, Franziska.

Continue.

Under the same name—though by then the directors were Weiss's widow, Franziska, and her brother Pinkas— the firm signed a contract with our grandfather for making potash. After our grandfather's death, this contract was renewed without my consent, and my sisters shared the profits from the burned forests among themselves.

Continue.

Later on, the firm was liquidated, and the creditors, among them my sisters, were left high and dry. All that's left of the whole business is acres of burned forest.

Where were you two days ago?

I went to take delivery of my belongings that I had shipped from Novi Sad: two cupboards full of bed-clothes and kitchenware.

Describe the cupboards.

Two old-fashioned single-doored walnut cupboards, which used to be highly polished, with removable vaulted cornices and stylized wooden roses; more precisely, bunches of roses centered around spiral orna-ments resembling the scroll of a bass viol.

Who drove you to Lenti?

Martin, a coachman.

What did you talk about on the way?

About garlic as a specific for warming the blood and improving the digestion; about high prices, shortages, and peach brandy.

Had this Martin ever driven you before?

Several times. In 1909, he drove me from the Lenti station to the village, and two days later, from the village to the station; again in 1914, the same two trips; just a month ago, from Lenti to Kerkabarabás; the day before yesterday, from Barabás to Lenti to Sziget; and today, from Barabás to Csesztreg.

What took you to Sziget?

I went to see the Rosenbergs.

Is that the same Rosenberg you mentioned once before?

No. That was Izsák Rosenberg, the miller and merchant in Baksa; this was Jakob Rosenberg, his younger brother, also a merchant.

What did you want from Rosenberg?

A loan. In a way, I was taking advantage of him, because I knew he couldn't refuse me; as proof of my destitution, I pointed out the window at the peasant wagon with my two cupboards on it. I admitted that I had started out without a copper to my name and that I wouldn't even be able to pay the coachman, who was waiting patiently for me in the wagon.

How much did Rosenberg give you?

Thirty pengö.

Why did you stay there so long?

He kept me. He told me to stay the night and either keep the coachman or send him back, because I could have his, Rosenberg's, wagon in the morning. I decided

to let Martin spend the night there because I knew
there was no one at home who would help him unload
my cupboards. You see, one can't really count on Martin;
if people hire him, it's mostly because his horses are
known to be intelligent. Martin is never sober, he sleeps
most of the way.

What did you do in the Rosenberg house?

I was very tired, so I went to bed early. It took me a
long time to get to sleep, so I tried to finish the letter I
had begun to my sister Olga in Szentadorján. It's a copy
of the one I've been carrying around with me for a long
time.

When did you become acquainted with this Rosenberg?

In the days when the firm of Weiss & Pollak was still
in business. The firm signed a contract with Rosenberg
senior, Izsák's father, and at about the same time my
late father, Max, was admitted to the firm at the suggestion of Rosenberg senior. Later on, the Rosenberg sons
invested the money they had made on potash in a glass
factory and hired some Czech glassmakers to run it.

Continue.

Weiss's widow, Franziska, later married Rosenberg
senior and continued to run her business in collabora-
tion with a relative of Rosenberg's, a Mr. Schreiner, a
master glassmaker. Quite a few journeymen and apprentices worked under his supervision, as well as ten
or twelve potash makers who burned potash for the
glass factory.

What became of Schreiner?

Schreiner borrowed money and invested it in forests,
for the most part young forests and coppices. Then one

fine day he woke up penniless, with the creditors on his neck. First a forest fire caused by carelessness destroyed most of his woods; then Weiss & Pollak were ruined by the appearance on the market of Bohemian and Italian glass, which were cheaper and better. Schreiner gave up the glass and potash business and fled secretly, first to Budapest and then to Zagreb; he finally ended up in Weissenbach. At the time when the firm went into liquidation, the forests had all been burned. All that was left to auction off was five glass kilns, a warehouse, the house in which the masters, apprentices, and potash burners had lived, a freestanding baking oven, and a stable suitable for eight or ten horses. The total value was estimated at about two thousand florins. On the same day, the remaining stock of glass products, fine and coarse quartz sand, and potash were inventoried and valued at something over three hundred florins, while the furniture, tools, and equipment came to about two hundred and fifty florins. I might add that the glassware, the ordinary glasses, vinegar and beer bottles, etc., were of poor quality. The methods used in those days were rather primitive.

Do Rosenbergs still own part of the forests?

To the best of my knowledge, no. I believe they got out of the potash business in time and sold the young forests, which had grown in the meantime, to the family of Count Esterházy.

Does Izsák Rosenberg hunt?

I don't know.

What are the relations between Rosenberg and your nephew George?

George gets his stock of glassware from Rosenberg.

They come from what's left of the inferior merchandise that the Rosenbergs kept in their cellars, or stuff of equally poor quality that they brought in from Budapest or Kanizsa.

What are the relations between Rosenberg and Mrs. Fischer?

Rosenberg collects Bohemian glass. He also owns a valuable collection of sacred objects, of ritual vessels and candelabra. As Mr. Fischer was a *shohet* and himself a collector of ritual objects, Rosenberg was understandably interested in Fischer's estate. To the best of my knowledge, he bought a good part of the objects from Mrs. Fischer, but the remaining five or six pieces didn't seem to interest him, though Mrs. Fischer once told me that she wouldn't part with them even if it meant starving to death. I personally think Rosenberg is only pretending to underestimate their age and value, because the last time I saw him he asked me whether the Fischer woman was still keeping (I quote) "that junk she regards as valuable" in her private museum.

So you've acted as an intermediary between Rosenberg and Mrs. Fischer?

Yes, long ago, about 1935. When Fischer was out of work, before he got his job as *shohet*, I offered to find someone who would buy a part of his collection on favorable terms, but he wouldn't hear of it. But even then, if I remember right, Rosenberg went to see them and looked at the things. Whether he bought anything, I don't know.

How many times did you act as an intermediary between them?

That was the only time. Later Rosenberg came to

Novi Sad on several occasions and attended to his
business himself. At that time he was still mobile.

Still mobile, you say?

Yes, he hasn't been able to walk for the past three
years. I mean, he's reduced to a wheelchair. I'm told
it's creeping paralysis, something of the kind.

Did he visit the Mayers before? I mean, while he was
still mobile?

I don't know.

Has Rosenberg any other hobby besides collecting
glass?

I think he used to collect stamps, but he hasn't
mentioned it to me lately. At one time, he would ask
me to save valuable stamps for him from foreign letters.
He used to take a great interest in Montenegrin stamps
from the reign of King Nicholas. He asked me to get
him some, but then I fell sick and I wasn't able to oblige
him.

Is he interested in radio telegraphy?

Not that I know of.

Has Rosenberg ever given you news and said he had
it from a reliable source?

No.

Think it over.

Well, he once said that he thought the law requiring
people to show documents proving they were citizens
and had paid their local taxes was the last measure the
government would take against us. But he didn't say
anything about a reliable source.

What are the relations between the Mayers and the
Rosenbergs?

Apart from business relations, Rosenberg for a time

maintained a kind of scholarly friendship with one of Mayer's sons, the one who is studying archaeology. Actually, Rosenberg tried to get Mayer to investigate the Semitic contribution to the archaeology and paleography of Pannonia.

Have they met recently?

I don't know.

Who else lives in the Rosenberg house?

His wife, Szilvia, who has been running the house since he became paralyzed; and the domestics: a stable hand, a gardener, and a maid who doubles as a nurse.

Who is the stable hand?

A man of sixty, the spit and image of Martin, the coachman. He helped Martin unharness the horses, and anyone could have seen that they were both drunk. Rosenberg himself told me that his stable hand never drew a sober breath.

And the gardener?

Name of Boris Abramovich Struve, a Russian born in Riga. He came to Abbazia in 1916 as a prisoner of war. When the war was over, he stayed on. First he opened a barbershop, then a bookstore, and then he set himself up as a tailor. For a while he had a small greenhouse in which he experimented with exotic fruits and flowers. He bought the seeds from sailors. I know he worked for some time as gardener and elevator boy in a hotel in Abbazia. That's where Rosenberg met him. To this day, he shaves Rosenberg at eight o'clock every morning, after which he prepares a special bath for him. He also looks after the garden, but doesn't seem to enjoy it.

How about the maid?

A spinster, going on fifty. She tyrannizes Rosenberg and his wife. The evening I had that conversation with him, she came into the room without knocking and wheeled Rosenberg out in his chair; he just smiled and shrugged, as though to tell me that that's the way it was. Her name is Rosalia. Rosenberg brought her, too, from Abbazia, where she was working as a chambermaid. I think she and Boris Abramovich were fond of each other at first, but now they can't stand each other. Mrs. Rosenberg told me that.

What was the reason for their falling out?

Rosa found out that Boris was corresponding with a woman in Riga, or rather that they had been corresponding until three or four years ago. It seems that this woman in Riga was Boris's common-law wife and had had a son by him. Rosa, who was forty-one by then, regarded this relationship as an unforgivable infidelity and tried to commit suicide: she took some of Rosenberg's tranquillizers, but not enough to kill her.

Is Boris Struve still corresponding with his common-law wife or his son?

They both disappeared around 1940. His son was accused of high treason for allegedly poisoning certain political leaders in Riga through deliberate medical malpractice, and was condemned to death. The sentence was commuted to a long term at hard labor in Siberia, where he probably died. His mother, who had been working as a hospital nurse until then, was also sent to Siberia and hasn't been heard from since.

Does Struve correspond with anyone else in a foreign country?

For a time he corresponded with a relative in Paris,

and it was through this relative that he heard about the death of his wife and son. But after that he stopped corresponding with him. Rosenberg told me that.

When did you meet Struve?

On my first visit to the Rosenbergs, about 1927 or 1928. At the time, Struve was employed by them as a gardener; he was replanting their big garden. He got rid of the *Gartenzwerge*, pulled up the cheap carnations, and put in French roses. He was an experienced gardener and I learned a lot from him. Unfortunately, I've never had a chance to make use of what I learned.

Have you corresponded with Struve since then?

He wrote me just once, about 1932, asking me to get him a book about Dutch tulips. I never answered his letter, I was prevented from doing so by the state of my health.

Why did you visit the Rosenbergs in Csesztreg that year?

I wanted to clear up the business of the forest. According to my sisters, the Rosenbergs were the chief beneficiaries from the burned woods and I wanted to talk things over with them. I came away empty-handed. The Rosenbergs simply washed their hands of the whole affair. They said that nothing illegal had been done and that it was no responsibility of theirs if their father had advised my father to leave his forests to the firm of Weiss & Pollak.

Did they give you any money on that occasion, as compensation, so to speak?

Yes. The totally symbolic sum of two hundred pengö.

Do you also regard the so-called loan you received from them today as partial compensation?

Yes, in a way.

Did Struve practice any other trade besides those that have been mentioned?

To the best of my knowledge, no.

In your previous statement you said: "Struve asked me to get him some spare part for his radio in Novi Sad."

Yes. A tube for an Orion radio.

Did you get it?

No. Certain unforeseen events made it impossible for me to think of such things.

What do you mean by unforeseen events?

The collapse of the house I was living in and the consequences of that catastrophe.

In an earlier statement you said (I quote): "I am convinced that the collapse of the house was caused by a rat." Is that still your conviction?

Yes.

Let's get back to Struve. Did he ask anything else of you before you went to Novi Sad?

He asked me to get him a good shaving brush, "for the master," as he put it. Since I myself do not own a decent shaving brush, I told him I'd try hard to get him one. Unfortunately, I found one neither for myself nor for him.

If a person is able to replace a radio tube, don't you think he must know something about radio engineering?

Not necessarily. That sort of repair—just replacing a part—can be done by any amateur.

Were you aware that this Struve was a gunsmith?

I've heard something of the kind.

Have you ever seen a workshop in the Rosenberg house?

No.

What rooms have you been in?

The entrance, the living room, and one of the two bedrooms. Actually, the room Rosenberg gave me for the night was the dining room. There was a couch in it.

Did you hear any suspicious sounds?

I heard no sounds of any kind. Before going to bed, I drank a bottle of Traminac with my host and I was so tired from the trip that I slept soundly.

Was Struve with you at the time? I mean, while you were drinking the Traminac?

No.

Where was he?

I think he went out to attend to the wagon and to settle Martin in. I only saw him at dinner. He was dejected and complained of a headache.

How did Struve and Poltaratsky get along?

I once asked him, Mr. Struve I mean, what he thought of Poltaratsky (that was two or three years ago). He said that personally he'd be glad to put a bullet through his head. I was amazed because this Boris, Struve I mean, is a peaceful, cool-headed man. I knew that at one time they had lived together in Novi Sad, like brothers, in good times and bad. They were generally regarded as some kind of conspirators or freemasons. Struve was supposedly Poltaratsky's orderly—I mean, that was the role he played when people were around. I believe there was some kind of intrigue connected with Sofia Nikolaevna, Poltaratsky's wife. The three of them, Struve, Sofia Nikolaevna, and Poltaratsky, were said to live in perfect harmony. So it probably wasn't jealousy that made Struve say he'd be glad to put a bullet through

Poltaratsky's head. That was clear to me. Boris himself confirmed my suspicions and explained the motives for his hatred. Poltaratsky was involved with the Trotskyists. I believe that was the reason for their rupture.

So you believe that, certain facts to the contrary, Boris Struve could not have been working for the Soviets?

Yes, I'm sure.

Have you any proof?

All indications are that he was already anti-Soviet at the time of his friendship with Poltaratsky, if not actively, then at least in his convictions. After hearing about the arrest and disappearance of his wife and son, he was quick to turn against the Soviets and Poltaratsky, though at the time for entirely different reasons. He wanted nothing more to do with either of them. His present psychological state is a consequence of both these developments. Rosenberg tells me he detects signs of alarming psychological confusion in him; that is, Boris. The headache he complained of that day was only a pretext. He has been going in heavily for theosophy and seems to be attending a spiritist circle of which his former friend Rosa is an active member. According to Rosenberg, Struve is trying to make a life for himself outside of this world.

Let's get back to Rosenberg. You say his only son disappeared?

I've never been able to find out exactly what happened to him. My sister keeps saying that I must never under any circumstances mention Rosenberg's son in his presence, and the rebarbative Miss Rosalia, the maid, said the same thing when she opened the door for me.

Did you know him personally?

I only saw him once. At that time, he was working in Novi Sad at the White Cross Pharmacy, run by Zsigmond Lukács. Later he worked for a time at János Grossinger's pharmacy. That was two years ago.

Who is Zsigmond Lukács?

He's an old friend of mine. He had a pharmacy on Louis Barthou Street. He was in prison in Petrograd for a while, then he was transferred to Belgrade. I've heard that he was beaten to death. They stuffed dirty rags into his mouth while they were beating him. Grossinger told me that.

Who is Grossinger?

Another pharmacist. He was in prison in Petrograd for a time; later he was shot as a hostage. I read his name on a bulletin board, along with the names of other hostages who had been shot.

Let's get back to Rosenberg junior. What happened to him? How much were you able to find out?

According to my sister's version, he hid for a while in Novi Sad, working as an anesthetist in a hospital. Someone seems to have denounced him. He took an overdose of morphine, but the doctors were right there and he recovered. Then he was sent to Budapest, where he had a nervous breakdown and committed suicide.

Continue.

In his frenzy, he knocked his teeth out and smashed his skull against the stone walls of his cell. Evidently under the influence of some drug.

Do you often leave your home?

Only when absolutely necessary, and then with the permission of the authorities.

On your walks in the woods, have you ever come across anyone suspicious?

Up to now, as I've already told you, I've only had two encounters in the woods: with my nephew George and with those hunters, one of whom, a certain Tót, has it in for me.

When did you leave Sziget?

The next day, the ninth.

Did Rosenberg urge you to stay longer?

I told him I was in a hurry to get home, and explained the reason for my haste: I had to be back in Novi Sad on the fourteenth at the latest, because of an official summons I had received from the local office for the registration of foreigners.

Did you have the documents they wanted?

My sister Netty has gone to Budapest on the same business. She will get some of the documents, the ones concerning payment of local taxes and those relating to the nationality of our parents, for both of us. At least, that's what we arranged before she left.

Did you see Struve again before leaving the Rosenbergs?

I didn't see him until I got into the wagon. Then he appeared behind the curtain for a moment, and I think he waved to me.

Did you stop along the way?

We, Martin and I that is, stopped for a shot of brandy to warm us.

Did you talk to anyone else at the café?

There was no one at the café just then, except the two of us, and Madame Clara, of course.

What did you talk about with her?

The weather, prices, the rise in the alcohol tax.

Did you pay her what you owed her?

I was in no position to do that.

Did you drop any allusions?

I don't understand.

Try to remember.

Unless you regard my attempt at a gallant compliment as an allusion.

What was the wording of your compliment?

I said something like this: I look forward to seeing you next spring, Madame Clara, if I am still here. That is . . .

What did you mean by "if I am still here"?

If I'm still alive. That's what I meant.

What is the meaning behind the code words "shoes" and "shaving brush"?

They refer to plain ordinary shoes and a shaving brush that my sister Olga promised me when I was staying with her. I was with her for a week.

To whom did these shoes belong?

They belonged to her deceased husband, Móric.

Have you seen these shoes?

Yes, they were on the shelf in the storeroom, with ten or a dozen pairs of women's shoes, galoshes, and boots.

Describe the shoes.

I'm tired.

Describe them.

They are gray, imitation antelope skin, I believe, with hard counters and rounded tips, size forty-four or forty-five, anyway they were too small, because I tried them on in a hurry, I didn't want Olga to see me. I could have squeezed into them with a little effort, especially as they have double soles, one of which I'm certain is cardboard. But when it comes to their looks, I don't like them at all, they are covered with perforations shaped like snowflakes, on both sides of the laces and at the toes.

Did you stop anywhere else besides the café in Baksa?

No, Martin can back me up, insofar as he remembers anything.

When did you get home?

About five in the afternoon.

Who helped you unload?

The coachman and I pushed the cupboards over the snow like sleds. That was my idea.

Did anyone else help you?

No.

Where were your wife and children?

When I opened the door, I saw they had left the house in a hurry.

What made you think they had left in a hurry?

The first thing I noticed was books and a cardboard schoolbag with straps, all lying helter-skelter on the kitchen table and on the wooden chest under the window. The books were open, the pencil box was empty. The bed was unmade, and the part of the wall that was supposed to be whitewashed while I was away had not been whitewashed; but there was a pail with a brush in it beside the wall, and I could see two or three brushstrokes. Obviously, she had suddenly been interrupted.

Did you go to your relatives?

No. I only asked Mr. Hermann, the neighbor whose windows overlook our yard, if by any chance he had noticed when my wife and children went out.

Who is Hermann?

A shoemaker. He has helped us out a few times, lending us one thing and another, potatoes, cornmeal, salt, that kind of thing.

What did he say?

That he'd seen some policemen at about ten in the morning, probably looking for me, and just after they left he had seen my wife rush out with the children. When I asked if he knew which way she had gone, he motioned vaguely in the direction of the woods.

Did you ask anyone else?

Near the wooden footbridge, I met Fani, a woman who says she is a sister of the "third order." When I came near her, she clutched the cord she has under her skirt, and fled as fast as her legs would carry her.

How do you interpret that?

I think she's not all there.

Did you ask anyone else?

I ran into the postman on the way and he told me he thought he had seen them a few hours ago rushing toward the Roman road. After that I thought it wiser to wait for her at home, because if she came back while I was gone, there might be another misunderstanding. Anyway, I was tired, and my leg hurt badly. It was dark by the time they got home.

Why didn't you go to your relatives for help?

It seemed to me that in such an emergency they might have volunteered information. All the more so as I was sure they were watching me from behind their curtains.

Where had your wife and children been all that time?

Hiding in the woods on the other side of the river. They had taken refuge in a shepherd's hut. They came home frozen and frightened to death.

Why didn't you respond immediately to the summons the police had left you?

My fatigue and the pain in my leg made it impossible for me to go out again that evening. So I went to see Mr. Fehér, the village mayor, and asked him for advice. He said he couldn't advise me in so delicate a matter, but was prepared to testify, if necessary, that I had been to see him that evening.

Had you ever spoken to Mr. Fehér before?

I first met him just after we arrived in the village. He said then that he would have preferred not to have me in his jurisdiction, because he wanted no truck with the police. The second time, it was he who sent for me in connection with what may have been too noisy an argument I'd had with my nephew George. God only knows what George had told him.

What's wrong with your leg?

In the course of some incident in the labor brigade, one of the supervisors seems to have kicked me in the shin. Luckily, the bone wasn't broken.

Have you got a doctor's certificate?

No.

Who treated your injury?

Dr. Jakob Herzog.

Where and when did you meet Herzog?

Herzog came to Kovin the day before I left for the second time. He worked there awhile as an intern. And I met him again not long ago in the labor brigade that was assigned to the brickworks.

Continue.

Seeing that I had a visible limp the day after that incident, Dr. Herzog came up to me on his way home and advised me to drop in and let him examine my leg.

Especially as I had complained of bruises, swellings, and unbearable pain. He was living on Greek School Street and I went to see him that same day. He examined my leg and told me I needed rest, but that as far as he could see there was no damage to the bone. To be absolutely sure, an X-ray would be needed.

Continue.

That's all.

When did Herzog disappear from the labor brigade?

A few days later. One morning he wasn't there for roll call. The guards were especially strict that day.

Do you know what became of him?

He hid somewhere in Budapest under a false name, he and his wife. When the police agents knocked on the door, they both took cyanide.

Who gave you the details of Herzog's death?

Fülöp Uhlmann.

Who is Fülöp Uhlmann?

An optician. He has a shop on St. Sava Street, but it was closed down recently. Uhlmann and his wife live in the courtyard of the same building. I asked him to repair my glasses after the incident, but he said his shop had been sealed with all his instruments and materials inside, and that he was waiting for permission from the authorities to start working again. Then he sent me to Jovan Benedek at 8 Danube Embankment, who replaced my broken lenses at a very low price.

Who is Jovan Benedek?

Benedek's mother is a Catholic from Sopron, and his wife is also a Catholic, name of Julia Almási, from Subotica. After two weeks in pre-trial custody, he was released. Thanks to the intercession of some influential

friends of his mother's, his shop was returned to him
and his license renewed.

Had you known Benedek before?

No.

Your relatives, specifically Gyula-George Boroska,
told the police that you went to Budapest.

Yes, I was planning to go soon, but they must have
known that I hadn't left yet.

What business have you in Budapest?

I shall try to get the Ministry of Transportation to
bring its influence to bear on the commission that has
reduced my invalid's pension, unjustly and illegally, in
my opinion.

Is that the only reason for your trip?

The denture that Löbl made for me pinches badly.
So I mean to consult a certain Barna, whose ad I saw
in the newspaper. Moderately priced dentures with a
ten-year guarantee.

Who is Löbl?

Löbl worked with me in the labor brigade. Then he
suddenly disappeared. Later I heard from Herzog, now
dead, who had been in pre-trial custody with him, that
Löbl had been condemned to death and hanged. He
was half dead when they took him to the gallows. One
of his heels was badly festered from stick blows and the
bone could be seen through an open wound on his
shin.

TRAVEL SCENES (IV)

[*61*]

The man is sitting next to the coachman in the front seat of the wagon. It is a kind of horse-drawn dray, loaded with furniture secured by two ropes. The man is holding a stick between his knees and turning the handle in his hands. The coachman has an unlit pipe in his mouth. Two huge Styrian horses are dragging the wagon slowly over the frozen snow, which crunches under the wheels. First they pass through a narrow street; then they turn left and debouch onto a large square. It is no longer snowing; the man raises his head, takes off his glasses, and wipes them with a corner of his handkerchief. Gothic buildings with stylized cornices pass slowly to his left. The big iron gate in front of the building is shut; so are the windows with their barred wooden shutters. The Gothic cathedral lies straight ahead. The man looks at the steeple clock and takes out his pocket watch, no doubt to set it. It is three o'clock. The cathedral door is open. The man sees a silhouette in the shadow of the portal, but cannot be sure whether it is a man or a woman. The silhouette seems to be moving, crossing itself and genuflecting several times in a row. In the background, through the open door, the man sees flickering candles, or is it only the play of light on the stained-glass windows, or a mere illusion? The square is deserted. Suddenly a man appears from behind a mound of snow. Leaning on a wooden shovel, he looks in the direction of the wagon. The man with the glasses looks back at the man leaning on the shovel,

then suddenly loses sight of him. The man with the
shovel looks after the wagon for a while, then he bends
over and resumes shoveling snow onto the pile. The
man in the wagon turns in the direction where he saw
the snow shoveler a moment ago, but can no longer see
him because the man is hidden behind a white hillock,
bent over as he scrapes his shovel over the crunching
snow. But this the man cannot hear. He hears only the
scraping of the wagon he is sitting in. Now he sees only
the dog, which, head hanging, has been following the
wagon for a time. Suddenly the dog runs off to one side
and starts jumping about clumsily, his legs sinking into
the snow. Some pigeons that have been quietly pecking
fly into the air, hesitate for a time, then settle on the
marble base of a monument. The man watches the dog
jumping about in the snow. Now the dog is close to the
monument. A man stands on the marble pedestal,
pointing his upraised right hand at the cathedral or the
dark sky. The snow on his shoulders looks like white
epaulets. The dog is very near the base of the monument, where two white pigeons are sitting; from a
distance, they look like specks of snow. They are evidently in no hurry to fly away, confident no doubt that
the dog cannot get at them. They stay like that for a
while, then they suddenly take flight, with a loud
flapping of wings. The dog follows them with his eyes,
then approaches the pedestal and lifts his hind leg. The
man looks after the pigeons, which circle irresolutely,
then fly higher and disappear into the window niches
of the Gothic cathedral or onto the cornice or into the
lacelike rose window over the portal. The man in the
wagon watches the dog, who retraces his steps through

the snow and returns to his old place five or six steps behind the wagon. The man says something to the coachman beside him—probably the address to which the furniture is to be delivered. The coachman nods and pulls gently at the reins. The wagon turns into a side street on the right. The two men drive on for a time without a word.

CRIMINAL INVESTIGATION (IV)

[62]

When did E.S. reach his destination?

He arrived at the East Station in Budapest at 5:20 p.m. (Central European Time), all of two hours late.

What caused the delay?

Snowdrifts.

What did the traveler regret?

Not having filled his briefcase with sandwiches or provided himself with more than one bottle of beer at the station in Novi Sad.

What infuriated him?

His usual inability to derive useful lessons from his empirical knowledge.

For instance?

Though frequent experience (empirical knowledge) should have told him that the trains on any number of lines (including Novi Sad–Budapest) often lacked dining cars, with the result that he was left suffering from hunger and thirst, he continued stubbornly and stupidly to trust in the heraldic emblem of the crossed knife and fork beside the train number on his timetable.

Cite another example.

Though he had often experienced the ruinous effect of liquor (empirical knowledge), he nevertheless started drinking whenever the occasion arose, as if it were the first (or last) time in his life and as if he had not, a day or two before, suffered all the consequences of his failure to learn from experience.

In the last cited example, what advantages outweighed

the so-called negative consequences, so that a new
experience demolished his knowledge of the consequences?

Intense emotional life as long as the drunkenness
lasts; a sense of strength, a surge of potency, increased
libido; rhetorical virtuosity gradually degenerating into
gibberish; a gift for idioms and figures of speech
(metaphors, metonymies, variations on themes, syncopes, puns, etc.); partial or total loss of cynophobia,
enhanced mobility, relaxation of the sympathetic nervous system; alternation between a sentimental (feminine) and an aggressive (masculine) mood; a sudden
flowering of sociable feelings toward inferiors as well as
superiors (in title, rank, income, and intelligence); ability
to fraternize with members of all professions regardless
of sex, social position, and religious denomination;
oscillation between euphoria and aggressiveness; sudden emergence of a memory of and facility for (known
and unknown) languages, accompanied by a gift for
linking them by means of puns, in such a way that a
shift of accent or a slight deformation metamorphoses
a word in one language into a word in another; a free-
and-easy attitude toward money and the salutary effects
of such an attitude; a sense of opulence, princely largesse
(drinks all around and munificent tips); sudden recol-
lection of songs (words and music) that had lain dormant
for years in the depths of the unconscious; a spontaneous exuberance that explodes in music and song; a
tendency to beat time on the tabletop with one's hands
and on the floor with one's feet, or simply by clapping
hands; sudden increase of vocal range from mezzo-
soprano to bass, coupled with the ability to sing notes

that are hopelessly beyond one's reach in a state of sobriety; improved ear for music; a strengthening of the vocal cords; change of vocal timbre (for the better); exceptional gift for improvising on hitherto unfamiliar tunes and rhythms (csardas, gigues, barroom ballads, romances); ability to hear one's own voice as the voice of a stranger inside or outside oneself; fluctuation of mood according to the rhythm and tone of the music; ability to re-create a mood with roughly the same intensity by playing the music over again; identification with the simple story or subject of a song and the associations it arouses (love, youth, death); pleasant feeling of warmth that rises like a miniature sun from the sympathetic nervous system (one is reminded of a woman who feels the first stirrings of life in her belly: blessed be the fruit of thy womb); ribaldries which, along with songs, jokes, and puns, liberate us through laughter; an urge to kiss the hands of waitresses, cash-iers, cloakroom attendants, flower girls, and respectable ladies, and at the same time to shower them with tips, thus giving evidence of refinement and a democratic spirit; a tendency to pour out one's heart to total strangers (women as well as men) in the hope of arousing feeling, compassion, amazement, or admiration, and, in the last analysis, catharsis; sorrow at the thought of man's mortality accompanied by a fugitive sense that the moment is immortal.

What negative experience was powerless to outweigh the advantages just mentioned?

One whose intensity he forgot as soon as the first symptoms of hangover (*Katzenjammer, másnaposság*) had passed: nightmares (old age, danger, death); painful

awakening from dreams, one's entrails burning with a
thirst like a forest fire that water can barely quench; an
intolerable headache that is not helped by aspirin; bitter
remorse over something one has done, still vaguely
perceived, but becoming more explicit as the mind
awakens and the events of the previous evening take
shape and form; the anguish of seeing oneself as
someone else, someone who squanders his money mind-
lessly, beats time with his hands and elbows on the
tabletop, kisses the hands of cashiers, waitresses, and
whores, talks a strange language that he himself barely
understands to people who don't understand it at all or
misunderstand it, improvises cheap puns, smutty jokes,
and obscene curses (*le vagytok szarva cseresznyemagos büdös
kurvaszarral*), or pours out his heart to total strangers
who are not in the least interested; the stench of stale
wine in his room, the smell of his own body, the vomit
and urine stains on the trousers he had thrown over
the chair beside the bed; the memory of his agonizing
retching, as he splattered his shoes and socks with fish
soup and greasy goulash. (And it's no use hiding his
head under the bedclothes and trying to go back to
sleep and forget the whole business. No use at all.)

What advice pertaining to hangovers did E.S. give an
unknown traveler (about forty years of age) in the
compartment of the Novi Sad–Budapest express?

The most effective remedy for hangover (*mein Herr!*)
is suicide.

Where did the traveler go from the station?

Because, owing to the lateness of his train, he could
not attend to any of his business, he hailed a cab and
had himself driven to 12 Dohány Street, third floor, an
address given to him by Rosenberg.

Had he made a note of it?

As a precaution, he had not written it down and had relied on his memory.

Why hadn't he stopped at the station restaurant to quench his thirst?

Because caution and experience counseled him to avoid, when possible, public places such as beer halls, dining cars, department stores, bookshops, libraries, public baths, markets, puppet theaters, circuses, parade routes, churches, buffets, synagogues, auction rooms, banks, and railroad stations.

What did the tired traveler hope?

That at the secret meeting place (12 Dohány Street, third floor) drinks and coffee would be served and that he might be asked to stay the night.

How was he received?

After he had stubbornly and repeatedly rung the doorbell of apartment 18 (*Barna I. fogorvoslásra jogositott áll. vizsg. fogász*), a woman in hair curlers appeared at the door of the adjoining apartment, told him that the gentleman whose bell he was ringing had not been seen for more than two months, and advised him to leave the building forthwith, or else she would call the police.

How did E.S. try to justify his presence?

By saying that Dr. Barna had been his dentist and had made him a denture which unfortunately was beginning to pinch.

Where, in defiance of caution and experience, did the tired traveler then go?

To the New York Restaurant.

What attracted him to that particular place?

The possibility of watching the passersby through the big plate-glass windows (in the winter) or (on sunny days) comfortably seated with a glass of beer at a table outside; the presence of artists and bohemians, among whom he often recognized faces from the newspapers or illustrated weeklies; the friendliness of the female personnel, especially the redheaded cashier, who regularly greeted him with a smile, and sometimes even inquired into the reasons for his long absence.

What change did he notice?

The redheaded cashier was not there, and in her place (behind the big, baroque, cathedral-like cash register) sat a corpulent lady who didn't even take notice of his presence.

Did he meet anyone that day at the New York Restaurant?

A certain Zöldesi (formerly Grünwald), a pianist whom he had met recently in Novi Sad, where he had been Miss Gavanski's piano teacher, passed by but did not return E.S.'s greeting, either because he did not recognize him or because he did not wish to recognize him; E.S. shook hands with Viktor Kolb, a pharmacist and native of Koprivnica, but Kolb soon left the café with the excuse that he was in a hurry; a Mr. Roder (first name unknown), former editor of *The Business Herald*, lifted his hat to him; Imre Vándor, owner of a small dry-goods store, did not return his greeting, although their eyes had met; a middle-aged lady (first and last names unknown) smiled at him in passing, and he replied by lifting his hat, but couldn't remember where and when he had met her; one István Szemere (occupation unknown) asked him for a loan of two pengö; a flower girl offered him anemones at two pengö apiece; a police agent asked politely for his papers.

Whom did he telephone from the New York Restaurant?

Otto Weiss, real-estate agent, residing on Thököly Street, but his number did not answer, though E.S. called three times in the course of an hour; Mrs. Ida Krauss, widow of the late Jenö Krauss, optician, but it appeared that the mistress had been "pleased to absent herself for several months and had left no address"; one Béla Gutmann, a railroader, who, as E.S. was told by a woman in tears (probably his wife), was, alas, no longer among the living; Zsigmond Móricz (namesake of the well-known writer), a notary, who claimed to be swamped and gave him an appointment for three days later; Clara Kohn, née Müller, a former proofreader for *The Business Herald*, who had gone out but would be back in half an hour at the latest (when he called for the third time an hour later, he was told that she had left town unexpectedly); Mr. Aladár Nagy, a lawyer, who, it turned out, had been sick in the hospital for some time; a Mr. Tassinger, bookbinder—no answer, though he tried twice; one Rachel (profession and surname unknown), who, he was told, had married and moved to an unknown address, probably in Buda; Ferenc Fehér, retired railroader, who invited him to dinner at nine that evening.

Why did he decline this invitation with thanks?

Because his train was leaving at 8:15 p.m.

Did his recent experience teach him anything about train travel?

No, but at least in his own eyes he was justified by the following facts: having spent nearly all his ready money on telephone calls, beer, chicory "cappuccino," anemones (which he sent to the new cashier), and cabs, and in no position, *vis major*, to borrow more, he was unable this time to fill his briefcase with sandwiches and beer and had to content himself with a small bottle of golden beer, which he kept in his pocket as his last (gold) reserve.

What thought preoccupied him while steel girders clanged and his train rolled slowly across the river, which flowed invisibly under a thick layer of ice?

The thought that this river extended like a long, throbbing artery from the Black Forest to the Black Sea, a distance of some two thousand kilometers, connecting peoples and regions, so that many nations separated by language, religion, and customs might regard one another as cousins and brothers.

What courtesy call did he pay before abandoning himself to sleep and oblivion?

On his way to relieve his bladder of the golden beer—which would flow in a golden stream—he made his way down the corridor of the first-class carriage (paradise lost), impelled by the nostalgic desire to recollect the land of Canaan.

What did he glimpse in the first-class (non-smoking) compartment?

There in the violet light of the compartment sat a lady in black, leaning her lovely head against the high plush backrest; a little girl lay sleeping on her lap.

What did this remind him of?

Of another (unless it was the same) lady, whom he had seen somewhere not so long ago on a previous journey in a first-class compartment, and who had vanished without a trace from his life, only to reappear now like a ghost.

What did he think possible?

That the two ladies in black were indeed one and the same lady, and that he had been fated to cross her path for the second time.

How might he have tested this hypothesis?

By (a) asking the one and only witness (not counting himself) of the first encounter (where? when? how?), since he himself was no longer able to remember the previous lady in black; (b) leaving to the one and only witness (apart from himself) the initiative of letting him know by a sign whether or not his suppositions were correct.

Did E.S. go through with this investigation?

No.

Did the one and only witness give him a sign?

The lady in black was sleeping with her mouth half open (as he was returning along the corridor) in the violet light of the first-class (non-smoking) compartment and was probably dreaming.

Dreaming what?

That a fine-looking gentleman with spectacles lifted his hat as a sign of respect and admiration, and that she responded with an encouraging smile; that, before anything could happen, this gentleman was expelled from the first-class compartment; that she saw him again for a moment, hurrying to the cab stand, to disappear forever (forever?) from her widowed life.

Where was E.S. going?

At a reduced speed of 70 kilometers an hour (because of the snowstorm), he was riding through the Pannonian night, over frozen rivers and streams, across bridges, over embankments, pastures, and meadows, through forests and valleys, sand dunes and snowdrifts, seas and memories, toward a faraway dawn that he himself could barely imagine.

Where did he find himself immediately after that?

After describing an enormous circle, his body (his mind) found itself in a cold room, where the feeble flame of an oil lamp (*ner tamid*) flickered.

What religious theme was concealed behind his interest in that lamp?

The theme of the Hanukkah miracle, when an infinitesimal quantity of oil burned for eight days in the menorah (after Judas Maccabaeus had conquered the temple in Jerusalem); which led him to believe, hope, and trust in God that his own bit of oil would burn until dawn, until daybreak, for if the oil lasted eight days for them (the Maccabees), why wouldn't it last eight hours for him?

What was he trying to prove?

He was trying with this trifling experiment to demonstrate empirically and with precision the possibility of a miracle (the first one).

When (by Central European Time) will the sun rise on the fifth day of the fourth month of the year 1942, at the letter writer's place of residence, if we take as our starting point Lendava, situated at one hour and six minutes east of Greenwich and at 46.5 degrees north latitude?

Nautical twilight will occur at three hours and thirty-three minutes, and civil (morning) twilight will last from four hours and thirteen minutes to four hours and forty-seven minutes.

Where does knowledge not only of the cyclic movement of the sun, moon, and planets but also of the cyclic alternation of day and night inevitably lead?

To the knowledge of death; for the mind of him who creates cannot escape the laws that govern the cyclic movements of the earth, the sun, and the planets.

Where was another cyclic movement represented?

On the color lithograph (gift of the late Móric), which its new owner brought from Novi Sad and which, under the high-sounding title *Das Stufenalter des Mannes* (*The Ages of Man*), provides a schematic picture of the ascending and descending stages of human life.

What does the frame of this picture look like?

A thin wooden frame covered with wormholes, black fly droppings, and patches of peeling gilt.

Describe schematically, step by step (without omitting the central motif of the Garden of Eden), all the motifs of the color lithograph *Das Stufenalter des Mannes*.

The Garden of Eden. In the foreground, slightly bent, an apple tree. Just below the crown, a single branch, distinct from all the others, protrudes, at almost a right angle to the trunk. An apple can be seen amid the rich green foliage. The sky on the distant horizon is a hazy blue. Along the curving, broken line dividing land and sea (in the background), deep bays and fjords, with jagged mountain peaks between them. A round red sun barely touches the highest peak. The long shadows of the mountains transform the blue of the sea into dark green, and draw a clear line between the blue and the green, as between two colors that do not mix, or at least not as readily and completely as the blue of the sky and the blue of the water on the distant horizon. From there, from the distant blue horizon, a flock of birds come flying. The brotherhood of all God's creatures. To the left of the apple tree, a lioness. To the right, a gray bear. At the back, a lion and a dromedary.

A little farther back, a stag and a doe, in an attitude of serene expectancy. Chickens are pecking peaceably on the Edenic dunghill. A flock of resplendent white geese can be seen amid the greenery. A snake twined around an overhanging branch darts its tongue out. The snake's head is exactly halfway between the heads of Adam and of Eve. Eve, as naked as the day she was born, has taken hold of the bottommost branch with her right hand. With her left hand, she holds out the apple to Adam. Her hair, in two luxuriant skeins, covers her breasts and shoulders and reaches down to her hips. Under the apple tree, Adam sits naked, with a green spray across his knees. He holds out his hand toward the apple.

Birth. The baby boy lies in a reed basket in the shade of the apple tree. His right hand, disproportionately small in comparison with his head, is resting on his chest. We do not see the child's mother, but undoubtedly she is nearby, watching over him.

Ten years. The little boy is brandishing a stick and running after a hoop. The full weight of his body rests on his left leg, his right leg is slightly upraised and bent at the knee; in his right hand he holds the stick with which he is driving the hoop. He is wearing a blue sailor's cap with ribbons, a gray sweater, and blue trousers. A white collar is folded over the sweater.

Twenty years. The young man has his arms around a girl. His hair is still blond, though perhaps slightly darker than ten years ago. Wide mouth, straight nose. The lapels of his dark coat are lined with shiny black silk. His long neck looks even longer than it is, because it has been squeezed into a high celluloid collar, over

which a white bow tie is knotted. The girl is wearing a
blue dress with flounces, and a cabbage bow at the waist.
Two earrings resembling drops of blood peer out from
under her combed-back hair. Rounded celluloid comb.
Slender, shapely hands. With her left hand, she presses
a flower to her bosom. She is wearing a white lace collar.
The young man's right hand is hidden behind the girl's
back. They are touching each other's fingertips, as
though about to start waltzing.

Thirty years. The man has just come home from work.
He is wearing a dark suit and a hat. Holding his briefcase
at chest height, he has opened it and is engaged in
taking out a gift-wrapped package with a big golden
bow. The woman is wearing a long, bright-red dress.
She has a child in her arms. Her hair is done up in a
large bun. A second, older child, a little girl of five or
six, is standing with her back to the viewer. She, too, is
wearing a red dress. She is pointing the forefinger of
her left hand at her father's briefcase. Near them lies a
paper kite, and a little farther away, a child's drum and
a headless celluloid doll.

Forty years. A man in a morning coat and top hat is
holding open a paper scroll. A diploma? A stock certificate? A court order? Below his high collar, a black tie
with a huge knot.

Fifty years. Gray suit, hat held in left hand. His right
hand is raised in an oratorical gesture. What is he
talking about? Politics? Finance? Art? An amorous con-
quest? Death?

Sixty years. Holding a cane, the man is descending a
staircase. He has turned to one side. Leaning on his
cane with his right hand, he is pressing his left hand to

his chest. He is wearing a hat and a long coat that reaches almost to the ground. His face is rather worn, his eyes protuberant, his whiskers are going gray.

Seventy years. Leaning on his cane with his left hand, he is holding a pipe in his right hand. He is wearing a cap, below which can be seen gray hair combed behind the ears. Despite his heavy sweater, he hunches his shoulders as though suffering from the cold.

Eighty years. Bowed and bent, holding a cane in his right hand, the man is descending the next step. He is wearing a dark dressing gown, gathered at the waist. Raising his head with difficulty, he looks off into the distance.

Ninety years. On the last step, the man turns around suddenly, as though with a last burst of energy. He is wearing the same, now rather faded, dressing gown, buttoned up to the neck, and slippers. He is bending down, as though looking for something on the floor. His sensitive eyes are protected from the light by a celluloid visor attached to his bald head with an elastic.

On what step was E.S.?

He was on his way from the fifth and highest step (not counting the zero mark, which is *still* in the realm of nonexistence) down to the fourth from the end (not counting the last, level with the zero mark, which is *already* in the realm of nonexistence).

NOTES OF A MADMAN (V)

[63]

Even Spinoza (*Tractatus theologico-politicus*) reduces certain supernatural phenomena and biblical miracles to their positivistic counterpart. It is not my intention to analyze his errors in depth, although, because I still regard him as one of the world's greatest thinkers and as a kinsman, I am tempted to examine his false inferences. But what argument can I pit against his proofs when he himself offers no positive proof in support of his theses? There is no better proof than conviction. Accordingly, my only argument against his positivistic contention that "this divine miracle"—the manifestation of Yahweh to Noah—"was simply the refraction and reflection of the sun's rays in the droplets of water [*sic!*] suspended in the clouds" is my contrary conviction (which itself, however, partakes of positivistic reasoning); namely, that *it was simply a dream, or simply what it actually was, to wit, Yahweh's spoken word and face.*

What, then, can be expected of one Dr. S., the psychiatrist, or of the members of my own family, who are not capable of understanding even the most mundane phenomena which no one could suspect of unreality, which, though amazing, are far from miraculous; for instance, the fact that *our goose was cooked* a long time ago. And when I say our goose, I am thinking of your, of our, little lives. Because even if you don't believe in visions, you could at least believe in the plain (positivistic) facts you find in the newspapers. These facts and these newspapers make it clear that our goose is cooked and

that before the Allies can lift a finger the Horsemen of
the Apocalypse will be on us—unless we perish first. Of
hunger, of despair, of fear. Maybe you'll ask me what
these famous Horsemen of the Apocalypse, these monstrous figments of my maddened brain, look like. Although I detect the irony in your voice, although I read
your thoughts, I will answer you without irony: they
will be four handsome policemen on white horses,
armed with rifles and bayonets, handsome mustachioed
provincial policemen on horseback, with cock's feathers
stuck in their black hats. Maybe there won't be four of
them, as in a deck of playing cards, but only two. And
maybe their horses won't be white. Maybe they won't
even come on horseback, but on shiny bicycles, or on
foot, for that matter. But come they will, of that you
can be sure. Already they are twisting their mustaches
and fixing their bayonets on their rifles. I hear the
neighing of their horses, and I hear the feathers on
their hats flapping in the wind.

[*64*]

Maybe this letter, this communication of mine, will
look—and even now, with the first streaks of dawn, it
is beginning to look—like a thing of vanity, *vanitas
vanitatum*. Doesn't my letter, doesn't all my past life,
look *even now* like a shadow of vanity? *Even now* that
everything has passed through the purgatory of night,
the purgatory of darkness, the filter of eternity, which
holds back only the crystalline particles of pure existence, the hard crystals of being (essence). The night
will expunge all the rest, and my letter will remain

unsent; at dawn, my manuscript will be a dead manuscript in the dead sea of time, a dog-eared papyrus in
the putrid swamp of the Pannonian Sea, or a *document*
in a sealed container of green glass, the key to which
has been thrown into the water, into the swamp, a
document buried in the dark foundations of the night,
in the crumbling foundations of being, a testimony
addressed to some distant future—*postumus*.

[65]

Therefore, by these presents, my previous will is
declared null and void. At variance with my previous
and now invalidated stipulations, *I do not authorize* the
use of any part of my body for scientific or medical
purposes. I am referring first and foremost to my brain,
which evidently aroused the keen interest of Dr. Papandopoulos, at whose suggestion I made my previous and,
I repeat, now invalid stipulation. By these presents I
bequeath my body to the FLAMES; as executors of my
last will and testament, I appoint the *Regeneration* Cremation Society, to whose care I entrust my mortal
remains. I authorize said society to defray the cost of
its services and the expense attendant on cremation
from my estate; to wit, the part of the family house that
is my property. After the cremation, I wish my ashes to
be taken, in the urn provided for that purpose, to the
railroad bridge and from there scattered over the waters
of the Danube. I wish this ceremony to be attended
only by my nearest and dearest; that is, my wife and
children, and a representative of the Cremation Society.
Instead of a funeral service or of any religious ceremony,

I would like someone to be paid for reading excerpts from the Psalms of David, preferably Psalms 44, 49, and 54, as well as 114 and 137, in any of the following languages: Hebrew, Latin, German, Hungarian, Serbian, Italian, Romanian, Ukrainian, Armenian, Czech, Slovak, Bulgarian, Slovene, Portuguese, Dutch, Spanish, Yiddish; this reader must be neither a rabbi nor a cantor nor a monk nor an ecclesiastic of any kind, nor must the solemnity of the moment when dust is united with dust be defiled by the bleating of any actor or singer. The best way would be to find some tramp, some *Luftmensch*, who just happens to be idling on the banks of the Danube at the moment when the company with the urn approaches the bridge, and pay him to carry out my last will; it makes no difference whether this person is sober or drunk, provided he knows how to read; what more can be asked of my generosity? After the Psalms have been read and my ashes scattered over the Danube, let the urn or amphora be smashed into bits and it, too, be thrown from the bridge into the water like a broken glass.

[*66*]

Thanks to suffering and madness, I have had a finer, richer life than any of you, and I wish to go to my death with dignity, as befits the great moment after which all dignity and majesty cease. Let my body be my ark and my death a long floating on the waves of eternity. A nothing amid nothingness. What defense have I against nothingness but this ark in which I have tried to gather everything that was dear to me, people,

birds, animals, and plants, everything that I carry in my
eye and in my heart, in the triple-decked ark of my
body and soul. Like the pharaohs in the majestic peace
of their tombs, I wanted to have all those things with
me in death, I wanted everything to be as it was before;
I wanted the birds to sing for me forever, I wanted to
exchange Charon's bark for another, less desolate and
less empty; I wanted to ennoble eternity's unconscionable void with the bitter herbs that spring from the
heart of man, to ennoble the soundless emptiness of
eternity with the cry of the cuckoo and the song of the
lark. All I have done is to develop that bitter poetic
metaphor, carry it with passionate logic to its ultimate
consequence, which transforms sleep into waking (and
the converse); lucidity into madness (and the converse);
life into death, as though there were no borderline, and
the converse; death into eternity, as if they were not
one and the same thing. Thus my egoism is only the
egoism of human existence, the egoism of life, counter-
weight to the egoism of death, and, appearances to the
contrary, my consciousness resists nothingness with an
egoism that has no equal, resists the outrage of death
with the passionate metaphor of the wish to reunite the
few people and the bit of love that made up my life. I
have wanted and still want to depart this life with
specimens of people, flora and fauna, to lodge them all
in my heart as in an ark, to shut them up behind my
eyelids when they close for the last time. I wanted to
smuggle this pure abstraction into nothingness, to sneak
it across the threshold of that other abstraction, so
crushing in its immensity: the threshold of nothingness.
I have therefore tried to condense this abstraction, to

condense it by force of will, faith, intelligence, madness, and love (self-love), to condense it so drastically that its specific weight will be such as to lift it like a balloon and carry it beyond the reach of darkness and oblivion. If nothing else survives, perhaps my *material* herbarium or my notes or my letters will live on, and what are they but condensed, materialized idea; materialized life: a paltry, pathetic human victory over immense, eternal, divine nothingness. Or perhaps—if all else is drowned in the great flood—my madness and my dream will remain like a northern light and a distant echo. Perhaps someone will see that light or hear that distant echo, the shadow of a sound that was once, and will grasp the meaning of that light, that echo. Perhaps it will be my son who will someday publish my notes and my herbarium of Pannonian plants (unfinished and incomplete, like all things human). But anything that survives death is a paltry, pathetic victory over the eternity of nothingness—a proof of man's greatness and Yahweh's mercy. *Non omnis moriar.*

LETTER, OR,
TABLE OF CONTENTS

[67]

Kerkabarabás, April 5, 1942

Dear Olga,

   I am answering the short letter you sent me through Babika at some length, because thank the Lord you have given me something to write about. My dear relations have provided me with ample material for a bourgeois horror novel, which I might entitle Parade in the Harem, Easter in a Jewish Household, *or* Hourglass *(everything passes, sister mine).*

   It's a pity for you that you did not come here, because you missed an Easter banquet that could easily have fed two Montenegrin villages for a whole week; indeed, the whole house could have been repaired for the outlay. My children, on the other hand, had cold milk for breakfast, lunch, and dinner in a cold house, though I prepared a modest Easter feast for them by bringing a kilo of pork—leg, chops, and innards—home from Baksa. But fate is a dog and gobbled it all up.

   The story of this cold-milk Easter began on March 5, on the Friday when we left you and came home to Barabás (or when, according to Netty, Maria, and George, you chose to throw us out).

   We returned home from Baksa on foot, in a bitter, icy wind, leaving our baggage behind us. It had evidently been planned that hospitality would end when we got back. So Netty did not get me (I'd have paid her of course) the things I most urgently needed, she did not even lend me kitchenware to tide me over till I could bring my own (though they have enough for three families). On the contrary, in spite of her promises, there was such a fuss when we asked about borrowing kitchenware that my wife had to run out and buy two pots, four cups, four teaspoons, tin plates, etc., at a cost of about eight pengö. Now we have kitchenware, but they make the same fuss about giving us a little cabbage or a few frozen potatoes, and even more about allowing us a tiny place on the stove.

The cold and excitement have started my wife bleeding abnormally, and it's only natural that the unfriendly treatment has made her more nervous than ever, and myself as well, for that matter. And our nerves haven't been helped by the constant snowfall and frost, which prevent us from going out or putting our place in order.

The flour you gave us is used up, we have no bread, I have to go away, but I can't leave my family here without bread. The trip is urgent, because all pensioned railroad employees have to report by March 5, for possible recall to the service.

Netty's family have been making crooked propositions. For instance, they wanted me to buy two hundredweight of wheat at a price of forty pengö; they said they would grind it without authorization and then I wouldn't have to worry about bread until the fall. When I rejected this offer, they made a still shadier one; they wanted me to buy one hundredweight of wheat for forty pengö and offered to give me their flour coupons; naturally, according to your sister Marie Antoinette, I wouldn't have to take the fine-ground flour—what would I do with it?—but only the bread flour. Obviously, I couldn't accept a deal like that, one worthy of Jacob, so I looked for some other way of helping myself. I had no bread for five whole days, and that, I think, was the beginning of the whole hassle. When I refused to make shady deals with them, your sister Maria (Rebecca) began to act like a demented cow!

Finally, on March 17, salvation came: Nandor and Berta

brought us bread, flour, beans, and potatoes. That took a big weight off our minds, because I was at last able to leave. As it's impossible at the present time to make the trip from Barabás to Novi Sad without provisions, I had to stop in at Berta's to fill my briefcase; otherwise, I would have died of hunger and thirst on the way. The next day, I left Berta's and went to Novi Sad, where I attended to my business and shipped my two cupboards after filling them with kitchenware and bedding (unfortunately, they have not yet arrived). When I finished packing and shipping the cupboards, the house where I was living collapsed like a sand castle. If I had stayed inside a moment longer, I'd have been buried under the ruins, to the great joy of my relatives.

From Novi Sad I wrote Netty twice, I told her to watch her step. I said they should wait until we had settled our accounts, if there were any accounts pending between us.

On March 28, I returned home safely and found everything apparently in good shape. It was a beautiful spring day and I was delighted to be able finally to put my little stable in order. I began right away to dig up the ground in the kitchen. The next day it was cold again, cruel wintry weather. The enforced idleness kept me prisoner in the one room, or rather in the kitchen, where the children were unable to study or even to play. My wife, curled up like a hedgehog (because of her bleeding, which went on and on because of the cold and the state of her nerves), huddled with the children by the stove, which was going out. I told my daughter to put a log on the fire. Just then your nephew George stepped out of the other room. When he heard what I'd said, he began to scream at the top of his voice that they "couldn't afford to heat both ends of the house." A provocation. I clenched my teeth and balled my fists, thinking of our forest that they had burned and converted into potash. I said *at the time they had done it because they didn't know what they were doing.*

Then your nephew George, outdoing himself in generosity, got us a ramshackle iron stove (which our grandfather had probably thrown on the dump) and decided to have it repaired (like those kettles that you gave the gypsy to mend for us; I saw them: the lead rivets stuck out of the pots like 6.35 mm. bullets). Netty said she had some tin at home, so if she sent the stove to be mended, it would only cost us a few pengö; we'd have a stove that would serve us until the fall, and then we'd have to return it to its owner. On Good Friday afternoon they pushed the stove through the snow, and Gyula asked me for seven pengö forty fillér for the mending. I looked at the stove and told him to his face that I didn't need that junk. That was the beginning of a general free-for-all; all together and each one separately, they lit into me. Netty started in: "Luftmensch! Luftmensch!" Then it was Maria's turn: "How can a man with a regular income have the gall to let himself be supported for months by other people?" And Gyula: "And where will you cook? I'm serving notice that you will not put a single pot on our stove, because I'll throw it off!" etc. etc. But this lunatic medley of voices did not shake my composure, I told your sister Netty that if they weren't ashamed, I certainly had nothing to be ashamed of. After that, I fled from the house. My daughter and my wife had already gone to bed (it was almost eight o'clock), but my little boy was horrified, he followed me out into the street and begged me not to go, because Aunt Marusja had said she was going to take the beds away and we'd have to lie on the ground "like animals." I told him not to worry, if she took the beds we'd sleep in the straw.

Then I went for a walk in the village to collect my thoughts and calm my nerves. I was still in a state of nerves when I got back. My wife was afraid they would really take the beds away, and another thing that worried her was that the day before, while I was in Porszombat, some policemen had come to check my papers (which I had just straightened out at the town hall in Baksa).

To top it off, I got another order that same day to report without fail to the railroad administration on April 14. What was I to do? The housing problem was still unsolved. If I went away, there would be no one to take delivery of the things I had shipped, there would be sixty pengö to pay for them, we had no beds, we had no stove, but the worst of all was having to leave my wife and children at the unmerciful mercy of those people. My poor mother used to say that "night is a good adviser," so, taking the advice of the night, I wrote the following letter to Netty: "My dear sister: I assure you in advance, and I shall end with the same assurance, that I have no desire to quarrel with you and your children. It was you who advised me to spend a few weeks with each of my sisters, you thought I would have recovered by the time I had completed the circuit. I accepted your suggestion. But then the situation changed so radically that I couldn't come alone, so instead there are four of us. The consequences have been disastrous, as I was soon forced to recognize. I have endured provocations and chicanery with superhuman patience, in the hope that you people would tire of what you were doing and that it was not your intention to twist the knife in the wound. It is not my way to abuse anyone's hospitality, so if you sign the enclosed acknowledgment, I will send you twenty pengö for your two weeks' hospitality, because, after all, I was your guest and not your children's. What you have done cannot be undone, but try not to pick another quarrel with me, because what matters most to me at present is my health and the health of my family; so every quarrel or insult would be one too many, for your brother may not be a saint, but it is certain that you have nothing to reproach him with. (Acknowledgment enclosed): 'I hereby acknowledge receipt of 20 (twenty) pengö from my brother, retired chief railroad inspector, in payment for two weeks' board and lodging for himself and his family. Kerkabarabás, 4. IV 1942.'"

After I'd given them this letter, there was another terrible scene. Your niece Maria-Rebecca went on for a whole hour. "If only I knew how I'd offended them"; "I'm damned if I've done anything to offend them"; "For two weeks he says they've been eating here!"; "For a whole month they've been eating here!"; "Herr General Inspektor is a grand gentleman"; "None of his sisters wanted them, and now we have to dance attendance on them"; "Who insulted them, that's what I'd like to know"; "What in hell do they want of me?"; "My husband may not be a chief inspector, but I'm no less a lady than that wife of his"; "At least we're not schmutzig"; *etc. etc. For a full hour she spewed out filth, and if her brother-in-law hadn't interfered, she'd still be at it, especially as Babika (by whom you sent your comforting letter) arrived in the meantime and would certainly have chimed in.*

Among other things you write: "I shall answer your letter in brief. I told Gyula not to give you the ham until Easter, because it's the country custom that there should be ham in every house at that time, and I wanted it to be like that in yours too," etc. (But the very next day, the day after your letter came, the day George arrived, they cooked a big ham and ate until they were ready to burst, I won't even mention the Hanukkah, I mean Easter, nuts.) But the ham that Netty, following George's instructions, put on my table on Easter Sunday was a mere stump weighing 2.4 kilos (in our part of the country, not even a Jewish upstart would call that a ham), but stump or not, I wasn't even able to cook it, because on Good Friday I was expelled from the kitchen. Further on, you write "briefly": "I heard Big Berta had brought you flour, that's why I didn't send you any bread, because I thought you had some." You didn't hear anything of the kind, my dear, it was I who wrote you that the "wicked" Brandlis were the first to bring me bread after I'd gone hungry for five days, whereas the "good" Groszes and Boroskas weren't ashamed to let the Rosenbergs and Mayers send me bread. About the shoes meant for me, or the shaving brush, you don't say a word.

And now that I've given you a small piece of my mind, let me get back to your dear relations and tell you how they spent Easter Sunday and how I spent it. While your dear sister Netty was serving up a Lucullan banquet that must have cost more than thirty or forty pengö, I, as I've already written you, and my family were having cold milk for breakfast, lunch, and supper in our cold chicken coop. The room was cold because they had taken away the stovepipe, and the milk was cold because they wouldn't let us warm it on their stove. And while we, after our "lunch" of cold milk, were reduced to crawling into sheetless beds, they were merrily drinking wine and guzzling fine chicken soup and eating chicken meat and cooked ham (not a stump), huge quantities of cake and pastry, etc. etc. That was my Easter 1942, and someday when we're alone I'll tell you about my Easter 1941. (Actually, I suspect that it's more than your nerves, or your sister Malvina's for that matter, could bear.)

But now I come to the biggest tragicomedy of all. It seems that your niece Babika, who had already provoked us, especially my wife, in Szentadorján, got even more steamed up "at home" when George told her about my "unmitigated gall" in turning down that ramshackle stove, though I "could have used it until the fall for only seven pengö and forty fillér." Your niece then asked him: "Why didn't you slap his face?" I swallowed that with the patience of a saint, I didn't say one word, all I did was tell Netty before she went to Budapest to make her children leave us alone, because if any of them lifted so much as a little finger against us, she'd have to come home for the funeral.

I think I've almost finished. My cupboards arrived today, carted from Lenti to Sziget, where I am continuing this letter. Tomorrow I shall return home, for by Sunday at the latest, that is, by the 12th, I must have the apartment ready, so as to be able to report to Novi Sad without fail.

When I got back from Lenti the next day, I was horrified to find neither my wife nor my children at home. The whitewashing had been interrupted, and I could see that the children had not been to school. None of the neighbors knew where they had gone, they had just seen them go, some said right, some said left. Your blessed relations evidently enjoyed seeing how upset I was at not knowing what had happened in my absence. Finally, just after dark, my wife came home with the children, dead tired and scared out of her wits. They'd been afraid to stay in the house, because the police had come looking for me again. I went to see the village mayor, who told me to report to the police in Czesztreg the next day. My leg hurt very badly, so I had to take a horse cart to Czesztreg, where I attended to all the formalities required by the investigation. If your dear children had properly informed the police during my absence, they would have spared me a great deal of trouble and expense. After all that, it was only natural for me to wire Netty to come home. I don't know whether she has arrived, because I had to leave Sunday (just now, I am in Novi Sad) to look for new lodgings after the collapse of the house. That's taken care of, and now I've moved from Bem Street to 27 Vitéz Street. I'm expecting a package from my wife, I'll leave as soon as it comes and hope to be back in Barabás by next Tuesday or Wednesday, after stopping for a day in Budapest.

Now I have something more to say to you. Once the house is in order, I'm going to invite you both, because we were all delighted with your nocturnal parade in pink nightgowns. (Let me whisper the truth in your ear: it was in just such diaphanous garments that those roses of Hebron who had waggled their asses too much were stood up to face the machine guns.)

Now I understand a good many things that escaped me before. Now I know why in October 1931 the Pannonian mud was impassable as far as Szentadorján, though the roads to Cetinje and Trieste were in good condition. Now I understand why the bus from Bakk to Szentadorján is so disgustingly expensive. I understand all that now. But I hope that one of these days you and yours will learn to understand not only that I am a husband and a father but also that I am fifty-three years old.

Getting back to the question you ask in your sweet letter: have I had the gray suit altered? My answer: I am waiting for you to send me instructions through George or Babika, waiting for you to tell me when country people wear a winter suit, because in town a man wears his winter suit all the time if he hasn't any other.

Now I have really finished my letter, and hope that in the future you will not give me reason to write you at such length and with so much bitterness, because this "little letter" is only a distillate of what I and my family have been through for the last three months. The mills of God grind slowly, yet they grind exceeding small.

I think I'll be home next week, I'll let you know. And since I never want to cross your threshold again, I wish you would come and see me, for I have some very important matters to discuss with you.

And now goodbye, or until we meet again.

Your loving brother,
Eduard

P.S. *It is better to be among the persecuted than among the persecutors.*

(Bava Kamma)

TRANSLATOR'S NOTE

I wish to thank Jane Bobko for her invaluable help and advice in connection with this exacting translation.

R.M.